NOOSE

A Selection of Titles by Bill James

DOUBLE JEOPARDY *
FORGET IT *
FULL OF MONEY *
HEAR ME TALKING TO YOU *
KING'S FRIENDS *
THE LAST ENEMY *
LETTERS FROM CARTHAGE *
MAKING STUFF UP *
NOOSE *
OFF-STREET PARKING *
THE SIXTH MAN AND OTHER STORIES *
TIP TOP *
WORLD WAR TWO WILL NOT TAKE PLACE *

The Harpur and Iles Series

YOU'D BETTER BELIEVE IT
THE LOLITA MAN
HALO PARADE
PROTECTION
COME CLEAN
TAKE
CLUB
ASTRIDE A GRAVE
GOSPEL
ROSES, ROSES
IN GOOD HANDS
THE DETECTIVE IS DEAD
TOP BANANA
PANICKING RALPH
LOVELY MOVER
ETON CROP
KILL ME
PAY DAYS
NAKED AT THE WINDOW
THE GIRL WITH THE LONG BACK
EASY STREETS
WOLVES OF MEMORY
GIRLS
PIX
IN THE ABSENCE OF ILES
HOTBED
I AM GOLD
VACUUM *
UNDERCOVER *
PLAY DEAD *

* *available from Severn House*

NOOSE

Bill James

This first world edition published 2013
in Great Britain and the USA by
SEVERN HOUSE PUBLISHERS LTD of
19 Cedar Road, Sutton, Surrey, England, SM2 5DA.
Trade paperback edition first published
in Great Britain and the USA 2014 by
SEVERN HOUSE PUBLISHERS LTD.

British Library Cataloguing in Publication Data

James, Bill, 1929-
  Noose.
  1. Actresses–Suicidal behavior–Fiction.
  2. Journalists–Fiction. 3. Brothers and sisters–
  Fiction. 4. Great Britain–History–Elizabeth II,
  1952–Fiction. 5. Suspense fiction.
  I. Title
  823.9' 14-dc23

ISBN-13: 978-0-7278-8318-6 (cased)
ISBN-13: 978-1-84751-489-9 (trade paper)

All Severn House titles are printed on acid-free paper.

Severn House Publishers support the Forest Stewardship Council™ [FSC™],
the leading international forest certification organisation. All our titles that
are printed on FSC certified paper carry the FSC logo.

Typeset by Palimpsest Book Production Ltd.,
Falkirk, Stirlingshire, Scotland.
Printed and bound in Great Britain by
TJ International, Padstow, Cornwall.

AUTHOR'S NOTE

Some material in this novel is adapted from a short story in my collection *The Sixth Man* (Severn House, 2006).

ONE

Twice tonight, within a couple of hours, he was invited back into his past. Invited? Frogmarched, more like it. Not a totally happy feeling. Recently, a novel had come out with an already famous opening sentence comparing the past to a foreign country. He'd agree. And not just foreign. Fundamentally and cantankerously hostile. Vengeful.

He had a call at home from Percy Lyall on the *Mirror* News Desk, the usual flippant but, behind-it-all, urgent tone. 'Here's a possible tale that's very much your sort of thing, Ian – a poignant mix of near tragedy, possible thwarted romance, glamour. Can you get over there? Needs sensitive but, of course, dramatic treatment. And it goes without saying, so I'll say it, depth. I immediately thought of you.'

'How right you were.'

'Daphne West,' Lyall said. 'Heard of her?'

Ian Charteris paused for a moment, or a moment plus. Yes, say three moments. The shock deserved that.

'Heard of her, Ian?'

Well, yes, sort of. She might be my sister. Might. We possibly share an amphibious father. Most probably. Certainly. But Ian didn't say any of this. 'Actress?' he replied. 'Television, stage, a film or two? Twenty or so.'

'A beauty. Starred very young, like Jean Simmons. Hang on. I've got some background cuttings here and very fetching library pix. Yes, born 1936, so, as you say, twenty.'

That would be about right. 'Near tragedy? How?'

'She's tried to kill herself. Standard method – gas, the ever-available, as long as the meter's stoked. Half in love with easeful death because a love affair of a different sort turned un-easeful and sank. She's in hospital, possibly OK now. But touch and go. Her publicity people, bless them, and their protectiveness and speed, are putting out the usual kind of horse shit: an accident – water boiled over, extinguished the flames, but the gas kept coming, as gas will. Daphne dozing nearby didn't notice. Tired after early morning wake-up for filming. Luckily, or maybe not, someone in the next flat smelled gas and after knocking and yelling got no reply so barged the door in. Stove immediately switched off. Windows swiftly, recuperatively, opened. The customary PR gab. Get the truth, would you, please, Ian? That's our business, isn't it – at least, as long as the truth is (a) gripping and (b) convenient for the paper. See if rolled towels were in place under door gaps, including the door of the break-in. The rumour is she was getting fucked on a reasonably regular basis by a big-deal theatre producer, Milton Skeeth. Could have been mistaken by the girl for something serious, the way girls do. *Man's love is of man's life a thing apart, 'Tis women's whole existence.* Byron. Heard of him?'

'Byron?'

'Skeeth.'

Oh, yes, indeed. Heard plenty. But that was added to the great unsaids. 'The name seems familiar.'

'It looks as though Daphne was only one of his bed mates. A lad in his position can move around among young, ambitious lovelies. He has parts to offer. His. Fay Doel. Heard of her?'

'Another actress – TV and so on?'

'Like that, yes. Skeeth lives at twelve Feder Road, Chelsea.'

Lived. Has lately long-term exited. But Charteris didn't say this, either. 'I'm making a note. Feder Road, twelve. Right, Percy?'

'Right. Perhaps Doel is there with him.'

Charteris knew nobody was at twelve Feder Road and wouldn't be tomorrow or the day after or possibly for weeks, months ahead. There had been what battlefield communiqués during the war called 'a tactical withdrawal'. Hoof it, in other words. From Ian Charteris, though, more silence.

Lyall said: 'Maybe West had been ditched. And so, despair. These theatrical people, they emote easily. They're trained to it. It's their long suit. And so, a decision to end it all. And so, gas.'

'Which hospital?'

'St Thomas's. Talk to her, if possible. Well, obviously. This is a voice from the almost Beyond. Lazarus, but prettier and with tits. Normally I'd give the tale to one of our staff people. But it seems so very right for you. They probably won't let us in to do new pix. She might not be looking her best. No problem. We've plenty in stock. An eyeful. Ask her what really happened. That's one of your flairs, isn't it – getting folk to confide, blub on your shoulder, reveal all? You sport that kind of sympa face and chummy voice. You could become an agony aunt when age sets in and your career starts to wind down. I want to hear the flagging of her gas-strangled heartbeat in your stuff, Ian. This calls for prose. This calls for prose that sobs and strums and reaches, above all, our lady readers. Some might have been thinking of gas themselves.

'Then recovery. I need to watch via your phrasing how near-deadly emptiness for a while colonized her lovely photogenic eyes   grey green in most of the cuttings, aquamarine once, but in the *Herald*. I want to share the pain and piquant hopelessness of a nice cast-off piece of thespian arse.'

'We don't actually *know* that, do we?'

'You believe her publicity people's version?'

'Was there a note?'

'You don't get notes with an accident. That's the thing about accidents – they come out of nowhere and don't give you time to write notes.'

'But if there was a note it would show definitely it wasn't an accident.'

'Probably the publicity people have been around to her flat and destroyed any note.'

'Conspiracy theory?' Ian said.

'What keeps journalism going.'

Hospital stories could turn out difficult. Although wards were, in a sense, public areas, open to visiting at certain hours, managements hated any Press scrummage around beds of the famous and would often try to exclude reporters and photographers, claiming hospitals had a duty to protect the privacy of patients. Maybe they did. But news aces had a duty to get the news and, as Percy said, to expose conspiracies.

Hospital security people were guarding Daphne West. When

Ian reached St Thomas's this evening he found reporters from the *Sketch* and *Mail* already hanging around Reception and trying to negotiate admission for a brief interview. So, the word about the star and her gas was out in Fleet Street. Ian gave his name and the *Mirror*'s and added his plea for an interview. They were told the requests would be passed on and up. Nothing happened, though. The *Mail* man left. It wasn't really a broadsheet tale. Tacky? TV obsessed?

At the end of another forty minutes, Ian and Greg Amber of the *Sketch* heard that one of them, and one only, might be allowed a quick visit to Daphne West. Ian and Amber agreed to toss a coin. Amber won. The arrangement was that whoever interviewed her showed his notes to the other afterwards. Ian felt nervy but thought it might be all right. Tabloid honour did exist, even if not standard issue. A couple of hospital officials accompanied them upstairs to the ward. Ian hung back, as stipulated. Amber walked with a guard on each side like a deserter on his way to be shot. He tried to do some amiable chat but they weren't having any. At the entrance to the ward they seemed to tell Greg to wait while the two went into what might be the sister's office and closed the door. Another formality? Or an invitation to Greg to nip into the ward and talk to Daphne without their approval, so there'd be no later reproofs for caving in to the Press?

From where he stood, Ian could see West in the second bed. She was sitting up, looking alert and very wholesome. This was not in any sense an ordinary moment for him. He tried to think brotherliness, in case she did turn out to be his sister. There wasn't really much doubt. He didn't understand why Greg went on waiting. The agreement could still be countermanded by someone bossy and non-cooperative in that room. Amber was experienced, tough, as pushy as any *Sketch* reporter. Did hospitals paralyse him? They were home ground to Ian. He walked past Greg to the side of Daphne's bed. 'Hello, Miss West,' he said, notebook ready.

'Who are you? Press? Is it as important as that?'

'*You're* important. Think of all the worried fans.' She had on a short blue silk jacket over what might be hospital pyjamas with faded red and orange stripes, not new. Ian found himself sniffing at her hair for gas. 'Are you all right now?' he said.

'Oh, fine, fine. What an idiot I was, though, causing so much fuss! Sorry. So, sorry.' A big, stagey, '*So* sorry.' At once then she started the boiling water flimflam, telling it with lots of face pulling and minor groans to indicate the extent of her stupidity. Yes, actress. Very successful young actress, so there *would* have been enough in the meter. He wondered if she worked out the explanation alone or whether, as Percy Lyall suggested, she'd had expert public relations advice. Her agent might already have visited.

Ian, of course, kept 'glamorous' in his head for the statutory description of her, but she wasn't made-up now, and at some moments between the gushes of self-mockery she seemed almost haggard and resentful at being alive still, as if sure suicide would have been her grandest performance yet. He searched for resemblances to his father. Was there something about the slant of those light-blue eyes, and an unusual depth from the bottom of her nose to her top lip – supposed to be characteristic of a comedian? Well, Dad was one, but without knowing it. Daphne's tale about the boiling water had its giggle aspect, too – the daft unlikelihood.

She seemed to become unsettled by the thoroughness of his gaze, though someone with her attractions should have been used to men staring. 'I look pretty rough, I expect,' she said.

'I've enjoyed a lot of your stuff on television,' he said.

'Oh?' She was thrilled and real pleasure sweetened her face, rather than the put-on, jolly, self-mocking chirpiness.

Ian said: 'Look, I might get thrown out in a minute. Can we talk about – about the gas? What's your first memory after waking?'

'My first memory? Oh, being slapped twice across the chops, to bring me round. And then the ambulance. Have you ever been carted off as an emergency in an ambulance?'

Yes, he'd been carted off as an emergency in an ambulance. And screaming for his mother. But this bedside meeting wasn't about him. He said, 'A siren? Flashing blue light?'

'*So* frightening, ambulances,' she said. 'Those terrible bright red blankets, and the shine on all the metal gear.'

'Is this stuff about the boiling water total garbage?' he replied. 'Your flunkeys have been along and told you what to say? They don't like "Star in suicide bid"? Not good for the image, is it? Not good for their percentage.'

'Flunkeys?'

'You're an investment. There'll be an organization behind you, won't there? A manager. An agent. An impresario. They have to look after their property – you.' Percy Lyall had spoken about Ian's empathy flair – spoken about it satirically, but with some truth there, too. Occasionally, though, in this game an amount of brutality – verbal brutality – had to take over: when time was short, for instance, and when you suspected you were being soft-soaped.

'No, it isn't like that. Not at all,' she said. Her voice had weakened, though, as if she'd been knocked off-balance by what he said. She wouldn't have been able to get her lines to people in the back row of the stalls.

'Is it a love affair? Something gone wrong between you and a man? Was it a serious relationship, at least from your point of view, and suddenly it's finished?'

She looked startled. 'Why do you say that?' she said.

'Has he disappeared, perhaps with another woman? The gas wasn't an accident, was it? As I see it now, you—'

'"Disappeared" with another woman?'

'Something like that.'

She stared about the ward, as though searching for Matron, to ask her, 'How come this rude, offensive, gutter reporter can get in here to torment me?' Aloud she said, 'What do you know?'

'It's a guess, a reasonable guess, that's all. "*Cherchez le gaz, cherchez l'homme.*"'

'What do you know?' She whispered the question. They'd suddenly entered an area of secrets, though there remained for now one secret she wouldn't be dealing with – her/his father.

'I'm asking, no more than that,' he said. 'This kind of thing – it's usually a matter of a fractured romance.'

'You see scores of such cases, do you? Professionally?' She turned away from him and began to sob.

'Oh, look, I'm sorry,' Ian said. 'I'd hate to hurt you, believe me.' He leaned forward over the bed and gently touched her hair. 'Look, Daphne, you and I might . . .'

He'd been about to cough the familial lot to her, or the familial lot as it might be, but those hospital security people plus a ward sister arrived at the bedside just then. They had Amber with them. They told Ian and him to leave at once. They said Ian was blatantly upsetting a patient and it couldn't be allowed. Her recovery would be set back.

'But we're only here to help,' Ian said.

'You're reporters. You're here to help yourselves,' the sister said.

'Out, please,' one of the guards said. 'Out now.'

In the corridor afterwards, Ian gave Amber all the boiling-water quotes and full atmospherics of Daphne's blue silk jacket, the old pyjamas, the way her face seemed to sag and crumple now and then, though no gas smell in her hair. Maybe they'd given her a full rinse.

'This is total, routine fucking rot, isn't it – her account of things?' Greg said. 'You can buy it by the yard from some protect-your-reputation firm.'

'Sure.'

'So, what's the real story? Man trouble? He's dumped her?'

'Not that I discovered,' Ian said.

'Is she up the duff? You wouldn't con me? I was the one who should have been talking to her.'

'Why weren't you?'

The ward sister came out from her office. She'd be in her mid-thirties, long-faced, auburn-haired, authoritative looking, not too friendly, good, enticing legs. Ian thought something had messed up to a major extent in her life, and being a ward sister with her own office and the power to vet visitors didn't totally compensate. You could meet people like this: grudge driven. 'That was quite a little shock when someone brought your names and the papers' names up from Reception. I've often seen your byline on reports – that's the term, isn't it, byline – and wondered,' she said.

'Wondered what?' Amber said. 'About me? About him?'

'Him. Whether he was the same one. The same Ian Charteris. I can see now the age is about right.'

Charteris felt a second, disturbing, frightening tug into the past. At least disturbing, and maybe frightening. First Daphne West, now this. But he couldn't work out yet what the sister meant. 'Age about right for what?' Ian said. 'Have we met before? I've done other hospital tales from here.'

She answered to Greg Amber, not to Charteris. 'Back in 1941 he got a man hanged, you know.'

'He *what*?' Amber said.

'He was a kid of eleven or twelve then,' the sister replied, 'and he got a man hanged. His words helped get a man hanged. They did quite a bit of hanging in those days.'

'No, I didn't know,' Greg said. 'That right, Ian?'

Yes, it was right. How did she know about it, though? Why should she care about it, though? Why should she blurt it now, though? 'A man got *himself* hanged,' Ian said. 'He stuck a knife into his brother because of money. All sorts saw it. Several described what happened.'

'But you told the story so well in court the jury was bound to convict,' she said.

'He's good with stories,' Amber said.

'It wasn't a story,' Ian said. 'Daphne West tonight is a story. The other was evidence. There's a difference.'

'What *is* this, Ian?' Amber said.

'You read about it in the Press at the time, did you?' Ian asked her. 'You must have some memory!'

She nodded. 'Yes I did read about it in the Press. But I knew about it anyway. It had touched my life.'

'I don't get it,' Ian said.

'You sent a man I loved, and who loved me, to the drop,' the sister said. 'He'd been swindled, and because he struck back against that duplicitous, greedy bastard brother he was hanged.'

'Oh, God,' Ian said.

'Is that right, Ian?' Amber asked.

'This is terrible,' Ian said.

'It's right all right,' she said.

Yes, it might be. 'Back then, he did tell me he was on his way to see a lady,' Ian said. 'You?'

'Me,' she said.

'An air raid had stopped him. We talked by the public shelter in our street. I was going to bring you a note from him to say what had happened.'

'Were going to, but didn't.'

'I couldn't.'

She spoke again to Amber: 'And this one actually went down to the prison to see the execution notice posted – so proud of himself, purring while the noose snapped a neck inside, glorying in it, squinting at the notice on the prison door eventually, saying it had been done nice and tidily. People made a fuss of him. His mother advertised him.'

'Were you there as well, then?' Ian said.

'As well?' she said.

'Oh, there was a woman present who scared my mother,' Ian said.

'Not me. Why would it be? But I had to be there.'

'You sent those postcards – the nine postcards?' He softened his voice. As Percy Lyall had said, Charteris could do that, and do it well.

'Postcards?' Amber said.

'There were anon postcards,' Ian said. 'But what happened to you afterwards?' he asked her. 'You moved to London?'

'Afterwards, this is what happened to me, in due course,' she said, giving a little wave, apparently meaning the hospital and her job.

'Have you got . . . well, a family?' Ian asked.

'Would I have?' she said, and walked away, back towards her office.

'I don't follow all this,' Amber said. 'What nine postcards?'

'Leave it. Daphne's the story.' That's how Ian would prefer it. He knew that however he wrote up Daphne West and phoned the words in, the *Daily Mirror* machine would shape it to the correct tabloid formula. In fact, when his piece led the paper next day, it struck Ian as one of the most brilliant and ruthless exercises in coding he'd seen for at least weeks. He did not claim complete credit – wouldn't want it; he'd have liked the report to be gentler with Daphne. Same genes? One or two gifted sub-editing touches had been applied, though.

By 'coding', he meant that the story appeared to say one thing but actually said something else, something much more risky and unpleasant. Well, naturally: if it were not risky and unpleasant no code would be necessary. Newspapers often went in for what might be called 'reverse writing' when the topic was legally dangerous. For instance, suppose the prevailing idea was that Mr A had murdered his wife, Mrs A; a reporter would ask Mr A, 'Did you murder your wife, Mrs A?' Of course, Mr A would reply, 'No.' And the paper could then say: 'Mr A denied yesterday that he had murdered his wife, Mrs A' – which meant everyone deduced that Mr A *had* murdered Mrs A, but the paper couldn't get done for libel.

The essence of the Daphne West story as published lay in two words placed reasonably close to each other during the opening few sentences. The words had alliteration, both beginning with g, but although the paper loved alliteration, it did not contribute all that much here, possibly nothing. No, but one of the core rules of tabloid reporting was this: if the adjective 'glamorous' – as in 'glamorous star of film and television', or 'glamorous model', or 'glamorous girl-about-the-night-spots' – yes, if the adjective 'glamorous' appeared somewhere near the word 'gas', as noun, or adjective itself, as in 'gas stove', the story's real message – immediately cottoned on to by the reader – was this: 'beautiful woman's failed love-affair suicide attempt', no matter what it seemed to say on the surface about a mere accident involving the beautiful woman and gas and/ or gas stove.

Naturally, Ian knew this convention and, besides, he didn't want to say anything too blunt about Daphne's attempt. Sis? He'd had to say something, therefore, without saying it. He had, of course, lined up 'glamorous' and 'gas' in his copy. But he hadn't done it with top skill. The sub-editing magic, or voodoo, recast his sentences, and managed to place 'gas' only just over thirty words from 'glamorous', rather than Ian's fifty, so that even someone fairly dim and interruptedly reading the paper while strap-hanging on the Tube, or washing up in a breakfast cafe, would get the underlying hints. Suicide, or a try, was a crime in Church and State law and plainly to accuse someone of it might be offensive and could be libellous. Even leaving the illegality out of things, it would be harmful to the career of a famous figure to suggest s/he despaired of everything and, therefore, actually and evidently despised the public and its adulation, or even despised the public *because* of its adulation, and would prefer sudden death, thanks very much. Thus, the code.

Another way to hint that what had happened derived from no mischance or carelessness, but from a boredom with – even contempt for – life, was to say in the story: 'All seemed to be going so brilliantly for her/him lately, yet a few more minutes' delay would have meant the end of this superbly promising career of the star from Such-and-Such and Such-and-Such.' Ian had written it like this, with Daphne West's name filled in and the stage, film and TV credits. It was an invitation to readers to look beyond the career glitter, and mawkishly wonder whether all that kind of stuff could really satisfy, because her love life must be rocky, just like any quite ordinary person's might be.

Tabloids relished – lived by – mawkishness but would have called it 'basic human emotion common to all'. The *Mirror* longed to strengthen the tie-in with a large part of the paper's ten to fifteen million daily readership, and gravely preached how a rise to money and fame could not necessarily satisfy. Subs liked to supply a moral and knew basic Scriptural teaching, such as 'What shall it profit a man/woman if he/she shall gain the whole world and lose his/her own soul?' Soul here having a wide significance, and meaning, among other factors, domestic and bed joy with a hubby or wife chosen for truly loving, not materialistic reasons.

Ian's story came out under the main headline 'TWO MINUTES FROM DEATH' plus beneath, in smaller type, 'TV Star's Miracle Escape', then 'by Ian Charteris' although it wasn't quite all his own work: subs didn't get bylines and were paid more in lieu. In the Daphne West coverage, a head-and-shoulders picture of her from the *Mirror* archive occupied three columns to the right. The report began: 'Glamorous TV, film and stage actress Daphne West told me yesterday from her hospital bed of the night she almost died alone and helpless in her luxury apartment. "If neighbours had not smelled gas and broken down the door it would have been too late. I could not be more grateful to them," whispered still-in-shock Daphne, star of TV drama series *The Whitfields* and movies *Loving* and *Mid-Atlantic*.'

To report lavish thanks for being saved was another tabloid device that indicated someone had been trying to kill himself/ herself and felt enraged with the damn nosy twerps who'd intervened and done the decent, life-saving bit. The sub-editor had rejigged Ian's copy, placing her quotation up near the start. This meant the reader could be whacked very soon with 'gas' after the opening 'Glamorous'. In Ian's version he had slackly used the second sentence of the story not for gas but to elaborate on the nature of Daphne's beauty – complexion, natural blondness, green-grey eyes. This could all come later.

The guts of the piece remained approximately his, though. At the fifth or sixth paragraph now it said: 'Twenty-year-old Daphne nervously tugged at her long, corn-coloured hair and described the accident with her gas stove that proved so nearly fatal. "I had put a saucepan of water on one of the rings intending the water to boil and remove some stains on the inside of the saucepan. I sat down in the kitchen to wait and must have dozed off. I have been working very hard on my new film, *Light Years*, and getting up at four o'clock every morning for weeks. The water must have boiled over and put out the flame. But the gas continued to flow and fill the room."'

In the afternoon, he had a telephone call from his father. 'I saw your byline on a *Mirror* story, Ian, about the actress Daphne West.'

'Yes, Dad?'

'Is she all right?'

'Oh, yes.'

'I've always taken an interest in that girl.'

'Yes?'

'Her career.'

'Yes?'

'A very talented kid. I've followed her successes. Did she have love trouble? That's how it sounds in the paper.'

'No, no, an accident.'

'Are you sure?'

'Absolutely.'

'When newspapers write about something in that way it generally feels like a suicide attempt.'

'Is that right?' Ian thought he heard a door open behind his father's voice and then a woman, almost certainly Ian's mother, yelled something aggressive and curt, but he didn't get the words. The phone at his father's end was put down with a real smack.

That sounded very absolute and final – topic closed. But, of course, it wasn't – the opposite, in fact. Why was the conversation hastily and definitively cut like that? The past had a lot of answering to do.

TWO

F ragments of that past – fairly important fragments – lay in Ian's childhood. Occasionally during those gone years it would be reasonable to say Ian starred – for instance, getting a man hanged. As the sister at St Thomas's Hospital had said, there'd been quite a fuss made of him because of his part in that incident. Children who got someone hanged were rare, even though hanging itself then was not.

But at other times in this period, it would be his father who captured the spotlight. Mr Charteris liked best to talk of those episodes. What Ian's father loved speaking to him about as a boy was ships. Mr Charteris described very exciting moments, and Ian knew some of them must be true. Ian used to listen and didn't get completely fed up, even though he had heard these memories before, especially that terrible sad stuff starting when the weight of the young woman's wet clothes pulled her under in dark water close to the pier. This tragedy happened a long time before the war and that air-raid shelter murder mentioned by the angry hospital sister. Ian's father was definitely the one who figured big in the pier event, but it would have mighty effects on Ian's life also, although he didn't realize it while only a youngster. It affected his mother's life too, as could be seen outside the prison that day following the execution in 1941, but he didn't understand this either at the time. Just after they'd read the door notice saying everything had been as it should be, his mother suddenly wanted to leave and go home. Eventually, he was able to guess at why his mother refused to linger in that crowd at the gates. He came to realize she had glimpsed a woman she loathed and feared and wanted no contact with.

As a boy, Ian would never show by making a face or yawning that he'd like a change from his father's ship stories, please. He believed he should be good to his father and try to enjoy the yarns about tides and spray from the bow so high it hit the wheelhouse. Every boy should be good to his father because fathers were so much older and really thought they were interesting when they talked about the same past things nearly every time they opened their gob. Ian felt certain his father did not deliberately try to bore Ian as a punishment for something, although he did bore Ian. His father thought he had to go over and over this stuff because Ian found it really thrilling, and he did, first time he heard it.

Ian realized he might be lucky in some ways. Not many boys had fathers who'd been in sea adventures and could talk about tides and spray from the bow so high it hit the wheelhouse, or a woman struggling in the sea where her soaked clothes dragged her down and down under the hull of the ship. When Ian thought of this he was reminded of something in a film called *Mutiny on the Bounty*, which he had seen in the Bug and Scratch, where the cruel Captain Bligh could punish men by having them thrown over one side of a ship and pulled on a rope under the vessel and out the other side. This was called keelhauling. Or if the captain thought someone had been really bad they would be pulled under the whole length of the ship, not just the width. The men on deck tugging the rope would try to get the man on the other end out from under the ship as fast as they could or he would drown. Captain Bligh didn't care. He had a lot of breadfruit to take somewhere and plant, and so he thought the crew should behave themselves. Even if the men did not drown they would be cut all over their bodies by being banged against the hull as they were pulled. Ian's father could tell a tale which was nearly as good as a film, Ian had to admit this.

His father worked on a sand dredger in the Channel because of the war. But before it started he had a job on a pleasure paddle steamer. Those ships stopped sailing after 1939. They would have used coal needed for the war effort, and, in any case, there might be dangerous magnetic mines dropped by German aircraft in the Channel. Instead, Mr Charteris had joined the crew of the dredger. It brought sand from near Flat Holm island, needed to make new airfields and shelters and defence posts. Of course, the dredger might get blown up by a mine, but there'd only be six men on board, not a lot of passengers. In any case, after a raid by German bombers the dredger used to go into dry dock to be what was referred to as degaussed. This meant the boat would be given some electric treatment that stopped it drawing magnetic mines towards itself. If a magnetic mine was pulled against a ship, one of its spikes would get broken and allow chemicals to mix and cause an explosion, blowing a hole in the hull. Most paddle steamers were 'mothballed' as soon as the war began – that is, kept in a dock or a river somewhere until peace came again. A few did other kinds of work carrying cargo, instead of passengers.

'The ships were known as the Masthead fleet,' his father would say. 'There were four. All pleasure paddlers are laid up now or converted to small freighters owing to what's known as "hostilities". I worked on one called . . .' He would pause and snap his fingers in a fond, encouraging way then. 'But perhaps I've told you that before, Ian, and you'll remember the name of the vessel.'

'You used to work on the *King Arthur*, Dad.'

'The P.S. *King Arthur*. The Paddle Ship *King Arthur*. In the old days, many ships, even the biggest, relied on sails. So, ships with engines powered by steam took the P.S. in front of their names, if they had paddles, or S.S. – meaning Steam Ship, if they had propellers. And later, when some ships used oil instead of coal, they had M.V. meaning Motor Vessel. But the *King Arthur* was steam, a paddle steamer, closed stokehold, burning coal at more than two tons an hour when flat out. It's as if I can see her now – a proud, bold-looking craft, two silver-painted funnels, the paddle boxes making her broad amidships, of course, sort of tubby, and on a good summer's day the decks crowded with passengers, off to a holiday in, say, Ilfracombe or Weston-super-Mare, or returning. Or just an afternoon and evening non-landing cruise around Lundy Island, sometimes a choir outing, with singing of famous pieces from *The Messiah* and *Chou Chin Chow*, which would resound above the noise from the engine room and the paddles digging into the waves.'

From adulthood, Ian would occasionally still look back to those days when Mr Charteris did his reminiscing, and could recall that as a boy he had a foolish, very limited idea of what words could do. He'd detested it when people said 'as if' and especially when his father did. Always what he considered rubbish came next. 'As' and 'if' – each of these meant not really, so two of them must mean *really* not really. Of course, his father couldn't see the *King Arthur* and her funnels then. Ian and Mr Charteris would be talking in the kitchen at home. His father might be looking at a cupboard or the sink, and they were nothing like a paddle steamer.

'"Weather and circumstances permitting" – advertisements for the trips carried this caution, Ian. The Bristol Channel can be diabolical. There might not be all that much of it, and some called it only the Severn Estuary, but the Channel could produce real mischief. A ship might set out in fine conditions and the barometer reasonable. Then, suddenly, a squall, or even a storm. Spray up from the ploughing bow so high it hit the wheelhouse. I say wheelhouse, but it had no roof or walls, just rails all round with tarpaulin lashed on to give the helmsman and captain some protection against the hurtling water. And, also during rough weather, the sea would sweep over and soak passengers' shoes on deck, but some of them didn't notice because all they wanted was to stand there chucking up into the waves, and feeling so rotten they'd like to chuck themselves over, too.

'Although these craft were called pleasure boats, sometimes the passengers did not get very much pleasure, Ian. And they'd be sick in the lounge and the dining saloon as well. Such a job, clearing up when we docked. It might be a quick turn-around trip, new passengers waiting, and you could not have public rooms in that condition, the prickly stench of recent ample vomit – often, admittedly, high-quality vomit, with a French touch from the dining salon: genuine *hors d'oeuvres*, steak tartare, Camembert. And not always neatly piled, but strung out in long, many-coloured, glistening lines on the floor and across the upholstery. People threw it up uncontrolled when staggering about with the swell, or against it, maybe having had, yes, a four-course luxury meal with all the trimmings, plus wine – perhaps *red* wine, usually dark red, but sometimes brighter, burgundy or claret.

'A ship could lose its passenger licence if an inspector came aboard and found wholesale, prevalent puke. This was understandable. The ship would not seem comfortable or homely. A pleasure boat had to look like a pleasure boat and smell like a pleasure boat, not a disgorge site. The *King Arthur* was over six-hundred gross tonnage. She could take a thousand passengers. Not all would be aboard and sick every trip, though still quite a quantity sometimes. But on a nice day, such a brave sight, the *King Arthur*! Unusually high potential horse power for such a vessel then. This would be quite a few years ago, now, Ian.'

'Horsepower meaning the energy used to drive the paddles.'

'And a speed touching twenty knots.'

'A knot, or nautical mile, is two thousand and twenty-five yards – more than an ordinary mile, twenty knots being twenty-three miles an hour.'

'There were races, Ian.' Mr Charteris would sound a little ashamed and confidential about this.

'Not proper races, with judges and a starting gun, Dad.'

'Races of a commercial nature to get first to where passengers waited ashore and pick them up, and collect their fares. That was the objective, Ian – collect their fares. The Masthead was not the only fleet. Hardly. Some did very well indeed. People who had some money meant to enjoy themselves after all the troubles of the Great War. Excursions in the Bristol Channel between south Wales and the west country, and vice-versa. Popular. That's what I mean about the racing. Competition. It wasn't supposed to happen – of course it wasn't. It could be dangerous, boats nearly ramming each other to get in ahead at a landing stage. But it did happen. You could call it greed, you could call it enterprise.'

'And so, that terrible bad accident,' Ian would say.

'Very bad. Not necessary. Never take the sea lightly, Ian. There's a lot of it, with its own way of doing things, such as swamping, battering, rearing high. The Bristol Channel might be limited, but it's joined to all kinds of other seas and oceans covering much of the globe. The decline of the Masthead operation started here. We won the race that day, but the death – it broke company morale, it put a pall over the fleet for a while. I think the company might have failed, even if the war hadn't come. I got this dredger job then. It wasn't any longer a time for cruising and enjoyment; it was a time for sand and gravel.'

'But back on that special day, you dived in from the port deck rail, determined to make a rescue.'

'Had to.'

'The woman's coat and other wet clothes tugged her down.'

'The sea there, murky. Hard to spot anyone at a depth. That's what I meant about the sea. It can be murky, it can be clean and clear, but it is always the sea and unmerciful, summer or winter. It doesn't just lie there between pieces of land. It's never still. Go and look at it. What you'll see more than anything else is movement. That's built in to the sea – movement.'

'We had a poem in school: "The sea, the sea, the open sea, the blue, the fresh, the ever free."'

'Not always blue or fresh looking, but ever-dangerous,' Mr Charteris replied.

'You had to go to what was known as a Board of Inquiry.'

'An awful time. But up until the drowning, you could say I was lucky to get a job on the *King Arthur*. Only a deckhand, though good pay, the work not too hard, and passengers usually in a nice holiday mood, unless heaving up sticky, odorous ex-fodder. Luckily, I'd been in the navy during the Great War, so I knew seamanship. I had to take the wheel sometimes, even in a storm. Important to fix her head or stern towards the weather, Ian, so she didn't broach on. I had to use all my strength to hold the rudder on course, even with the paddles driving her straight forward. The ship would sort of fight me, like an enemy, but knew it couldn't win against my steady force and skill. I was lucky to have these aplenty, oh, yes, part of my nature.'

'"Broach on" meaning a ship did not keep her bow or stern to the weather but went broadside on, and the wind and big waves hit her there, made her helpless, got into her engines, and maybe rolled her over, capsized her.'

'Each voyage we ran safety drills with the lifeboats. Think what it would be like if the worst happened and we had to get a thousand people to safety in big seas. We'd swing one of these lifeboats out on davits every trip, to make sure the lowering mechanism worked, and we'd show passengers their emergency stations. Of course, they thought it was all a bit of a game, a slice of amusing drama to liven up the trip, but it wasn't, I can assure you. "Only the Bristol Channel," they'd exclaim, perhaps laughing. There's nothing "only" about the Channel, Ian.'

'Davits – small cranes that took lifeboats down to the sea if the ship was going to sink.'

'The Board of Trade had naturally thought a lot about the *Titanic*, destroyed by an iceberg in 1912 with many lives lost. They tightened precautions. I'm not saying there'd be icebergs in the Bristol Channel! But ships could sink for other reasons. Our lifeboats were ahead of the paddle box on the port side.'

'Port is left when going forward, right starboard. Port lights red, starboard green.'

'Plus some of the benches where passengers on deck could sit were made so they would become life-saving rafts with ropes to hang on to if the ship went down.'

'These were what's known as "double-purpose".'

'Generally for relaxing on and chatting together, but also a safety measure. And then, a smaller lifeboat at the stern. This could be lowered quicker than the others, and was for the kind of emergency when someone went overboard, or if a line fouled the rudder. We got the stern boat into the water fast on that bad day, but not fast enough. This was 1934.'

'The dark water.'

'I want you to think of those two paddle steamers approaching Penarth pier, Ian, the *King Arthur* and *The Channel Explorer*. These are rivals.'

'No love lost.'

'*Channel Explorer*, owned by the Pearson company of Bristol and Avonmouth and part of its *Ocean Quest* fleet, gross tonnage five hundred and fifty, maximum speed claimed as twenty-one knots, master, Captain Lionel Corbitty, buckets of deep-sea experience before taking *Explorer.*'

'Age, forty-eight, nickname "Top-dog Corbitty". He thought he ruled the waves, like Britannia.'

'Scratch golfer.'

'Big-headed.'

'The skipper of the *King Arthur*, himself a bit of a Great I-Am. Perhaps they all needed some of that to become captains. It's called "dash". Like Drake and Nelson. Remember Nelson putting his telescope to his blind eye and saying, "I see no ships," although enemy vessels were bearing down on him. Or Drake snoozing in his cabin while the Spanish armada approached. They were sure of themselves, believed in themselves. They'd make their decisions, give their orders, confident they had things right. Edgar Dominal – in that tradition. And Top-dog. "Britannia rules the waves." So, the two ships make for the pier, both bound eventually for Ilfracombe and Minehead. About a hundred passengers waiting. Luggage, fishing gear, prams, summer hats, parasols, everything festive. Tickets to be bought as they boarded whichever ship. They're each coming from the east.

'So, say you were on the pier there, Ian. You'd see those two vessels, bows pointed your way, black smoke trailing thick from the funnels, the fires primed high for speed, paddles hammering down at rapid rate under their boxes, turning the water white, flags stretched sternwards in the wind, bold and gaudy.'

'And another poem at school about a ship,' Ian said: "'Whither away fair rover, and what thy quest?'"

'Quests are, indeed, what ships have. The quest for both *these* ships is to get to the pier first. They're alongside each other but about half a mile apart, *King Arthur* best placed for the pier, because in closer to the coast. The distance is shorter, more direct. But the *Explorer* has that extra speed – is *supposed* to have that extra speed, twenty-one knots, not the *King Arthur*'s twenty.'

'Twenty-one knots being over twenty-four miles an hour.'

'Corbitty probably wanted to show that the *Explorer* did have an extra knot. Some considered it just blab and sales blarney. On the bridge he would put the engine room telegraph to Full Ahead for both paddles, but as well as that, he'd be on the voice pipe, shouting to the chief engineer down below for every whisker of push. Paddlers could take

risks dangerous for propeller-driven ships. Paddles helped
with the steering. You could get a change of course quicker
than from a rudder alone, by stopping one paddle while the
other kept working, or by using them at different speeds, or
one going forward, the other in reverse. And if both paddles
were put hard into reverse they could stop a ship in a shorter
distance than a reversed propeller, or even a reversed double
propeller on a twin screw craft. That's obvious, you must
agree, Ian.'

'Well, yes, Dad.'

'So, Ian, a fierce race that day. Not unusual. Nobody would
have admitted it, of course, and nobody admitted it at the
Inquiry. Racing was against regulations. Rightly against regulations. It meant playing with passengers' lives. That's how
the authorities would regard it. Rightly regard it. But a captain
like Corbitty – he'd think regulations were there to be got
around. Or they were for other captains, not the great Corbitty,
who'd seen so much deep sea. Audacious – that's probably
how he thought of himself. Seamanlike, alert to hazard, but
audacious. Edgar Dominal would not put up with that from
him, wouldn't be cowed by his swank, though. Edgar Dominal
could be stubborn. Most likely he would call it steadfast or
un-panicked.'

'He wouldn't consider giving way to Corbitty.'

'Plenty of passenger business to be had around the Channel,
but also plenty of ships chasing it hard. And if you didn't
chase it hard, and often get it, your firm died.'

'As happened to several.'

'It cost money to keep those ships working – the crew's
pay, coal, dock charges. And the only way to get money was
fares, plus the catering. That day, the *King Arthur* had docked
in Newport overnight and called at Cardiff on her way to
Penarth. *Explorer* was coming from Bristol, on the other side
of the Channel. So, we had that inner position now, under the
Penarth Head cliffs. To Dominal it must have seemed certain
he'd arrive first. The published timetable put us at Penarth
fifteen minutes before *Explorer*, although Corbitty might ignore
that. His nature would be to ignore it. The *Explorer*'s call was
mainly for setting down some of its passengers from the West

Country, not for picking up – except stragglers who'd missed the *King Arthur*. Or some might especially want to go on the *Explorer*, maybe to try its speed and see if she got across the Channel quicker, even though she might leave Penarth *after* us. Dominal would not like that, and nor would the crew on *King Arthur*. He could be a nuisance and a show-off but he was our captain and we had to give him loyalty. This is how a ship works, unless there's a mutiny.

'Some passengers had come aboard the *King Arthur* in Cardiff, including a young woman, Emily Bass, and her family and several friends. This name would become important. Remember it, Ian – Emily Bass. Our passengers could see it was a race, naturally, although it wasn't supposed to be, and they were excited – thrilled – yelling up to Captain Dominal to get her going faster and also yelling at *Channel Explorer* across the gap between the two ships, telling Corbitty he was beaten and should give up. Cheek. People on *Explorer* shouted back. The insults could be heard all right above the din of the paddles, same as with the *Messiah* etcetera. But it was harmless – no proper dislike, just a sort of holiday game to both ships' passengers.

'Not to Corbitty and Dominal. Like gladiators. They'd be mostly gazing ahead, with no time to look at each other. They stood on the bridge of their ships, giving orders to the helmsman, one hand ready on the lever of the engine room telegraph to alter speed. There was going to be some tricky manoeuvring. Each of them thought he could handle it. Neither would doubt it of himself. Maybe each thought he could handle it better than the other. Neither would want it to go around the Bristol Channel ports that he – Dominal or Corbitty – had lost his nerve and come second out of two. This was the kind of tale that would get repeated and repeated, maybe with some trimmings, to make things even worse for the defeated one. We had a saying, Ian: "The captain's on the bridge" – meaning everything was under control because the master had charge. If the captain on the bridge failed, though, that saying would lose its force – lose its force for the also-ran.'

'The bridge being where the wheelhouse was, and the engine telegraph and voice pipe.'

'Now, the piermaster at Penarth has a problem, hasn't he, Ian?'

'Flags.'

'It's his job to hoist one to show which should come in first. He has a box with the particular flags for each Channel paddle steamer. The *King Arthur*'s is silver coloured, like the funnels of the fleet, with a white lighthouse on it sending out golden beams. The *Explorer*'s is dark blue around the edges.'

'And a map of the world that showed the five oceans in red, to remind everyone *Explorer* belonged to the Ocean Quest fleet.'

'Not easy for the piermaster, Ian. Oh, the rules would say he's in charge and can hoist whichever flag he wants. But he would be unsure which ship was ahead of the other – just these two prows bustling on towards him, carving their way towards him, rushing towards him, and about level pegging. He knew the timetable said the *King Arthur* should precede *Explorer* and take all the passengers who wanted to board the Masthead ship. But he also knew about Corbitty and the sort he could be once he thought someone had crossed him, such as a Penarth piermaster. Corbitty was a *ship's* master, and he would consider himself very much more important than master of a pier, because piers just stood there – they didn't have to be navigated through the waves and tides faster than rivals. Ships' masters sometimes retired to become piermasters, like out to grass as they say about horses.

'Corbitty had been cracking his boat on at twenty-one knots and he would expect the piermaster to realize this must be because its captain wanted to beat the *King Arthur.* He would believe the piermaster could tell from the *Explorer*'s bigger bow wave that she was going faster than the *King Arthur.* So, if the piermaster put up the *King Arthur*'s flag it would be an absolute offence to Corbitty and his ship and her special speed. That's how the piermaster must have thought. Corbitty could get very unforgiving and rough. If you'd been deep sea you didn't like people such as a piermaster messing you around.'

'The piermaster waited too long with the flag.'

'He dithered, Ian.'

'Perilous.'

'This was a lapse of duty, a bad shortcoming.'

'Eventually, the piermaster did decide. But *only* eventually, Dad.'

'He chose the *King Arthur*'s flag. As was correct. As was timetabled and published. Oh, yes, the piermaster had the printed official information on his side. He might not have Corbitty, though. I don't know if you can pull a flag up the pole with your fingers crossed but if you could he'd have been doing it! I was probably the first one to see it rise, before it unfurled fully in the wind and became obvious. And I realized I could be the first so I shouted – bellowed – up to the bridge and Captain Dominal.'

'You called out to your captain, "Permission for us to come alongside now showing, sir!"'

'Shouted it twice, to make sure. And then some of our passengers saw it, too, and began to clap and cheer. And a bit more mockery and triumphant shouting from these folk to those on the *Channel Explorer*.'

'This was the beginning of the terrible events.'

'Oh, definitely.'

'Turning triumph into something else.'

'The young woman – Emily Bass – is on the port side of the *King Arthur*, looking towards *Explorer*, really lapping up all the fun, especially because it looked certain we would succeed. That's the kind of person she obviously was, keen on fun, very natural to the young, and attractive in them.'

Ian said: 'She might not have seen the pier flag from there, but she'd hear the cheering and clapping and guess *King Arthur* had won, or was going to.'

'She was full of excitement and mischief and noise, Ian – calling across in a jolly, winner's way at the rival vessel. I was forward on the other side of the ship.'

'Ready to fling the mooring line to the pier, so they could pull in the heavier hawser tied to it.'

'I didn't see or hear her yelling at *Explorer*, but this came out in the Inquiry. And the rest of it.'

'The things leading to disaster.'

'The *King Arthur* didn't have solid bulwarks, Ian.'

'Bulwarks being the sides of a ship above the main deck.'

'What the *King Arthur* had instead was a broad metal rail at about four feet above the deck, and beneath it three spaced cables making a sort of safety fence. Now this woman, Emily Bass, was petite, and she must have thought they would hear her and see her better on *Explorer* if she could get extra height to shout her teasing. The thrill of it all seemed to take away her judgement. That can happen to people. I wouldn't say especially to women – that might not be fair – but it does seem to affect women the most. She climbed on to the first cable – about one foot above the deck. She must have decided this wouldn't do. She still wasn't high enough to be properly noticed from the other ship and heard. She stepped on to the second cable, another foot up. Her friends should have stopped her. But several of her party, including her parents, had gone starboard to watch the approach to the pier. Some pals did remain close by. They were as excited as she was, though, and one of them had climbed on to a cable as well, so as to be seen from the *Explorer*, but only the lowest.

'This woman, the friend of Emily Bass, told the Inquiry there was what she called a kind of "holiday fever". She said she'd tried the second cable, but didn't feel safe and came down to the one below. Anyway, nobody advised Emily Bass to be sensible. If a member of the crew had seen her, he would have made both of them get down on to the deck, but we were all on the starboard side, because that's where we'd be needed when we reached the pier.'

'Ropes. The mooring hawser.'

'Now, what became clear at the Inquiry was that Corbitty saw this woman, Emily Bass, from where he stood on the *Explorer* bridge and realized at once that she'd climbed into a very hazardous position if the *King Arthur* should rock or sway a little as she approached Penarth pier. He waved hard at her and also called out, telling her to get down. *Explorer*'s helmsman confirmed this at the Inquiry. But Emily Bass only laughed at Top Dog, seemed to think he was cross because the *King Arthur* would be first, and wanted to stop her enjoying this idea so much. Corbitty immediately put the *Explorer* engine room telegraph from Full Ahead to Dead Slow Ahead Both – obviously recognizing now that the *King Arthur* should go in first, and that *Explorer* must lie off and wait, for the sake of the woman's well-being.

'As I mentioned, Ian, at the Inquiry nobody spoke of a race, except for one member of the Board, who asked if there had been anything of that nature, and received a very clipped and definite "No" – was told such behaviour would defy regulations, and therefore could not possibly occur. It would be irresponsible. He had to say that. He had to lie. Of course, there *had* been a race, but Corbitty must have seen the danger to that woman leaning out over the rail, and called off his challenge. He was a captain and competitor but also a professional and a gentleman. He accepted that the race must be abandoned so as to cut the risk to Emily Bass.'

'The *King Arthur* had been making for the pier unusually fast, because of the threat from *Explorer.*'

'Not *much* too fast, Ian. A little. Dominal knew he could rely on good stopping power from the two reversed paddles. That's how he was going to play it. I'd seen him carry out that kind of action several times before. He had the experience. But, Ian, you see, a sudden change from Full Ahead Both to Full Astern Both on a paddle steamer will always cause a kind of profound shock to go through the whole hull of a ship, and affect her steadiness for a moment, only a moment. There's a definite strain on the structure. Perhaps it's something like jamming the brakes on in a motor car. The driver can't be sure how the vehicle will behave then. With a ship, it's worse. She might suddenly and briefly develop a list – a tilt – to one side or the other when suddenly asked for that kind of abrupt change. This will be especially true if the port and starboard paddles are not absolutely matched in timing. Even a difference of half a minute between reaching maximum power will cause a ship to pitch slightly and briefly to one side. Paddle steamers gradually got phased out and the Bristol Channel pleasure craft became propeller driven. But that's how the paddlers were then – liable to lurch.'

'It's known as yawing,' Ian said. 'And this is what happened to the *King Arthur.* And this is what happened to Emily Bass.'

'Dominal signals to our engine room Full Astern Both because his ship is almost at the pier. He knows he has won.

The chief engineer gives him that big reverse surge at once – has been expecting the telegraphed order. Paddles as brakes. Dominal doesn't want to go backwards, but to halt. Once the *King Arthur* is stationary he'll telegraph Stop Engines. The Inquiry heard that tests showed the *King Arthur*'s paddles could, in fact, be very slightly out of unison – not enough to cause bother normally, but dangerous on the day owing to a pile-up of special circumstances. When he signalled for Full Astern Both, one paddle was fractionally behind the other in responding. This had an effect. It made a wobble more likely, and more marked.

'That woman, Emily Bass, because of where she stood on the port side second cable, had the top of the rail at somewhere between knee and thigh level, Ian. It meant she had no proper balance if the ship skewed. Corbitty had spotted that, and cut his speed, evidently hoping Dominal would see he'd won, and could therefore take the *King Arthur* in gently to the pier, coming down gradually from Full Ahead Both to Half Ahead, then Slow, then, on the opposite side of the dial, to Slow Astern Both, Half Astern, and, finally, ease her into Full Astern, with no abruptness or stress on the hull.

'But Dominal had let the *King Arthur* get a little too close to the pier for that sort of careful, stage-by-stage, standard run-in. The ship stopped at the landing point, with no damage to the pier or vessel, but she did do a momentary minor dip to port – yes, minor, only a few degrees, but, on account of the way Emily Bass had climbed, enough to fling her into the sea between the two ships. She was like a stone shot from a catapult. She had no hope of control.'

'And then, Dad, as the *King Arthur* swings back to normal upright the ship sucks the water in under her port side, making a sort of whirlpool, and this is something else to pull Emily Bass down – and anyone trying to save her.'

'I was still forward on the other side handling the ropes for mooring us to the pier, and didn't know about her at once. I did know the ship had "done a shudder" as we used to call it, but that was more or less normal when a paddler went suddenly into Full Astern from Full Ahead. We didn't worry. And we'd had so much yelling from both vessels that nobody could tell there'd been a change in what that meant. But some of it now was distress shouts from her friends.

'On Slow Ahead the *Explorer*, a little further out, had gone past us and I could see the whole length of her near side. Captain Corbitty was on the starboard bridge wing, staring down at the sea near the *King Arthur*. He wore dark blue uniform and a gold peaked cap, very smart, very Corbitty, but he pulled the cap off and let it fall at his feet and then started to undo his jacket. I realized two things then, Ian. First, someone must have gone overboard from the *King Arthur*, and second, I saw that Captain Corbitty meant to dive or jump from the bridge wing and attempt a rescue.'

'Your mind raced.'

'It did.'

'You thought it wasn't right.'

'In a certain way I thought it wasn't right.'

'Because until now Captain Corbitty had been a sort of foe, and yet he was the only one ready to go in after one of *your* passengers.'

'Well, not a foe, exactly. Say, a rival.'

'A different ship.'

'He was taking responsibility for the danger to one of our passengers, not one of his own. It made me feel ashamed, Ian. I was still forward on the starboard side, but I ran across the deck and along to the spot which Corbitty had seemed to be staring at. Several of the woman's friends stood at the rail looking down at the sea, calling her name, screaming that someone was overboard. Captain Dominal, on our bridge, must have heard this. He came out on to the port wing to see what had happened. He understood instantly and shouted to me to get the small, stern-mounted dinghy into the water. This was the sort of crisis that boat was meant for.'

'But you thought it would take too long.'

'Other crew members could do that. Dominal's reaction was the standard reaction. I don't say this amounted to an obvious mistake. No. In some situations he would have been absolutely right. But, as I think you know, Ian, I am one who will not always be satisfied by the obvious, the laid down method of tackling a situation. I am one who will form his

own, personal response to a problem. I certainly don't want
to overplay this. It's simply how I am. Others are made differently, and it would be vain and foolish to think less of them
for that. But I decided, personally decided, that fellow crew
members could launch the stern boat. The moment required
something else from me, something quicker, in fact, something
immediate. Demanded it.

'I was at exactly the right place. This is something of a flair
of mine. I tend in some mysterious, instinctive fashion to put
myself into a position where, if there are difficulties, I can
deal with them. Again, I don't wish to swank about this. It is
a subconscious urge. I cannot explain it, or expect credit for
it. Simply, it is me, Laurence Charteris.'

'Although you were on the starboard side your flair and
subconscious urge told you to get to the port side.'

'I'm used to such promptings. I couldn't see Emily Bass,
but I knew this must be the spot, because her friends had
gathered there at the rail. And I knew also because Captain
Corbitty must have seen her fall and, even while he undressed,
had his gaze directed to one patch of water. I ignored Dominal's
order. This is no small matter at sea – to disobey the captain.'

'In *Mutiny on the Bounty* they used to keelhaul sailors for
that.'

'But I would have felt guilty if Captain Corbitty had gone
in alone. I began to pull off my own clothes, then climbed on
to the deck rail and dived.'

Ian became used to – very, very used to – the unvaried way
his father always ended the account of things. He would tell
the story as far as the couple of tense seconds while he stripped
to his underclothes, climbed on to the *King Arthur* deck rail,
stood poised for a moment, then dived. At any segment in this
tale, if his father had suddenly lost his voice, Ian would have
been able to continue with more or less exactly the right words
and clever, well-tried pauses. But, always, when his father had
reached the deck rail and the dive, he'd say hardly anything
more.

Instead he'd hand Ian a scrap album already open at the
spread of pages two and three. This book contained cuttings
from newspapers dealing with the rescue, and the death. Mr

Charteris had glued them in. Ian could never decide whether his father chose this way of finishing the tale because he did not want to be boastful, or because he *was* boastful, and thought that if several newspapers called him brave he must have been, so all he had to do was show the cuttings. On the whole, Ian, the child, considered his father had quite a stack of boastfulness in him, although he wasn't tall. Ian also considered that his father had been very brave. Nobody would have criticized him if he hadn't dived, but, instead, done what the captain instructed and gone for the stern dinghy. Yes, his dad could be brave, and his dad wanted people to know about it.

Ian had read the many cuttings so often he could have recited them also, without the print in front of him, but he always behaved as though this was the first time he had seen them, because of pity for his father and the way he needed to be praised and glorified for what he did. Ian would follow the newspaper paragraphs slowly, line by line with his finger, pretending to be scared of missing any of it, and he'd show quite a load of admiration and wonder. He thought his father expected this.

And when he had first spoken to Ian about events on that bad day, and first showed him the scrapbook, Ian really had felt admiration and wonder. And the second and third time, also. But then quite slowly there came an alteration. However, Ian knew it would be cruel to close the scrapbook too soon, or not to look at the shreds of newspaper at all, because this might show he had seen these cuttings enough to make him sick of them and to wonder whether his father was really proud of himself, too proud.

The scrapbook contained nothing else, and several pages at the end remained empty. It had seemed a waste to Ian. His father should have torn out pictures of film stars from magazines, or sportsmen, and filled up the rest. But Ian knew his father could be crafty. Perhaps he'd be afraid some people might be more interested in those later pages than in the ones about him. By putting only stuff in the scrapbook concerning the rescue, Mr Charteris greatly helped anyone looking at the pages to think only about those events and him. There were

times when his father didn't mind helping others, especially
to discover great things about him.

Because of time, some of the cuttings had begun to turn
yellowy and the glue underneath browny, so several of the
words were not easy to read because this browniness came
through and stained the print lines. Ian thought of the browniness of the sea where the trouble occurred, making it hard to
find anyone under the surface, different from a swimming
bath. Many factories and mines tipped works waste into the
Ely and Taff rivers, which carried it to the Channel. And there
was sewage. Penarth was a holiday place, although the sea
looked so dirty. People didn't seem to care. They swam there.
But they'd just be swimming to get a swim, not looking for
a sunk body between two paddlers.

Ian had realized at the time, of course, that this accident
was important for South Wales newspapers, taking up many
pages where they described events, and also giving Inquiry
reports. In the cuttings on the scrapbook's first pages there
were pictures as well as the words, though only pictures of
the two ships. But the cuttings on later pages came from
newspapers two days later, when there had been time to arrange
things. These contained a photograph of his father and Emily
Bass standing at the exact place on deck she'd been flung
from, and which he'd dived from.

His father had on the uniform crew wore – dark trousers
and a navy or black jersey with 'Masthead Fleet' written across
it in white, and a black hat with a small peak, like a tam, that
wouldn't be blown off in gales. Emily Bass's fair hair was in
a bun on top of her head, and she wore a summer dress deco-
rated with flowers. But Ian knew that at the time of the accident
she had on a warm coat, because the boat trip could be breezy,
or even really windy. The coat plus her other clothes would
get very heavy in the sea. Ian thought she looked quite a clever,
adventurous sort of woman, maybe the kind who would climb
up foolishly towards the deck safety rail and scream teasingly
at another ship going at twenty-one knots.

In the picture, Emily Bass and his father both seemed
serious, staring straight at the camera, the deck rail behind
them. This seriousness was what came to people who'd been

in the water for not just an ordinary swim but because of a
bad and very foolish mistake, especially a girl or woman. But,
of course, enthusiasms and excitements could take hold of
people and make them behave out of the usual – out of the
usual for themselves, not just out of the usual, especially if
they were usually adventurous.

One page in the scrapbook also had a picture of Captain
Corbitty, but it had been taken previously, perhaps when he
first arrived from deep sea to command *Channel Explorer.* He
was in his officer's uniform and cap and stood on the starboard
wing of the *Explorer*'s bridge, gazing forward. Perhaps at that
time he'd been taking the ship full speed ahead and feeling
pretty proud.

What Ian thought of as the main cutting from the *Western
Mail* came earlier:

TRAGEDY AT SOUTH WALES RESORT
– Respected paddle steamer captain drowned
– Young woman saved
– Great bravery of crew member
*The well-known captain of a Bristol Channel paddle
steamer was drowned yesterday when courageously
attempting to rescue a young woman who had fallen from
a ship into the sea. She survived, saved by another sailor.*

*The tragedy happened at Penarth, one of South Wales'
best-loved resorts. Two paddle steamers were involved
–* King Arthur, *of the Masthead fleet, and* Channel
Explorer, *an Ocean Quest vessel. The ships were close
to each other, near Penarth pier waiting to pick up and
land passengers.*

Captain Lionel Corbitty of the Channel Explorer
*apparently saw the woman passenger fall from the deck
of the* King Arthur, *having climbed to a dangerous
position on the deck rail. Captain Corbitty dived in from
the bridge wing of his ship to try to save her. It is
believed that while attempting to locate her under water
he struck the hull of the* King Arthur *and was concussed
prior to drowning. A member of the* King Arthur *crew
also dived in and managed to locate the woman and*

bring her to shore where she was given first aid and recovered.

The body of Captain Corbitty was found by coast-guards half a mile out into the Channel two hours later, having been carried by the notoriously strong Bristol Channel tide. They gave artificial respiration in their boat and later on Penarth beach, but Captain Corbitty did not respond and was declared dead by a doctor just after midday. The rescued young woman was Emily Bass, aged 23, of Marlborough Road, Cardiff. She and a party of relatives and friends were enjoying a trip to Ilfracombe to mark the birthday of her mother, Mrs Doris Bass, also of Marlborough Road, Cardiff.

Emily Bass's rescuer was Laurence Charteris, 38, married with a young son, a crew member of the King Arthur, of Hunter Street, Cardiff. Passengers from each ship praised his courage and life-saving skills yesterday. Both vessels continued their voyages to cross-Channel resorts after a considerable delay. Speaking aboard the King Arthur *when she returned to Newport last night Laurence Charteris said: 'The young woman had disappeared beneath the surface but I knew where she'd gone under. I dived and hoped to find her, although the sea was murky.*

'I think Emily had been pulled under by the King Arthur *righting herself after she had listed slightly to one side while manoeuvring towards the landing stage. The sea was sucked in beneath the side of the ship, and then rushed back again. This must have swept Emily free and I caught a glimpse of her face at a depth for one second. I knew I must act quickly before she sank further and became lost to sight. I reached out and was able to grab her coat and keep hold. I brought her to the surface, then used the life-saving stroke to take her to the* King Arthur *stern dinghy, which had been emergency launched in accordance with standard practice for someone overboard.*

'Crew in the dinghy lifted her from the sea and applied artificial respiration, successfully, thank heavens. I swam

back to look for Captain Corbitty between the two ships.
I had seen him about to dive or jump into the sea just
before I did. I feared he might have realized Emily would
be pulled under the King Arthur *and had gone to her*
aid, but found himself pulled under, also, and not released.
I believe this is what happened. It is a tragic loss. He
will be greatly missed by his family and by all who knew
him around the Channel.'

The final cutting in the scrapbook reported parts of the Inquiry.
The chairman said about Ian's father:

'This crew member of the King Arthur *put the safety of*
a passenger above considerations for his own, personal
safety. His action was in the great tradition of bravery
at sea – the acceptance of risk for the sake of others.
Captain Corbitty of the Channel Explorer *showed this*
same courage, this same respect for the traditions of the
sea worldwide. Tragically, it cost him his life.'

In the last paragraph of this cutting, Captain Dominal made
his denial that the ships had been racing. He said:

'This idea is unthinkable. It was a terrible accident caused
by a combination of unfortunate factors. The pleasure
steamer service of the Bristol Channel has lost an excel-
lent officer.'

A couple of years after this, Ian's father said there would be
a ceremony to unveil a memorial to Captain Corbitty, and that
Ian could come with him to see the event, if he liked. His
father would be invited, of course, because he had done a lot
to make the accident not as bad as it could have been, although
still bad. Ian said, yes, he'd like to go, but he worried because
his father's voice didn't sound good when he spoke of the
ceremony, sort of making fun of it. He often made fun of what
other people were up to, as though he found them rather stupid,
or not as sensible as himself, anyway. Ian used to think there
might be people not as sensible as his father, but he hadn't

met very many. Most probably it would anger his father if someone got a lot of fuss and a memorial. He didn't like others getting a lot of fuss, even though dead, as was evidently necessary for a memorial. People still alive never had memorials. They didn't have to be remembered. They were here.

Ian's mother had said she would not be going to the memorial ceremony. Much later, of course, he realized why she wouldn't attend. At the time he thought it was simply because Ian's father could behave in a ratty, difficult way when there was a crowd. Ian had sometimes seen how ratty his father's rattiness might get – his eyes gone very narrow through rattiness, and no blinking, just a ratty gaze. But Ian felt he ought to say, 'Yes, Dad, thanks,' when his father invited him, because Mr Charteris probably thought he was being kind and he'd be hurt if Ian refused. That would look as if he'd hate to be present in case his father did something in his own ratty way to ruin things. Perhaps Mr Charteris would behave all right. He might tell himself that the Corbitty family and the council had obviously thought very carefully for a long while about the idea of a memorial, and it would be cruel to kick their special day to bits. Yes, one side of Mr Charteris might tell himself this, but would the other side – the ratty side – be listening?

A crowd of about thirty had gathered by the time he and Ian arrived. 'And here's Emily,' Mr Charteris cried. 'Married now, I hear, but invited, naturally, and still Emily Bass to my mind.' Ian thought his father looked really pleased and all right, as he greeted her. 'Emily, this is my son, Ian, who loves tales of the sea.'

She was small, pale, pretty, still shy looking, still clever looking, her fair hair cut short now. She said: 'Isn't this a lovely idea, Ian? I feel so special – a ship's master sacrificed himself for me. For me. I will always feel such gratitude and respect for that name, Corbitty. Also, of course, for your father.'

Ian saw strong rattiness begin to take over parts of his father's face, most parts, which was usual for full rattiness. He stared at her. His stare had no blinks. He would not like being mentioned second, after Corbitty. He remarked to Emily: 'Yes, a great man, Captain Corbitty.'

'Certainly,' she said.

'I got you out, you know,' Ian's father replied.

She said: 'Often I speak to my husband and my friends of the undaunted captain who flung himself into the dark, dark sea in a valiant though doomed effort to save me, while also mentioning your father, Ian, naturally. It's really fairly unusual to have a distinguished man die for you, isn't it? Off came his cap with gold braid on it, I believe. Oh, such an occasion then, and such an occasion now.'

'I got you out, you know,' Mr Charteris remarked again. 'Many a newspaper cutting I have at home describing this, haven't I, Ian?'

'Many,' Ian said.

The memorial to Captain Corbitty was an inscribed flagstone cemented into the pavement right at the entrance to Penarth pier. Ian's father carried a very good wreath of roses and greenery. He was the kind who would consider it a duty to spend quite a lot on a wreath, so it would not look cheap against anyone else's. And a wreath meant somebody was dead and wouldn't be a pest around the place any longer, so the flowers should be regarded as a kind of giggle. At first, he held the wreath in one hand low down by his side. Ian thought it was best like that because flowers didn't really go with his father's kind of face, or not fresh flowers anyway.

Although the Captain was buried ashore, people attending the ceremony had been asked to bring a wreath if they could, and, at the end of the little ceremony, to cast it on to the waves from the end of the pier, showing respect and sadness, because, of course, the accident had happened in the sea. Ian thought his father looked quite all right with the wreath, as though he often carried wreaths and kept them down by his side. Mr Charteris got some true grief and regret into his face, and into the slow, sort of heavy, solemn style he walked on the pier, which seemed to show that sorrow had taken a lot of his energy, with only a small amount left for moving about and carrying the wreath. Ian felt frightened by this big show of pangs. He guessed his father had something really rotten ready to spoil the do.

The tide was up. A square piece of blue curtain hid the

memorial at first. Ian watched the vicar in charge today bend
now and uncover it, with a big, important swirl of his arm.
Ian could read quite well by now and saw what the inscription
said: 'Captain Lionel Corbitty died near here in August 1934
while selflessly trying to rescue a young woman from drowning.
His family wholeheartedly remember a very gallant sailor and
gentleman.'

The dog-collar man made a short speech saying how
pleased he was that the Corbitty family had decided to
commission this stone, and that the local council had agreed
it should be laid there. All those coming on to the pier would
be bound to see underfoot the commemorative message.
Particularly he hoped youngsters would observe it, then ask
their parents to tell them more about the very brave, self-
sacrificing man.

'And, speaking of youngsters,' he said, 'I think it would be
a grand idea if to conclude matters now it were the children
present who cast the wreaths out on to the waves, symbolizing
the link between a noble past and their own beckoning future.'

People applauded and some grown-ups handed the wreaths
to their children immediately. Ian's father didn't seem to
want to part with his. Dog-collar approached, though, and with
quite a large smile and creepy voice said, 'I expect you wish
to make your own, individual gesture to the Captain – so
understandable – but this will be a unique opportunity, don't
you think, for your boy to become part of the fabric of our
community and its admirable history of which you are
a considerable element?'

After a while, Ian's father seemed to feel silly clinging on
to the wreath and handed it over. In a small, slow procession
with other children, Ian carried it to the end of the pier. A
folding card with writing on it was tied to a carnation stalk.
He wondered whether his father didn't want Ian to read it.
This could be why Mr Charteris had meant to drop the wreath
from the pier himself. The card was in a small, transparent
cellophane envelope that florists gave with a wreath so ink
messages would not run and blur in the rain at a grave or
funeral. When Ian was hidden from his father by the children
behind him in the procession he quickly opened the envelope

and read Mr Charteris's words. Luckily, none of them were too big for him.

'Remembering Top Dog Corbitty today, who failed twice. (One) he lost the race and (two) he idiotically fucked up his try at rescue by getting his head banged by a boat.'

Ian carefully pitched the wreath and its accurate card on to the smooth surface of the unclean sea and watched them float slowly away, bobbing gently on the swell, quite a waste of money. He felt glad he'd had the chance to read those words, and liked to think of currents carrying them to who knew where, far across the world, such as Japan or Africa, because, as his father had said, the Bristol Channel might not be a major piece of sea but it was connected to many other seas – even oceans. He thought they showed his father was still just as he usually was – alive, ratty, ready to spot others' mistakes and even tidily number them off years later, not at all in need of a wreath himself yet.

THREE

Those incidents with his father at the centre would have all kinds of strange results, some close to disastrous. And then came other incidents where Ian himself was central: at the prison gates and, of course, what had happened before, to bring him and his mother there beneath the high stone walls – the stuff the ward sister at St Thomas's spoke of.

At first, on that morning, things had seemed fine to Ian. A warder in a navy-blue uniform and with his peaked cap on came out through the small door cut into the bottom of one of the main gates and fixed a notice. Ian reckoned that anyone could have told from the way the officer walked that this notice must be something serious. Of course, the people grouped and waiting outside the gates *knew* it would be serious. That's why they had come. The warder's legs and arms seemed too stiff and he did not look at any of the people around. Although the notice was almost too high for Ian, he did manage to read the typed announcement. It said the hanging had taken place at eight a.m.

The warder used four drawing pins, and for a while nobody in the crowd had a proper view of the notice because the back of his head and the cap got in the way. Then, though, he disappeared into the prison, still walking that stiff and very solemn walk, and Ian went forward a little and could make out the plain, hard words. The notice was signed by the governor and by a doctor in black ink over their typewritten names. Ian thought this showed matters had been done right. It made things seem tidy.

The talk in the crowd outside the gates was quiet and OK. His mother mentioned to some people that without her son this hanging might not have taken place at all. 'It's true,' she said. 'If anyone were to ask me how the investigation that led to this execution started, I would point to Ian.'

As an adult, he was ashamed of it now – his part in getting someone killed – but he knew he'd felt important. 'Oh, yes,' she said, 'Ian was a witness. He had to go to the court, although he's only eleven. It was very unusual for a boy of that age to be a main witness in such a big trial, but they made a special rule to allow him. It was in the interests of justice. That's how I heard it described more than once – oh yes, more than once. Mr and Mrs Bell from the chip shop and myself also went into the box, of course, to say what we'd seen that night in the public shelter, but Ian did it so well that the judge gave him considerable praise. Considerable. Ian could provide the evidence because he was there when it happened. Close. Very. I was there when it happened, too, and my other boy, Graham, younger, but they did not need him in the court because Ian had said everything and it was clear.'

Ian felt people looked at him in a surprised and rather admiring way. He saw they found it all unusual. Some of them really stared, but he understood why. They were not used to boys getting someone hanged by the neck until dead. He didn't smile when his mother spoke about him, and how he had set things going that had ended here outside the jail. He thought it wouldn't have seemed right, because a hanging was not something amusing, although it was in the interests of justice, obviously. All of it was in the interests of justice – the jail, the wall, the warder, the gates, the death.

One of the women his mother talked to said she thought hanging too good for some. She nodded her head towards the prison gates to show she meant the man in the notice, which was all he was by then, a man in a notice. 'Knives. Dirty. Foreign,' she said. 'Someone uses a knife, he deserves to get the noose, or worse. Maybe a flogging with the cat-o'-nine-tails first. Not him now, because he's dead, but a message for the rest. The cat-o'-nine-tails cuts into their skin. Such beatings are very memorable and can be described in the Press.'

Another woman his mother talked to knew a lot about hangings. It might be her hobby, Ian thought, such as studying books and newspapers about it. She said the prisoner would fall through the trap and then they'd wait until he was still, totally still, 'no jigging about with his legs', because,

obviously, that would show he still had life left. She told them
he might spin or swing on the rope but that was different
from jigging. The jigging came from inside him, his nerves
still able to work. But the spinning or swinging could be
caused by the wind, even though the hanged man was undoubtedly dead. Sometimes people said, 'He'll swing for it',
meaning get hanged. This used to be especially true in the
navy when people who mutinied were hanged from what was
known as 'the yard arm', which was high up on a mast, and
sea breezes would make the body sway about. The woman
told them there was a story where a wife had murdered her
husband and kept frightening herself with the memory of
something she'd read in the newspaper about a hanging: 'the
drop was fourteen feet'. This meant the killer went through
the trap door and fell those fourteen feet until the rope caused
a stop and his neck was broken, or her neck in some cases
because women, too, could murder, perhaps with poison or
a kitchen knife.

The woman explained that the group present in the jail yard
at the scaffold couldn't see whether his face still twitched after
it happened because there'd be a bag over it. This was to stop
him watching with deep fright for the moment when the
hangman pulled the lever that opened the trap. The bag was
a sort of final kindness. Also, it meant the witnesses didn't
have to watch what happened to the murderer's face when the
rope ran out and did the jolt. This could be exceptionally
unpleasant for those observing. There had to *be* observers, so
it was known everything was carried out right, in the interests
of justice, but their feelings should be taken into account.

Eventually, they'd bring him or her down for the doctors to
make sure he was dead. This would be after a few minutes if
it went properly. Hanging should not be about strangling but
about snapping the neck to cause a quick death. The job of
executioner had its skills. It might seem simple, just to put
the noose around the neck and pull a lever for the drop, but
things could go wrong if there was clumsiness. She said not
to believe tales that one hangman whispered to the prisoner:
'Have I got noose for you?' This was a crude, cruel joke. She
said that unfortunately the bowels might discharge at the

moment of the neck snap because all control was gone, and the prisoner might have had quite a breakfast, which was another special kindness offered.

As soon as they'd agreed, someone had to go up to the Governor's secretary on special early duty to type out the notice. Hangings were always in the a.m. Or they could have the notice done already, say the day before, but not signed. The woman said she found this strange because the notice declaring the prisoner dead had already been typed out while he or she was munching egg, bacon and mushrooms at breakfast, sort of 'dead man – or woman – eating'. But, of course, the notice didn't have any signatures on it at the time of the breakfast, so really it didn't count till later, after the breakfast had been finished, and so on.

The signatures could not be written until the doctors decided he was definitely gone. Lastly, the governor gave the piece of paper to the warder and ordered him to bring it out and put it on the gate. The woman said this was what was known as the official announcement, on account of the famous rule that justice had to be not just done but *seen* to be done.

This did not mean all the people could watch the actual event, though they used to be able to in history, such as at a place called Tyburn. Instead, now, everybody could read the statement outside. This was why the crowd had come to gaze at the prison walls and the gates and then the notice. Luckily, it was in the summer holidays or Ian would have been at school and not able to come here with his mother. Graham had gone to play at a friend's house.

Ian used to say the man would be hung, but his mother told him paintings got hung, men and women got hanged. He learned you had to get a more particular word for a man or woman on the end of a rope than for some picture on a hook. She worried about picking the correct words, and about correct pronunciations. She didn't want to sound what she called 'pig-ig', meaning pig ignorant and rough. Ian's mother explained to the women that Ian had been in the newspapers when he went to court. They printed all his first names, she said. That was the way they did it in courts and the papers, not just Ian but Ian Timothy Edward Charteris, to make sure of his identity.

'Crucial – identity,' she said. 'And names. So that everything tied up nicely.'

But then, while his mother was talking about the knife that was used in the murder, and which several observed before and after the stabbing, she seemed to notice someone at the edge of the crowd who really upset her. Ian wasn't tall enough to see who it was because of the people around him, but he could tell his mother had become shocked and angry. She had a way of letting her jaw slant down a bit when she felt like this, and crouched forward slightly. It reminded Ian of newsreel pictures of a boxer coming out from his corner ready to clobber. 'We'll go now, Ian,' she said, and took his hand to draw him away. 'It's over. I think we've seen enough here.' It was said in her refined, un-pig-ig voice, but with a certain amount of blare stitched into it.

'What's the matter?' he said.

'A woman I don't want to meet,' she said.

'Which woman?'

'One I don't want to see or speak to.'

'Who? Why?' Ian said.

'She has no right to be here. It's close to a disgrace.'

'Why? The people here are only a crowd in the street. Anyone has a right.'

'She shouldn't be here. It's insulting, and hurtful.'

'How?'

'Insulting. Cheek.'

'But who?'

'We're going.' The woman who knew so much about hangings wanted to talk some more about them but Mrs Charteris said: 'No time for that, I'm sorry. We have to leave – urgently.'

The woman made a 'hark-at-her!' face. 'I listened to you going on about your son, didn't I?' she replied. 'Now if someone else wants to talk, nothing doing – *so* hoity-toity.'

When his father came home from working on the sand dredger later in that day, Ian told him about the notice on the prison gate and the crowd. 'But we couldn't stay very long because Mum saw someone, a woman, who she didn't want to meet.'

'Who?' his father asked, but he said it in a strange, weak sort of voice, as if he knew who, but had to ask, and had to pretend he didn't know which woman.

'Someone I didn't want to see,' his mother said. 'You know who.'

'Oh,' Mr Charteris said.

'I don't know who it was,' Ian said. 'I couldn't see. There were too many people.'

'Your father knows who.'

'Do you, Dad?'

'You get all sorts at that kind of event I should think,' he said.

'Yes, all sorts,' his mother said. 'Absolutely all sorts.'

She spoke like she was talking about muck. In the crowd this morning she'd said: 'We'll go now, Ian,' and they went home on the tram. His mother wouldn't talk any more about the hanging or the woman and in a while Ian gave up asking questions.

FOUR

That encounter with the hospital sister brought unpleasant memories of all this back to Ian, of course, and once he'd phoned over his story about Daphne West to the *Mirror*, he went home on the Underground and thought some more about those events of 1941. Obviously, the episode at the prison gates wasn't something that could stand alone. What had led to the trial mentioned by his mother and to the hanging?

What had led to them was the knife murder in the public air-raid shelter in the street where the Charteris family lived. It was still there, naturally, at the time of the execution. The war went on. They had walked past the shelter when they left the tram after that trip to the prison gates. But there had been no trouble like that in it since the terrible incident. These shelters were meant to keep people safe from bombs and anti-aircraft-gun shrapnel, not to get someone stabbed to death in. But this is how it had been.

That night at the beginning of January 1941, up at the other end of the big public shelter, an argument had started between two men Ian did not recognize. Most of the people in the shelter were neighbours, but not these two. They stood face to face, close, too close – not like friends but full of hate, trying to stare each other out. Everyone else in the shelter sat on wooden benches around the walls. There'd be about ten in the shelter altogether, including the two men. Ian sat with his mother and his brother, Graham, and Clifford Hill from the house next door. Clifford was fifteen, older than Ian and Graham.

Occasionally, Ian could pick out some words of the men's argument above the big noise of bombs and anti-aircraft guns outside. The quarrel seemed to be about money and nothing to do with the German raid. Mr and Mrs Bell sat near them. Ian thought Mr Bell must have shut his chip shop on the corner of Barton Street when the bombs started. Ian and his friends

called him Mr Chip Shop, but not to his face, out of respect.
He would not want to stay open when bombs were near. All
that glass in the shop windows could get smashed and pieces
skim around. Most people put strips of brown paper on the
windows of their house to try to stop the glass going into
dangerous flying splinters if there was a blast from a bomb.
But you could not do that with the big front window of a chip
shop.

Ian stared towards the arguing men. He couldn't see them
properly, but thought the way they spoke showed they definitely
did not come from these streets. They were too old to be in
the army, one about his father's age, the other a little bit
younger. The shelter had one central, poor, yellowy electric
light. Smoke from burning houses drifted in through the shelter's open doors at each end. Usually the street shelter smelled
of pee because people would slip in there for one, out of sight
of the houses. The bitter burning smell took over, though.
Even pee that had been well soaked into the bricks during
many months could not put up a fight against the stink of
burning houses in the next street – timber, clothing, mattresses,
sheets and blankets.

Now and then the smoke almost hid the men. Ian thought
sometimes they did not look real. They were like shadows or
dark pictures of mysterious characters in one of his adventure
books. They made him think of that unusual word, 'looming'.
He'd found it the other day in a story and liked the sound
when he spoke it to himself, the double o and the m, nice and
round, but also frightening. When something loomed it might
not be nice at all. He could work out from the story what
'looming' meant – something quite big, not very clear and,
maybe, dangerous would slowly appear. Every so often each
of these men would loom out of the smoke and shadows.

Near him on the bench, his mother watched them for a few
minutes, then turned her head away. He could tell they frightened her – the sharp hate in their voices, but also poshness.
She liked *some* poshness, but the men's poshness seemed to
hide very bad temper, and did not hide it very well. Mrs
Charteris wanted to pretend they were not there, not even as
shadows or pictures. She seemed more afraid of these two

men than of the raid and Jerry bombs that whistled and screamed down and exploded outside. People said if you heard the whistle you'd be all right. It was the one you didn't hear that would do you. This seemed to Ian just something people wanted to believe because, otherwise, the sound of the whistling could really scare you – you knew something was coming and you knew it couldn't be far away or you wouldn't hear it so well. The other thing was, how could you know whether people killed by the bomb had heard it coming or not? They couldn't tell you. He'd noticed that grown-ups invented all kinds of tales to comfort one another now life had become dangerous, tales such as Hitler really liked the British and was only bombing them because he wanted to make Mr Churchill ask for peace and a meeting and then everything would be OK. Maybe they'd divide France up between them.

Ian, his mother, his younger brother, Graham, and Clifford from next door, had run to this big, public street shelter because they did not like it on their own in the house as the raid and the whistling and explosions went on and got worse. Their metal Anderson shelter was flooded. It had been sunk into a shallow back garden pit and always flooded after a lot of rain. Although his mother had wanted the company in the Barton Street shelter, now she must think these two men were a new danger, extra to the Blitz. She put her face close to Ian's and whispered, 'Just ignore them.' He heard it all right. A pause had come in the din of the bombs and guns.

Maybe she thought that if the men saw Ian looking at them, and noticing how they loomed, they would forget their argument and turn on him, although just a kid. She'd think they would not like his curiosity. His mother could be like this sometimes. She believed that if you did not take any notice of something bad it might go away, like the bird that buried its head in the sand and thought it couldn't be seen because it couldn't see. Mothers were stupid sometimes. Mothers got very frightened. They needed to be looked after,

Of course, the bombs sounded bad and you had to take notice of *them*, and the sight and harsh smell of burning in the next street, and the glass bits under their feet from blown-out windows as they ran to the street shelter from the house.

But these two men – they might get tired of arguing if people
ignored them. Or, if the pause in the bombing outside went
on, perhaps they would leave the shelter and try to get somewhere else, such as to the pub or a lane where they could fight
if they wanted to, and one of them did sound as though he
wanted to fight.

Graham sat on the other side of their mother, his face turned
in against the top of her arm, as if he wanted to sleep or hide.
He was seven. Clifford Hill sat next to Ian. Clifford was with
them for a special reason. When the bombing started, he had
been by himself in the Hills' house. His mother and father
had gone out to see *Down Argentine Way* at the Regent this
evening, a cinema sometimes called the Bug and Scratch.
Clifford had seen it already and he hadn't wanted to go again.

When the bombing got worse and very close, he had become
scared in their house by himself. Their Anderson had flooded,
too. So did everybody's. Clifford began yelling, to see if anyone
was in the Charteris house. Ian, Graham, and their mother had
crawled for shelter under the big wooden kitchen table, and
just sat there on the mat. In a quiet few minutes, Mrs Charteris
got out from under the table, unbolted the kitchen door to the
back garden and shouted to Clifford to come in if he wanted
to. Clifford climbed over the wall between the two gardens
and the three made room for him under the table after his
mother had bolted the door again.

Ian's father would be on his way home by train from Newport
after a day's sand dredging on the boat in the Bristol Channel.
A lot of sand was needed these days for street air-raid shelters,
runways for planes and pillbox defence posts. Mrs Charteris
said the train would most likely be stuck somewhere because
of the raid. His father had told them to get under the kitchen
table if the Anderson was no good and a bad raid came. But,
after a while, when the bombing seemed to go on and on, his
mother said it might be better to be with other people. And
there was not really enough room under the table for four if
the raid lasted a long time. The public shelter stood quite near,
on what used to be a grass island in the middle of Barton
Street.

They got out from under the table and, when there was

some peace for a few minutes outside, his mother opened the front door and the four of them hurried to the big shelter. Kids had drawn love hearts with boys' and girls' names in them when the cement was still wet on the outside of the shelter a few months ago. Ian had liked the idea that those hearts would stay there until the end of the war and the shelter was torn down, unless it had a hit before then. The kids liked to think the love hearts and what they meant would last longer than just drawing hearts with chalk on an ordinary wall. Ian hadn't done a love heart because he was a bit too young to have the kind of girlfriend whose initials he wanted with his own in cement.

Searchlights swung about in the sky, hunting the bomber planes for the guns to shoot at. He thought that in peacetime these lights would have been very exciting and pretty, but now he had the feeling they were just useless. They never seemed to find Jerry. Although the anti-aircraft guns boomed and boomed, they might be firing anywhere into the darkness, hoping they'd get the enemy by luck. Houses on fire in the next street, Larch Street, lit up Ian's own street – a strange yellow, red and blue light, with black smoke at its edges. Everybody knew that if the bombs made a fire it would be seen through the blackout by the next gang of German pilots tonight, who'd use it for a target.

As they reached the shelter, Ian heard a cracking sound, then a funny rushing, roaring, and he thought this must be a Larch Street house as it collapsed. That noise didn't seem as bad as all the banging of the bombs and the anti-aircraft guns. It was gentler, not so crackly, not hurting the ears. It reminded Ian of when he saw and heard a big waterfall on an outing to the Brecon Beacons. But he knew it would not be like that for anybody in the house when it came down on them. In fact, he changed his mind. That sound was *worse* than the explosions from guns and bombs because it meant somebody's house had got it, and maybe the people in the house had got it, too. He thought of the guns and bombs as being like fireworks. Or he tried to.

Now, the two men still argued. They didn't seem to take much notice of what was happening outside. All they thought

about was each other, and they thought about each other with
true hate, anyone could tell this. In some quarrels the hate
could be very strong at the start, but then it would die away.
Things would get back to the ordinary. This didn't happen
with these two, though. They would move even closer, as if
they meant to fight, and then back away, but still grunting and
muttering about money, and doing their looming.

One said half the money should be his, that this 'stood to
reason', but the other replied that he was the one who found
it and that was that, finders-keepers, and in any case, it was
all gone now. Ian did not know which money they spoke about.
He thought it must be a lot if it made them posh-snarl so
badly, and not caring who heard. No, they didn't, and there
was swearing. The man didn't say just finders-keepers, but
finders-*fucking*-keepers. That was a terrible word, but Ian definitely heard it – things outside had gone quiet once more.

The men's voices seemed different from the ones he was
used to around here – more like the headmaster's in the
grammar school, where Ian had started last year, or even like
people reading the News on the wireless. One of the men
turned his back on the other. It looked as if he would walk to
the doorway of the shelter and at last try to see how the raid
was going. Maybe he suddenly got fed up with the argument,
or felt sick of looking at the other man and did not believe
him worth talking to any more. That's how it seemed when
he turned his back – not just to walk away, or find out about
the raid, but to tell the other man he was not worth talking to
any more. It had to be a rude thing to do. It was what his
mother would call 'a pig-ig thing to do', but she didn't say
that now. He knew she didn't want to say anything that might
get one or both of these men more cross.

Everybody knew turning your back on someone might be
rude. With kings and emperors and sultans, their court people
would walk backwards after meeting them, so as not to turn
their backs. It was respect. But during quarrels people were
often rude, because they wanted to hurt the other one, not
always by hitting them, but by an action such as not taking
any more notice. Perhaps the man who turned his back would
go. Although the siren had not sounded All Clear yet, the

raid might be finishing. For the last few minutes Ian had not heard any bombs and the ack-ack of the anti-aircraft guns had gone silent, so there would be no great lumps of jagged shrapnel coming down. These were pieces of metal that used to be the smooth, strong cases of anti-aircraft shells but had been ripped into chunks when these shells exploded in the sky. Some of this shrapnel had very sharp, spiky bits that made Ian think of the mouth and teeth of a shark he'd seen in photographs.

These pieces were supposed to hit aeroplanes and their crew and cause crashes, of course. But if they missed they would fall into the streets and lanes and would be dropping very fast. They were dangerous. This was one reason air-raid wardens had tin helmets. Some boys collected shrapnel. They thought that after the war there wouldn't be any anti-aircraft guns firing, so shrapnel would not be around in the streets and lanes. It would become rare and would help to show what war and raids had been like. Ian collected army badges instead. He knew regiments and their emblems and mottos. If the war lasted another seven years he might have to go into the army himself. Because of these badges he'd know quite a lot about the different parts of it. He'd most probably try to join the Royal Artillery. He would be used to the sounds of guns if there were more raids like this. Of course, he knew something about bombs and bomber aircraft, too. Perhaps he'd decide to join the Air Force.

Now that it had become quiet outside, with no shrapnel or bombs falling, Ian thought the men might go, or one of them, anyway. Perhaps his mother was right, and as long as nobody took any notice of the two this trouble would end. But then Clifford said: 'He's got a knife.' He did not whisper. He just said it in an ordinary way but with some throaty phlegm, trembling, and Ian could hear it, although his mother and Graham were between him and Clifford. Ian looked at the two men. One man seemed really angry because the other one had turned his back. He felt insulted, you could tell. Although Ian did not know their names at this time, he discovered what they were when the newspapers did reports on the stabbing, of course, and at the trial. When Ian was describing things to

the court the judge told him to say, 'The man I later learned
was Martin Harold Main', or the other one.

The man who had turned his back probably knew it would
make the other one more angry. That might be why he did it.
He wanted to be rude. It was like telling Mr Main he didn't
matter. This did not mean Mr Main was right to do what he
did. If he had been right he would not have been hanged after
the trial, and that notice put up on the prison gates. This was
obvious.

The man stepped forward two paces very fast and got his left
arm around the neck of the one who had turned his back. The
man with the knife pulled the other one hard against himself.
They both had black or dark overcoats on and now they were
together like that and in the smoke they looked like one big,
thick shadow of a creature with two heads. The one who had
turned his back tried to struggle and shouted something, or it
was nearly a scream, but Ian could not tell if there were words.
It might have been just a shout of surprise or perhaps he had
been trying to say something but could not because of the arm
inside the overcoat sleeve pressing so hard against his throat.
He might be able to get enough air to let him screech, but not
enough for shaping the screech into words, not even the one
short word: 'Help!' He could not fight free.

Anyway, perhaps he knew that calling for help in this shelter
would not work because everyone would be too scared to go
for the man with the knife. The raid outside with the whistling
bombs and the fire and the broken glass had made them frightened enough and they would not look for an extra fright, such
as trying to get the knife off this man. The posh way the two
men spoke might also stop anyone in the shelter interfering
because these two sounded as though they were used to doing
things the way they wanted and would not put up with any
bother from ordinary Barton Street people and such like.

Through the smoke around the two men Ian thought he did
see something shine. It was in the right hand of the man who
had not turned his back. His other hand and arm stayed around
the neck of the man who had turned his back. The man who
had not turned his back said in a loud voice, but still posh,
'You shouldn't have had it all. Shouldn't. He said the

'shouldn't' really strong, twice, and stronger on the second go. It seemed to sound right along the shelter, past Mr Chip Shop, and then past the four of them. This one seemed to have plenty of breath for words, even though he must be using part of his strength to grip the other man like that on his throat and not let go. But the 'shouldn't' came out with real power. He meant it. But it wasn't just that he meant it; no, he wanted all in that shelter to know the other man 'shouldn't'. This was a message to travel the total length of the shelter. Nobody in the shelter could miss hearing this 'shouldn't'.

The right arm of the man who had said 'shouldn't' went forwards and backwards four times, or maybe five, and Ian thought he saw that shining thing again and the man who had turned his back just slipped down and lay on his side by the other man's feet on the floor of the shelter. Even if Clifford hadn't said, 'He's got a knife,' Ian would have known then it was a knife that went forward and back. The man with the knife had given up his hold around the neck of the other one so he could drop. Ian saw that the bottoms of the shoes of the fallen man did not look at all dirty or worn. This newness made him think again that these two men were not from this part of the town.

Of course, if the man on the floor had taken a lot of money from somewhere, he might have spent part of it on shoes. He had said the money was gone, which showed he had spent it on certain items, perhaps such as shoes. Ian did not know whether the shoes of the man with the knife were also new. If both the men came from a posh part of the town, it might be the thing for everyone there to have new shoes. Many thought good shoes very important, not just for keeping feet dry but to look classy when polished up.

Before the big raid tonight, Ian and his friends had used the public shelter as just somewhere to play in. There had not been any bombs near their street until now. Girls and boys kissed in here and so on, away from grown-ups, and played chase through the shelter. It had a door at each end in case of being trapped if it was hit, and the locks had been broken and then mended and then broken again and left broken. When they built the shelter in 1940, just after Ian began at the grammar school, he had not written a love heart in the wet cement with his finger but 'Britons never shall be slaves'. He had taken that saying from the song 'Land of Hope and Glory'. He put those words there because Hitler said he would soon be ruling Britain. Ian wanted to give him a message. The cement went hard and the letters must stay for years and years – until the end of the war when the shelter would get knocked down because of no more raids, and Hitler would have been smashed by the army, navy and Royal Air Force.

Now, because of the raid and this man lying on the floor, and Clifford Hill saying 'He's got a knife' in an ordinary way but phlegmy and trembling, the shelter seemed to Ian quite different. It was not a place to pee in or play and kiss and get feels in, but to hide from the bombs and shrapnel in and watch two men become really angry about something to do with money, and one of them turn savage. The other man, the one not flat on the floor and most likely dead, went and sat on a bench. 'He's got the knife in his hand,' Clifford said. 'Blood.' Cliff was still trembling. Everyone in the shelter had had a shock, but it seemed worse for Clifford. It had been a very bad evening for him – in his house by himself when the raid began and now this man with the knife.

'Ignore him,' Ian's mother told Clifford. Ian could see the knife clearly now. The man held it down against his trouser leg in his left hand. It looked like an ordinary pocket knife but big. He did not fold the blade back. Blood would drip on his clothes and shoes, and he did not seem to care. Perhaps he had decided the other man must get stabbed like that because of the money, and now it was done and he could not be bothered to worry. Maybe some people were like this when they became angry about losing money. Ian thought the man would run away after doing what he did, but he stayed there, although outside everything still seemed better and safe. Mr Bell, the chip shop man, said someone should go and fetch a police officer, stabbings being a crime even in the middle of an air raid.

'Yes, the police,' his wife said.

'I agree,' Mrs Charteris said. 'Well, you go, Mr Bell.'

Mrs Bell said, 'No.'

Mr Bell replied he had to keep guard.

'Yes, he has to keep guard,' his wife said.

'Guard what?' Ian's mother asked.

'This is a situation where someone to keep guard is very necessary,' Mrs Bell said.

Ian thought that Mr and Mrs Bell meant somebody must guard the one with the knife and make sure he didn't escape. But Mr Bell was very wheezy and thin. He should eat more of his own fish and chips. He would not be able to stop the man if he wanted to go or if he became angry with someone else. He still had the knife open. Mr Bell said Ian should go. There'd be police in Larch Street because of the bombs and fire there. Perhaps even the mansion had been hit or the Gospel Hall.

'Sure to be police in Larch Street,' his wife said. 'They would be worried about the mansion and I think the Gospel Hall Sunday school were having their after-Christmas party there this evening.'

'The lad can wear this in case of shrapnel,' Mr Bell added. He had a grey, metal helmet by his side on the bench. Ian went and put it on. It was too big but Mr Bell tightened the strap under Ian's chin. He began to feel grown-up and necessary, as though he had become someone else. He liked that. Although the helmet was heavy, Ian didn't mind. It had to be thick and strong to stop the shrapnel which might be sharp and falling very fast. Or if a building collapsed near you bricks might fall and hit your head.

'No, Ian,' his mother said. He could tell she felt she'd lost him because of the helmet, as though he had put on army uniform and gone to the war.

'It's necessary,' Mrs Bell said. 'And a doctor will be needed too.'

'That man doesn't need a doctor,' Mr Bell said.

'A doctor to say he's dead,' Mrs Bell said.

'Doctors will be busy tonight, dealing with the injured,' Mrs Charteris said.

'Just the same, he has to be certified,' Mrs Bell said. She nodded towards the man on the floor.

Ian said he'd be all right and would come straight back

from Larch Street. If he found a policeman, the copper would know what to do about a doctor.

'He'll be all right,' Mr Bell said. 'The other boy, the older one, has some shock.' He meant Clifford. Ian felt proud to be doing something with a helmet on that Clifford could not do, even though he was older at fifteen.

'Well, *you* go, if you're so sure it will be all right,' Ian's mother said to Mr Bell.

Ian said Mr Bell had to be a guard. Ian knew Mr Bell would be no good at it, but he kept quiet about that, or he would have seemed cruel to someone who had lent him a grown-up's helmet. And Ian wanted to go to Larch Street and look for a policeman just to show he could do it, even though the raid might start again.

'That helmet suits your son,' Mrs Bell said. 'When the raid is over you and the boys can come to the shop for chips *and* fish free.'

'Yes,' Mr Bell agreed.

It was very cold. Ian went through the lane to Larch Street. All of one part of the street was down or burning and half the big mansion at the far end of the street had also been torn away. Ian could make out a bed and a wardrobe upstairs, where the wall of the room had gone. He saw a fire engine and two ambulances. Flames from one of the houses lit up the smashed mansion. Five or six firemen were pouring water from hose-pipes on to the blaze. The water froze in the gutters. The builder of these streets had put up this big home for himself, known as a mansion, with a high wall at the back and the River Taff right in front, just before its mouth into the Channel.

Ian thought the builder must know now it had been foolish to place that mansion there, especially if he was inside when the bombs began. A big ammunitions factory stood opposite on the other side of the river and the bombers must have been after that. Spies might have told them it was there. Even at night and in the blackout the German pilots could see the river. The airmen used it to find the factory and only just missed. They got the mansion and some smaller houses in Larch Street on the other side of the water instead. The builder had put the mansion there because he wanted a view of the river. But German bombers had a view of the Taff from up there, too, guiding them – the way rivers looked on a map, a line, seeming to wander, but clear.

The mansion was at the Taff end of the street, so the people there could get that pleasant sight of the water when it was peacetime. The Gospel Hall stood at the other end. It wasn't damaged. Ian had been to the Sunday school there a couple of times. He had been made to go so the house would be quiet for Mr Charteris to have his sleep in an armchair after the big Sunday dinner. He gave Ian twopence for collection. But Ian hadn't liked the way they talked in the Gospel Hall of needing to be 'washed in the blood of the Lamb'. He knew this was picture language only, but it still made him feel a bit sick. They said there that if you were washed in the blood of the Lamb you'd become whiter than snow. He couldn't really understand this. Anyway, although he went on taking the twopence for collection from his father, he didn't go to the Sunday school. He had a wander about instead. In the summer, he'd put one of his boys' magazines in his pocket, such as *Adventure* or *Hotspur*, and go and read some tales in the park until the time he knew Sunday school would be over.

A lot of the children from the Christmas party seemed still stuck in the building tonight because of the blitz. As Ian passed, they were singing a chorus, maybe meant to blot out the sound of the bombs and guns. 'Yes, we shall gather at the river, the beautiful, the beautiful, river.' That seemed to him a dopey piece to be singing here tonight. Rivers brought bombs.

Ian saw a policeman without his helmet on who was helping look for people in a wrecked house. It was half gone, beams and slates from the roof piled up on the floor of the front room. One wall of this room was down. Ian could see a piano in there looking all right, an open book of music stood on the holder, ready for playing. In the light from the fires he could read the title of the music, a song called 'Red Sails in the Sunset'.

One of Ian's friends, Doreen Spire, lived in Larch Street, but Ian did not know which house. It was not the mansion. She was one who wouldn't let you touch her anywhere. There were some like that, even though the shelter was usually so private. Probably, their mothers had been on at them about keeping their legs closed or boys would talk about you and have no respect. Most likely Doreen's parents went to the Gospel Hall where they would be fussy about that kind of thing. You were not supposed to get a handful until married if you'd been washed in the blood. He said: 'I think a murder. In the big shelter – Barton Street. Committed with a knife. Many witnessed it. They are all still in the shelter.'

The policeman asked how many. His face had ash on. It looked like warpaint smeared over an Indian brave in a cowboy film. He was taking a rest with a cigarette.

'How many what?' Ian said.

'How many dead?'

'Well, one,' Ian said. 'A murder. This was all very unexpected.' He thought he'd better explain it like that.

'There's three here. And four next door and three next door but one. We think three, and the cat.'

'Murder,' Ian said. 'About money, not the bombs.'

The policeman replied he might come in a minute. Ian watched while two air-raid wardens and an ambulance man brought out a woman's body on a stretcher under a blanket. He could see her stockings. They had slipped down her legs and were wrinkled and creased near her shoes. It was definitely a grown-up woman, not Doreen. She did not wear stockings like that and the legs were too thick, much thicker than Doreen's, which were slim and quite long. Ian had paid attention to them regardless of how she wouldn't let anyone do anything. This looked like the kind of woman who would play and sing some number like 'Red Sails in the Sunset'. The policeman asked how it was that Ian had a helmet. Ian said it was Mr Chip Shop's.

'A kid of your age shouldn't have a helmet. They're not for kids. Helmets are not toys.'

'It was important. I had to come. He might run. Or go for someone else with the knife. My mother and brother are still there, and Clifford Hill. Clifford couldn't come because there was only one helmet and he's already a bit scared from being by himself in their house at first. His parents went to see *Down Argentine Way*. It upset him to be on his own in their house.'

'Went to sea down Argentine way? Didn't our boys make
the German pocket battleship *Graf Spee* scupper herself in that
area? We had three ships there, smaller than the *Graf Spee*,
but they did the job. This would be HMS *Exeter*, HMS *Achilles*,
HMS *Ajax*. South America? That's a distance. And they left
the boy at home?'

'He had already seen it.'

'What?'

'*Down Argentine Way.* In the Bug and Scratch.'

'Right,' the policeman said. 'I think that's all we'll find
here.' He put his helmet on. They went back through the
lane. The man was still sitting on the bench with the knife
in his hand near the other man on the floor. The policeman
crouched and looked at the body. 'You did it?' he said to the
man on the bench.

The man held out the knife in one hand. Yes, blood, as
Clifford said. The policeman took a handkerchief from his
pocket and wrapped the knife before putting it on the bench.
'Evidence,' he said. 'Did you see what happened?' he asked
Ian.

'Yes. That one on the floor turned his back and—'

'All right,' the policeman said. He brought out handcuffs
and fixed them on the wrists of the man sitting on the bench.
The man let him. He did not fight or struggle or anything like
that. The policeman said he would go back to Larch Street to
tell the sergeant he had to take this man and Ian to the police
station. 'You're a witness, although you're young.'

This was definitely true. 'Yes,' Ian said.

'We were all witnesses,' Mr Bell said.

'Yes, but this boy came to fetch me,' the policeman said.

'I had to stay to protect my wife and the rest,' Mr Bell said.
'This was a matter of sharing risk.'

The policeman said to Ian: 'You and the suspect can both
wait outside now. The raid's over. It's calm. We mustn't have
this fellow frightening the other folk. I don't think he'll run.
He's not the sort. Anyway, in cuffs he'd look like a looter of
bombed houses who's escaped and people would really go
after him. They've heard of looters. They're not at all fond of
looters.'

Ian and the man stood near the words about not being slaves that Ian had written in the cement. The fires in Larch Street were still high enough to light up the message. 'What money?' Ian asked the man.

'Yes, money. It's always about money, isn't it?'

'What is?' Ian said.

'Trouble. Conflict. He found the money in our mother's house when she died. All the money. Behind volumes on the book shelves. That was just like our mother. She wouldn't use banks. She had read about banks going bust in America in 1929. She didn't trust them. Do you know what I mean when I say "going bust"? Collapsing through debt.'

'I was born in 1929,' Ian replied. 'I didn't realize about the banks, though.'

'He knew it – the money store. She was a widow. No will. I believe she didn't make a will because she thought we'd agree to take half each. It would seem natural to her. That money's an inheritance, for dividing, isn't it? This was quite a few years ago. I've only just found him.'

Ian would have guessed from the way he talked that this man's mother was the kind to have volumes and book shelves. Not just for hiding money but for reading and referring to, such as history or *The Practical Home Doctor*, which Ian's parents had at home for splinters or ingrown toe nails. Most likely the man's mother didn't have a maid, though, because she would find the money behind the volumes when she was cleaning and you couldn't tell what she would do then, such as take some of it. But, of course, the maid might be a very honest maid and would dust around the money without pinching any of it.

'But I shouldn't be telling you all this – a kid in a helmet,' the man said. He had a square face with a tiny dark moustache, a bit like Adolf's. You'd think men would shave off that kind of moustache now in the war, or let it grow bigger. He had on the dark coat and most probably good shoes, a white shirt and a tie with silver stripes on red.

'I was the one Mr Bell picked to go. And his wife. We'll get fish and chips later, if there's still time to light up. If not we can go there tomorrow, I expect, including Clifford Hill, because he was with us, and it would not be fair to make him do without, even though he didn't go to Larch Street for the policeman.'

'Even so,' the man said.

'Is he your brother?' Ian asked.

'He took it all. Spent it all. Or he *said* he'd spent it all. That might be just to stop me getting at any of it. You can't tell me that's fair.'

'No, not fair, but stabbing somebody to death is quite serious.'

'The hate came over me.'

'Why didn't you run while I was away fetching the copper?' Ian replied. 'Nobody could have stopped you. They wouldn't have tried, even. They wanted to get rid of you. They'd have been glad. They're all afraid. We're not used to this sort of thing, a raid and then a murder. The two together upset people.'

'Oh, I don't know. Where would I run *to*? What did the constable say – I'm not the sort?'

'You mean you'd be like Cain, after he killed Abel? Fleeing but nowhere to hide?'

'You go to Sunday school, do you?'

'My father needs a sleep in the armchair on Sunday afternoons. I'd say he deserves it, because he's out dredging sand for most of the week. He thought I'd better go to Sunday school so the house was quiet for a while. I got a bit fed up with it, though.' He didn't mention using the collection money for sweets.

'It's quite important to have a father, to help keep the family together.'

'Yes, I know. My father thought we could all get under the kitchen table in a raid, but my mother wanted company, I think. The table had fat legs with curls of wood on them, but they might not have been able to stand it if the house was hit.'

'This part of the city's been targeted, I think.'

'Near the docks and the ammo works,' Ian replied. 'I don't think you live around here.'

'Used to when I was young. Quite often, I come on the tram to see a lady friend. It could be a wedding matter soon. I'll propose.' He laughed and went down on one knee alongside the concrete, his wrists handcuffed together in front of him. It was a kind of joke. He seemed very jolly although he'd just killed his own brother. And had handcuffs on. 'Or I would have – if this hadn't happened. She's a nurse.' He stood properly again. 'But tonight the raid starts before I reach where she lives and I have to get into the shelter here. And whom do I run into? My brother. Luck. Good? Bad?'

Ian thought he was the kind of man who'd say 'whom' like that. 'Known as a coincidence,' Ian said.

'When my brother scooped the money he disappeared. He knew I'd be looking for him. He must have taken a place around here to hide. It's not the kind of district I'd expect him to be in these days – especially when he had that money. I always bring the clasp knife when I come this way to see the lady. Protection.' He frowned and paused. 'Oh, look, sorry, you live here, don't you? I just meant that if I . . .'

'It was an accident we were in the shelter, too,' Ian replied. 'Not enough room under the table when Clifford came from next door. I expect if my father had been at home he would have made us all stay under the table, never mind how crowded it was because of Clifford. Yes, fat legs looking strong, but only wood. It was completely my father's idea – the table. I'd say he's not always very clever. There are often problems in families, aren't there? If the house fell down that table wouldn't be any use. Rubble, bricks – they could smash a table regardless of thick legs. I'm glad we came to this shelter because I saw in Larch Street how a house could just tumble – even a mansion – so much really heavy stuff. Why do you see a lady here if you don't like this part of town any longer?'

'She's still the one I want.'

'What will happen to her now?'

'That's a problem, yes.' He stared at Ian. 'Look, would you take her a note for me? She'd most likely give you half a crown.'

'Have you got a pencil and some paper?' Ian said.

'In the inside pocket of my jacket. A notebook and fountain pen.' He couldn't reach there himself, because of the handcuffs.

'Shall I look?' Ian said.

'You'll have to, and write it.'

Ian put his hand under the two layers of clothes, the overcoat and the jacket and tried to search. He could feel the man's fast heartbeat. But the policeman, pushing a bike and with his helmet on, came back just then.

'What's happening?' he said.

'He wants me to let somebody know what's gone wrong.'

'Let who know?' the policeman said.

'It's a friend. A lady,' Ian said.

'You'd better leave it,' the policeman said. 'You're interfering with an accused. He'll have to be searched, in a proper fashion, according to regulations. I don't want you going through his pockets. You've been helpful. Don't spoil it. I still think it's wrong of you to have a helmet, but we'll forget that. But going through his pockets is a different matter. Very.' He leaned his bicycle against the wall under 'Britons never shall be slaves' and went into the shelter for the wrapped knife. He came out and put it into his saddle bag. Ian gave Mr Bell's helmet back. Ian, the policeman and the prisoner began to make for the police station, the policeman pushing his bike. They had to go back through Larch Street on their way. People were out on the pavements now, looking at the damage, watching the firemen. The frozen water had spread out into the middle of the street. It was difficult to walk. The sharp smell of burning irritated Ian's nostrils like scorched dust. When one group spotted the policeman and Ian with a man in handcuffs they began to shout and shake their fists and spit. One of the women screamed that he must be a dirty looter like she'd read about in the London blitz, and a good job the police had him. 'No, you're wrong, he only murdered his brother for the money,' Ian shouted. 'It was behind volumes, but his brother had an idea he'd find it there because banks collapsed.'

At the police station, the officer told an inspector what had happened in the shelter and in Larch Street. The inspector took a writing pad and said a knifing was still a knifing, on a blitz night or any other. 'This boy can give a witness statement, can he? Then we'll make charges.' He asked Ian his name and address and began to write down details.

That was it: 'charges'. This meant he would have to say in court what he had seen. Although Clifford had been the first to spot the knife, Ian thought he would be the one they'd want to say what happened, because he'd been around to Larch Street as well as in the shelter, and he'd talked with the man who'd be charged. He wanted to ask the man for the name and address of the lady so she wouldn't be left wondering where he was, but they'd taken him to another room to answer questions.

When Ian went home after the police station, his father was there. The train from Newport had stopped a long way from Cardiff station because of the raid and he'd had to wait in it, as Ian's mother guessed. His mother had told him what happened, and Mr Charteris was ratty because they hadn't stayed under the kitchen table, which was his special idea for taking cover when the bombs came. 'Why did you have to go to the street shelter?' he asked Ian's mother. 'We don't have to rely on something for the general public. We have our own way of handling things. Now look at the result. The family's involved in a dirty murder. I spend great efforts keeping our reputation on top, but you wouldn't stay under the table.'

'The one with the knife said he was only visiting. He'd come to see a lady,' Ian replied.

'Yes, I expect he had. I know their sort,' his father said.

'I'm sure you do,' his mother said.

'He has considered a wedding. Their mother had volumes and book shelves,' Ian said.

'Anyway, we're not *involved*,' Ian's mother said. 'We saw it, that's all.'

'It sounds like involved to me,' his father said. 'Our boy at the police station so late. At a police station in the middle of the night! What sort of family has one of their children at a police station in the middle of the night? And instead he could have been at home here decently under the kitchen table. There'll be statements. I've heard of that sort of thing.'

'Mr and Mrs Bell are going to open the shop and we can have free fish and chips,' Ian said. 'Clifford too. I had Mr Bell's helmet.'

'Don't talk to me about fish and chips,' his father said. 'This is a bigger situation than that. It stands to reason that things would have been completely different if you'd stayed under the table.'

'Not completely different,' his mother said. 'There'd still have been the trouble in the shelter.'

'Completely different for *us*,' his father said. 'For *us*. It was because I knew rows about money and a knifing might occur in a public shelter that I told you to go under the table at home in a raid. *We* don't need free fish and chips. We provide for ourselves, thank you very much. Are we going to be beholden to someone who runs a fish and chip shop, not just for free fish and chips but because our son wore his helmet?'

Sometimes, even when a child, Ian thought his father was half mad. Ian's mother would argue that Mr Charteris, despite it all, undoubtedly meant well, and to comfort her Ian pretended he agreed. *Did* agree a bit. 'He means well' was one of his mother's favourite phrases, equal to Ian's dad's 'it stands to reason'. For her sake, Ian would never have replied that, if his father meant well, yet behaved as he did about some things, he must now and then be off his head.

'We didn't *cause* the trouble in the shelter,' Ian's mother said. 'We didn't even take part in it or understand it. We heard of a disagreement about money, that's all. It was private to the two men.'

'Oh, yes, you did take part in it,' Mr Charteris replied. 'Ian went for the bobby and you say he talked to the man – to the murderer himself – outside the shelter, just the two of them. How will neighbours regard that? When they're trying to describe Ian in the future they'll say things like, "You know the boy – the one who had a nice chat with a murderer out in the street while Larch Street burned."'

'I feel sorry for the woman waiting for him off the tramcar. What will she think when he doesn't turn up?' Ian's mother said. 'She'll imagine he's been hurt or killed in the raid.'

'I don't care what she imagines,' he said. 'It's not to do with us.'

'And then she might read about this crime in the newspaper and see his name – see he's been arrested,' Mrs Charteris said. 'This will be *such* a shock.'

'I don't want us mixed up with people like that,' he said. 'That's why I told you to stay under the table, the gas stove nearby for cups of tea.'

When Ian had grown up and looked back at the home situation he could understand something more of his mother's attitude. She had married Ian's father and, because of the money conditions, and the general habit of the time, would be bound to him, regardless. This governed her outlook. And by then Ian knew there might be more for her to put up with than the arguments about the kitchen table. She had to take account of Emily Bass, that trophy saved from the sea by Dad, and who was liable to reappear now and then.

In hindsight, much later, Ian could also see that when his father said 'it stands to reason', he would frequently be referring to a special form of reasoning – his own, based on something ancient. At university, Ian would learn about an old form of debate known as the syllogism. This gave a framework. The two people disputing would each put forward two propositions which could be argued over, but which eventually ought to lead to an agreed solution. Ian supposed his father's thinking had gone like this:

(a) In a public air-raid shelter during a raid there could be all sorts, because it *was* a public shelter. This surely would be agreed on both sides of the debate.

(b) If all sorts went into the shelter some could be good, but some could be very bad and could even have knives. This, also, would have to be accepted as a possibility by the two sides, though not so obvious as (a).

(c) Therefore, conclusion, stay indoors under the kitchen table and hope the house was not hit by a bomb, bringing upstairs and the roof down, and smashing the table and everybody under it. This also had a claim to being sensible. After all, there were a lot of houses and not all that many bombs, so a direct hit could be regarded as uncertain, or *very* uncertain. That meant that the kitchen table rated as a perfect shelter as long as this shelter didn't actually have to shelter anyone.

Ian felt that items in his father's reasoning should have been put in a weighted sack, taken a decent distance and dumped with a good splash in the dock. In retrospect, Ian realized his mother couldn't have risked that attitude, though. She had to concentrate on the times he made some sense, or his choice of her as wife would lose value, wouldn't it? She'd attracted a nut case. Plus, she'd have the prospect of cohabiting with an off-and-on extreme oddball until one of them died. She *did* have this prospect but wouldn't want it defined by Ian, thank you. His mother believed bad things could get worse if you described them. 'Words bring extra' was another of her sayings. She reckoned it came from the Old Testament, but Ian had never been able to find it, not even with a concordance. In fact, he didn't think the word 'extra' appeared anywhere in the Bible. It was not a Bible sort of word.

Anyway, Ian could understand that if you'd been stuck on a train in the bombing it might upset your brain. Also, it could be that his father considered they should have their own individual kind of shelter – the table – not use a public one, or have a shelter similar to everybody else's, because his brother, Ian's uncle Ron, and his family did have an unusual kind of shelter, and Ian's father would not want to get left behind by a brother who was younger. Uncle Ron worked in a docks firm that made sea equipment and he'd turned a big, cast-iron navigation buoy into his air-raid shelter, with a door on hinges cut out of one side. Ian had been in the shelter and thought it great. Voices clanged and echoed. It reminded him of getting into the ark for salvation from the flood in the Bible, though not even iron would give salvation from a direct hit. Also, he considered it a bit like going into Aladdin's cave, without the treasure. He noticed in school that one of the masters seemed very interested when they were talking in class about what difference the war made to civilians and Ian said one thing was his uncle had a buoy against his shed in the garden.

Then, things began to happen to do with the Barton Street shelter that made Ian think his father might not be completely daft and wrong about the kitchen table after all, especially when those rotten postcards started to arrive. The newspapers had heard of the murder and a reporter from the *South Wales*

Echo came to see Ian at home. They had a front door which was half wood at the bottom and half glass at the top, but not clear glass. It had twirly bits in it, so the light came through but anyone on the doorstep could not stare into the house. From inside it was possible to tell the shape of somebody visiting, and you would recognize anyone you knew. If it was a stranger you could see whether it was a man or woman or a kid, but not the face properly. This glass part of the front door had stayed OK during the raid, although some other windows and door panes in the street were blown out by blast, and there'd been pieces of glass on the ground when they ran to the shelter.

They did not know this reporter from the *Echo*. Ian's father was at home because of the tides, and when he heard the knock at the door he came out of the living room into the hall and looked through the door glass to see who was there. Ian followed him, in case it might be a friend calling. He could see from the way his father's back and shoulders seemed to go all stiff that he thought this man outside was bound to be some sort of pest. 'I told you,' he muttered.

'What, Dad?'

'Going out to the street shelter.'

'It might not be about that.'

'Of course it's about that. Have you ever come across this bloke before? Did we ever have blokes of this sort calling here previously?'

'Which sort, Dad?'

'This sort, of course. The way he stands there facing the front door, as if he's got a right to.'

'Well, he's only knocking. It might be collecting for the starving in Africa. If he's calling he has to face the front door in case it's opened and someone in the house asks him what he wants.'

'I know what he wants. People like this, they stare in through the glass as though they think we're all hiding and won't open.'

'Will we?'

'What?'

'Open.'

'Excuse me, but there's no law I heard of that says we have to open to someone staring in,' his father replied.

'No, but will we?'

'Who is it?'

'I don't know, Dad. I can't see him properly.' It was not just the twirly glass making it hard to get a look. His father was standing in the middle of the hall, staring at the door, and Ian had to try to peer around him, past his body.

'There you are then,' his father said.

'What?'

'If it was someone we knew we could tell.'

The man outside crouched a little and put his face against the glass so as to get a better gaze into the house. He knocked again, this time on the glass with his knuckle, not using the proper door knocker.

'There you are,' Mr Charteris said.

'What?'

'The cheek. He thinks it's fine for him to mess us around.'

'He can see we're here, I expect, and he's wondering why we don't open the door.'

'That's what I mean,' his father replied.

'What?'

'Cheek. He thinks because he knocks on the door, and even on the glass, that we've got to jump to open it. This is what happens when you get mixed up with people in a public shelter. I ask you, Ian, what does "public" mean? I'll tell you. It means for anyone and everyone. We got no way to affect that mixture. In the house, under the kitchen table – that's privacy. I have no objection to Clifford coming in as well. He's a neighbour. We couldn't control his parents if they badly wanted to see *Down Argentine Way*. It was just a good, friendly thing to say he could come under the table. Staying there would undoubt-edly be the correct thing to do.'

Ian's mother must have heard the knocking and came out of the kitchen into the hall. 'What is it?' she said.

'I blame you for this,' Mr Charteris said.

'What?' she said.

'Have you ever experienced anything like this before?' he said.

'What?' Mrs Charteris said.

'Knocking first with the knocker, then on the glass. He

doesn't care which,' Ian's father said. 'I've observed his behaviour.'

'Why don't you answer?' Mrs Charteris said.

'Which will be just what he wants,' Ian's father said.

'Well, that's obvious,' Mrs Charteris said, 'or he wouldn't be knocking the door.'

'I won't play his game,' Ian's father replied, 'not at my time of life. In the past, maybe, when I was younger, but no longer.'

The man drew back from the glass and gave a small wave with his right hand, inviting them to come forward and open the door.

'Did you see that?' Ian's father said.

'What?' Mrs Charteris said.

'Like a signal – an order. The way you would call a waiter. I can't believe the neck of it. Most likely he was snapping his damn fingers, but we couldn't hear.'

'He won't be able to understand why we're standing here,' Mrs Charteris said. 'He can probably tell there are three of us, four if Graham comes in from the back garden.'

'Of course he can tell there are three of us,' Mr Charteris said. 'That's why I said "cheek". He thinks he can order us about in our own house – three or thirty-three, he doesn't care; he thinks he's entitled.'

The man bent forward again and this time he spoke through the letter box. 'Hello. Sorry to disturb. Is there an Ian Charteris here? Could I have a word with an Ian Charteris?'

'Ah! Didn't I tell you?' Mr Charteris said.

'What?' she replied.

'This is to do with that shelter, although I'd spoken often to you about the kitchen table,' he said.

'I'm from the *Echo*,' the man said.

'This is disgraceful,' Mr Charteris said.

'What?' his wife said.

'Hunting us down in our own property,' Mr Charteris said. 'This is barging in, the way the Press always does.'

'I thought you liked the Press,' Mrs Charteris replied. 'Your scrap book. The cuttings.'

'This isn't to do with that,' Ian's father replied.

'Of course it isn't,' Mrs Charteris said. She pushed past her husband and opened the door. 'Yes, Ian Charteris is here. What's it to do with, please?' She spoke with her special, refined voice again, so as not to seem pig-ig, even though they hadn't opened the door at once.

'Well, with a murder,' the man said.

'I knew it, I knew it,' Mr Charteris said. He punched the hall dado rail with his fist three times quickly. Ian's mother hated fist work against walls or furniture. She considered it as showing too much excitement, like foreigners, especially in hot countries where people got so steamed they forgot control. She went to the spot on the dado rail and brushed it with her hand, as though to give it comfort or make sure her husband hadn't contaminated it by getting his skin broken open in the blow and leaving blood. 'First, down the police station in the middle of the night, and now this,' Mr Charteris said. 'They want to know everything and spread it. Don't tell me they won't spread it. Why are they called "reporters" if they're not going to spread it? They're going to spread it to people who buy the *Echo*.'

'Spread what, Dad?' Ian asked.

'Oh, yes, spread it,' his father replied.

'Yes, I heard Ian went to the police station so late. That's why I'm here, really,' the man said.

'We're not at all inclined to take this matter further, thank you,' Mr Charteris said. 'We're certainly grateful for the interest shown by you and your paper, but we have decided not to proceed. I believe I've heard of a right to silence, and that's what we wish to apply now.'

'We can't write very much about it, because someone has been charged and it's a matter for the courts,' the man replied.

'Well, that's that then,' Mr Charteris said. 'Thank you very much.'

'But I heard about the police station and going for help in Larch Street,' the reporter said. 'We can describe that. You've got a boy who's a hero. A child braving the blitzkrieg in the best British tradition. It would be nice to have that presented in the paper and kept for all time as a cutting, don't you think? Someone said he was wearing a helmet. Have you got that somewhere? It would make a great picture to illustrate bravery

even at a young age, and defiance of the Nazis. The paper
likes to help with morale of the citizens.'

Ian knew his father would hate to hear someone else in this
family, not himself, described as a hero, and he would dislike
mention of the cuttings because that proved there was a scrapbook. Most probably he'd think Ian might want to use those
empty pages at the end of the book to stick cuttings about
him, Ian, this meaning people would not be able to concentrate
fully on the *King Arthur* incident.

'You're Ian, are you?' the reporter said. 'Aged eleven?'

'Certain matters are definitely suitable for the Press,' Mr
Charteris said, 'but other matters are not. That stands to reason.'

'My name's Cyril Buck. I'm Local News for the paper. Of
course, we reported a lot about you, Mr Charteris, some years
ago, concerning the rescue. You are a family that seems to
give us first-class stories!'

'Yes, those events got some attention in the newspapers, on
a national, as well as a local level,' Mr Charteris said. 'Many
folk still refer to the events of that time.'

'Your son obviously takes after you. I mean for bravery and
determination,' Buck said.

'I don't think of what I did as bravery,' Mr Charteris said.
'I don't care for the word "hero", though it was, I admit, much
used. What I did was necessary, that's all.'

'And perhaps, also, what Ian did,' Buck said.

'It was an unfortunate matter,' Ian's father said.

'In which way?' Buck said.

'They wouldn't normally have been in that shelter at all.
We have private provision, perfectly sufficient.'

'The Anderson?' Buck said. 'Often they flood if the floor
isn't concreted.'

'I don't say public shelters are unnecessary,' Mr Charteris
replied. 'Obviously, people from outside the area might get
caught in the street by a raid, and they should have somewhere
to take refuge.'

'That's what the man with the knife had done,' Ian said.
'Off the tram. The trams could not keep going. Too dangerous.
So this one pulled up near the shelter and the man and perhaps
some of the other passengers and the driver and conductor

went into the shelter.' Ian tried to keep this bit of talk going so his father couldn't have all the conversation to himself, as he loved. Although his body seemed stiff and twisted because of anger the words came out non-stop and smooth. Ian said: 'The man was going to see a lady, but the raid prevented this. Or made him postpone it. But, then, a sudden shock: who's in the shelter but his brother? They didn't seem to know that verse from the Bible, "Let brotherly love continue." I don't even know whether it ever started. Or perhaps they were OK with each other when boys, but then comes this squabble over their mother's money.'

'You'd better come in. It's extremely cold out here,' Mrs Charteris said. The 'extremely' she did very refined – in fact, Ian thought, you could say *extremely* refined. There was a lot of work on the em part of extremely when she said it, like extreeem-mmly. She might have heard someone do it like that in a play on the radio about rich people, or even royalty. Such people would say, 'Extreeemmmly glad to make your acquaintance.'

Cyril Buck took off his hat and stepped into the hall. He was tall and skinny, more than fifty, not young enough for the army, with a big nose that would take up too much space in a submarine. He looked all right for Local News. He had a notebook with the pages held at the top by circles of bright wire. Ian's father didn't get out of the way for him at once, as though he thought it was a mistake to let him into the house – someone who'd been knuckle-thumping the door glass and now talking too much about Ian and not enough about Mr Charteris himself. But then he did shift and they went into the living room. Mrs Charteris made tea. Cyril Buck unbuttoned his overcoat but didn't take it off. A red and blue woollen scarf was around his neck. He sat down.

Buck said: 'The walk through the lane to Larch Street, Ian – that must have been dangerous.'

'I had the helmet,' Ian said.

'If I'd been here, things would have been completely different,' Mr Charteris said. 'I was absent on certain war work and delayed. Pardon me, but we are not allowed to tell of the nature of that work. As the posters say, "Be like Dad, keep Mum" and "Walls have ears", meaning spies.'

'It would have been hard to get five under the table,' Ian said.

'Which table?' Buck said.

'People can panic at stressful times,' Mr Charteris replied. 'A rush out to a public shelter, for instance. It's understandable, I suppose, but to be avoided if possible.'

'We can't write about the actual stabbing,' Buck said, 'because that would be like saying he was guilty, and it's for the court to decide this, although he obviously is. But maybe Ian could just describe all the rest of the evening. This will really interest people. What colour was the helmet?'

'Greyish.'

Buck made a note. 'Did it have "WARDEN" written on it?'

'It was Mr Chip Shop's.'

Buck laughed and wrote this down.

'It's a nickname given by the children, you understand, owing to him having a fish and chip parlour at the end of the street, which you may have observed,' Mrs Charteris said. 'His real name is Mr Bell.' She had a small chuckle, nothing too loud or violent.

'People like Mr and Mrs Bell are all right in a public shelter as local residents, but you can't tell who else might be there, as these events certainly prove. I know there's a war on and things can be rather different from the normal, but just the same,' Mr Charteris said.

'Can you write about the mother who had shelves and volumes?' Ian said. 'Is that not allowed, either?'

'Books are all very well,' Mr Charteris said. 'There's *The Mill on the Floss* or *A Tale of Two Cities*. They're not the be-all and end-all, though, are they? I'm definitely in favour of books and turning pages in succession to one another. They are just a single aspect of matters, however.'

'What were you feeling as you walked through the lane to Larch Street wearing the greyish helmet?' Buck asked.

'Cold,' Ian said.

'But in an emotional sense,' Buck said.

'The smell of burning,' Ian said. 'And sad to see the mansion.'

'Serves him right for building such a big ugly place there,' Mr Charteris said. 'They never mixed.'

'Who?' Buck said.

'The people from the mansion – not with the rest of us around here. And a big wall at the back, like a palace. Snooty. Well, I heard the wall's down now and half the back of the mansion.'

'We have quite a clippings file on the Charteris family in the office,' Buck replied. 'The young woman you saved was from Cardiff, too, wasn't she?' He turned back a couple of pages in his notebook. 'Emily Bass of Marlborough Road, in those days. And there are pictures. Do you ever hear anything of her, I wonder?'

'You wonder, do you?' Mrs Charteris said.

'But most probably she married and has moved away. She was a pretty woman, wasn't she?'

'It depends what you mean by pretty,' Mrs Charteris said.

Ian thought the reporter suddenly seemed to feel he shouldn't have started on talk about the rescue and the young woman. He looked sort of worried and his long face and uncheerful nose made it worse. Ian was sorry for him. Mrs Charteris had become rather snarly, although Ian didn't understand why. There were times when she could become more snarly than refined. He thought it must be a strain for her being married to Mr Charteris, and this was bound to show itself now and then.

Someone else knocked at the door. 'This is really getting beyond a joke,' Mr Charteris said.

'What is?' Mrs Charteris said.

'The upshot,' Mr Charteris said.

'Of what?' Buck asked.

'This is the upshot – all this,' Mr Charteris said, 'people hammering on the door, including the glass part.'

'It'll be Gordon, our pictures man,' Buck said.

'Pictures man?' Mr Charteris said.

'They'll want a photo of Ian for the paper,' Mrs Charteris said.

'I don't think that's at all necessary,' Mr Charteris said.

'Straighten your tie and smooth your hair down, Ian,' Mrs Charteris said. 'People will be interested in him, Laurence.'

'I don't want them interested in him,' Mr Charteris said.

'Are you jealous, or something?' Mrs Charteris said.

'I won't smile, because it's a serious matter,' Ian said.

Mrs Charteris let the photographer in. The reporter told him a short version of Ian's story. 'Where's the helmet?' the photographer said. He was nearly as old as the reporter.

'Yes?' Buck said.

'*Now* do you see what I mean about the shelter?' Mr Charteris said.

'What?' Mrs Charteris said.

'This is, as I said, the upshot,' Mr Charteris said.

'What is?' Mrs Charteris replied.

'This helmet,' Ian's father said. 'They want a picture of him in the helmet for the paper. And you said you were not involved with all that disgusting stuff in the shelter. Do you still think so? If you're not involved why would they want a picture of Ian for the paper? They don't go about taking pictures of people who are not involved. The Press concentrates on those who *are* involved.'

'It won't do any harm,' Mrs Charteris said.

'It will tell the story of his courage,' the photographer replied. 'You've heard that saying, "one picture is worth a thousand words". This picture will illustrate his brave role, despite his age.'

'I'll go over and ask Mr Chip Shop for the steel titfer,' Buck said.

Next evening the *Echo* had a long account of Ian's actions in fetching the constable and going to the police station with him on the night of the raid. A large photograph of Ian wearing the helmet appeared in the middle of the type. Underneath this picture were the words '11-year-old raid hero of Barton Street'.

Two mornings afterwards came the first postcard. It had one word on the back in capital letters – 'SQUEALER' – and no signature. Mr Charteris brought it into the kitchen where Ian, Graham, and Mrs Charteris were sitting at breakfast. Ian's father put the card in front of his wife with that side of it up. She looked at it, then turned it over. It was addressed, also in capital letters, to 'IAN CHARTERIS, POLICE SNEAK, BARTON STREET, GRANGETOWN, CARDIFF'.

'No house number,' Ian's mother said.

'Not needed,' his father said. 'The postman knows who he is and where, because of the damn *Echo*.'

'The paper didn't give the house number, did it?' she said. 'That's why it's not on the card.'

'Not needed,' Ian's father said. 'Didn't I tell you?'

'What?' his wife said.

'Going to the public shelter. There was bound to be an upshot. This postcard is the upshot.'

Ian decided he hated upshots, if this was one.

'It's evil,' she said.

'Brought on ourselves,' Mr Charteris said. 'Brought on *your*self. It wasn't necessary for these things to happen.'

'Oh, tell Hitler it wasn't necessary,' Mrs Charteris said. 'Did I ask him to come bombing? Did I ask him to get those two men into the shelter so one could kill the other?' She turned the card back over with the stamp and Ian's address in view. 'The franking says posted locally,' she said.

'Of course it was posted locally,' Ian's father said. 'This is from somebody who knows the situation.'

'Which situation?' she said.

'Our son with the police.'

'What else could he do?' she said.

'What else could I have done, Dad?' Ian said. 'Someone had to fetch the policeman and then go to the station, because of being a witness.'

'That's it, exactly,' Mr Charteris said. 'What else *could* you do? But you shouldn't have been there at all, and then that question would not be required. There wouldn't have been an else *for* you to do; just sitting quietly under the kitchen table.'

'These capital letters – it's like a ransom note in kidnap films in the cinema,' Mrs Charteris replied. 'It's so tracing is impossible. We can't even tell whether it's from a man or a woman. But we should give it to the police.'

'No more police,' Mr Charteris said.

'Why not?' Mrs Charteris asked.

'We're tangled up in all that enough already. Think of that postman. He can read the card. It's not private like a letter. He talks to his friends about it. The tale spreads everywhere.'

'He'll know it's unjust,' his wife said. 'And so will everyone else.'

'Talk,' Mr Charteris said. 'What do they care whether it's just or unjust. They can gossip about us.'

Over the next week there were three more identical cards, and then another three after Ian gave evidence in the trial. Another three came following the hanging. These were not the same as the earlier ones, though. They said: 'SQUEALER. PROUD OF YOURSELF NOW?'

FIVE

So, these were some of the foundations of Ian's life. A lot rested on them as he grew up. And, of course, there'd be other foundations before he reached his *Mirror* days, his Daphne West and the gas days, and nights, his Suez days. In their turn, his *Mirror* days and the Daphne West and the gas days and nights and the Suez days would themselves become foundations for what followed.

After that little ceremony at Penarth pier, and then the hints and unexplained behaviour of his mother in the jail execution crowd, it was years before Ian had contact with Emily again. Emily née Bass – *rescued* as Bass. It came as a big shock. He didn't recognize her at once, nor she him: after all he'd been a child at the Corbitty memorial. Now he was in his twenties, with a degree, and wearing Royal Air Force uniform. By then – 1952 – there was a new war on. World War Two had finished in 1945 on his sixteenth birthday.

Naturally, Emily had changed, too. At the memorial ceremony she was shy and a bit silly, he'd thought, going on about herself as object of a tragic attempt at rescue by the captain. That had made him sympathize with his father, which didn't often happen. As his father had said – and said twice, Ian recalled – he, Laurence Charteris, had got her out from almost under the *King Arthur*.

He didn't recognize her at once. When they met tonight, she was hosting a party, a routine kind of thing for her, he gathered. She dominated. All shyness had apparently been ditched. In fact – an odd thing to say, a melodramatic, purple thing to say – there were moments when he felt a sort of hidden power reaching out from her, even a sort of sinister, unscrupulous power.

Ian and several of his fellow officer cadets had been invited to the do as part of the social side of their training course. The RAF liked to behave occasionally as a kind of finishing

school for its incoming leaders. They had to be shown how
to behave in off-duty situations. They would get eased up
gently into the officer class. A certain smoothness and polish
were inculcated. Emily circulated and, during some general
chat, she and he had each gradually begun to realize who the
other might be. 'This is terribly strange,' he said, 'but I think
I know you from way back. Aren't you—?'

'You're his son! Laurence Charteris's son! My God!' she
said. 'The wreath! You know, I've still got that hilarious note
in the envelope that went with it. Your father wrote it – so
wonderfully himself!' Ian might not have agreed with the
'wonderfully', but certainly his father was himself. There
wouldn't be much competition from others to be him. She
turned and called her husband over. 'Look who's here, Frank.'

'Who?' he said.

'One of your officer cadets.'

'That much I can see.'

'A special one,' she said.

'Yes?' her husband said.

'His father saved my life,' she said. 'The paddle boats.
You've often heard the tale. Me, full fathom five.'

'Once or twice or twenty times, yes,' he said. 'And the
wreath and the comment with it in the dinky little
envelope.'

'But you must look after this soon-to-be officer,' Emily told
him.

'I look after all of them. Which course are you on?' he
asked Ian.

'White, sir.'

'We always have one of these ice-breaking occasions for
new intakes,' Emily said. 'As commandant, Frank has to get
to know people. But there's never been anything as brilliant
as this before. I should have looked at the list of guests. Your
name would have hit me. What luck! I'm not always here,
you know. I spend some time in London – for my work. But
tonight, here I am. Grand!'

Ian felt buffeted by her gush. It came near to effusiveness,
seemed out of proportion. Perhaps that's what being hitched
to a Group Captain did for her. Yes, some enormous changes

had been made. He wondered what her work might be. Perhaps she'd say in a little while. 'Called up, were you?' she said.

'Yes.'

'Not career RAF?'

'No,' Ian said. 'Two years' conscription.'

'You'll do excellently, I know.'

'Well . . .'

'I *know* you will.'

National Service had arrived for Ian in 1951. He'd just finished his degree. Taking a university course allowed you to delay entry. He'd been drafted into the Royal Air Force Regiment, not aviators but a kind of army division of the RAF, its duties to guard aerodromes. The Regiment might be needed in the Korean War and was expanding fast. To Ian, it seemed more like the infantry than the Air Force. The Regiment bothered a great deal about appearances, liked boot toecaps to be really agleam, and required troops to march with 'bags of swank'. These were not a priority in the rest of the RAF, where a sort of seeming casualness – even a mild, gentlemanly scruffiness – was encouraged among officers. Flying crew killed people from a distance. The Regiment might have to kill people close. Militariness and pride in it were good – part of the mental armoury. A couple of days ago Ian and the rest of his unit paraded with these bags of swank and fixed bayonets one February morning in the nearby town to mark accession of Queen Elizabeth the Second. It was exceptional for troops to march through the streets with fixed bayonets. Accession of a monarch did rate as exceptional.

Ian's officer training for the Regiment took place on an almost abandoned airfield originally laid out in 1940 at the start of the Second World War. Lincolnshire, winter and very cold. And it was now, at this cadet unit, that he bumped into Emily Stanton, who had been Emily Bass and, as he discovered, Emily Something Else in between. She was on her second marriage. Members from all the training courses were invited in at some stage to meet the commanding officer and, perhaps, his wife, for a session of civilizing drinks and conversation in the Mess.

Group Captain Frank Stanton, the CO, and Emily circulated separately, chatting to their young guests. Grinning, affable,

assured, she'd approached Ian almost at once: 'Excuse me.
I've made a bit of a beeline for you. Please don't take fright.
I heard your accent when you spoke to one of your friends
just now. Cardiff?'

'I thought I'd got rid of it.'

'Why should you? I haven't. But some despise it, I know.
Caaardiff, as it's said. And the famous rugby ground, Caaardiff
Aaarms Parrrk.'

'You're Cardiff?'

'Marlborough Road. You?'

'We moved to Barton Street from Hunter Street.'

'Hunter Street,' she muttered. This second address seemed
to intrigue her, make her a bit breathless for a second. At that
stage he still didn't understand. She pursed her lips and slightly
frowned, as if doing some kind of quiet calculation. 'Look,'
she said, 'I was famous in Cardiff and thereabouts for a while.'

'Yes?'

'You'd have been a whippersnapper at the time – about four
or five.'

'Famous for what, please?' he said.

She seemed to become devious. 'Do you know the pier at
Penarth?'

'Of course. It's still there.'

'And the passenger steamers in the Channel?'

'The *King Arthur* and the *Channel Explorer* for instance?'
He gazed at her and began to snigger as the realization and
recognition came gradually to both of them. She'd called to
her husband. A smile stayed on her face but her eyes popped
in astonishment. 'Hunter Street. Oh, Lord! So, the service will
have to promote you to squadron leader at once.'

'At least,' her husband said.

'Right – on a two-year stint, are you Officer Cadet Charteris?'
She spoke in a mock military voice. 'National Service used
to be only eighteen months, didn't it? But now there's Korea.'

'Yes,' Ian said.

'Might you sign on for a longer career with the RAF at the
end of your time?'

'I don't think so.' He'd been thinking about newspapers,
journalism.

'You'd be, what, twenty-two, three?' Emily said.

'Two.' She must be just over forty, he thought, still slight. Her hair had darkened slightly from when he last saw her pictures, but it had no grey, or no visible grey. Although she'd had a drink or two and was slightly flushed, her skin looked unlined. She had a round, lively face and friendly but unfoolable pale blue eyes.

'Yes, about five when it all happened – the two ships?' she said. 'And later you were one of the stars at the memorial service with the wreaths, weren't you? And are you Korea bound?'

'Darling, he wouldn't know that. Nobody knows that at this point in their training,' Stanton said.

'Married? Girlfriend?'

'Girlfriend. Rather off-and-on.' Yes, his relationship with Lucy had its deep, recurrent difficulties lately.

'Does she understand you might be sent to Korea?' she asked. 'Is that what puts her off?'

'I'm not sure what it is,' he said.

'Did Emily tell you she actually still has the envelope and note?' the group captain asked.

'Do you remember it, Ian?' she said.

Of course he remembered it. His father's personality was in those farewell words – lively, unforgiving, inventive, effortlessly cantankerous and mean. But somehow Ian felt he should act dumb. 'A note with the wreath?'

'You and the other children threw wreaths into the sea from the pier to commemorate Captain Corbitty. You've forgotten? But you were only a lad. It's a long time ago.'

'I think I recall the wreath. Not the note. Would I have looked at it?'

'The wreath didn't drift far. It was washed up at Penarth on the next tide,' she said. 'Someone recovered it from the beach and must have realized where it came from. Most people in Penarth knew about the memorial ceremony. The message in the envelope was rather disrespectful, even cruel.'

'Oh? Who on earth would write something like that?' Ian said.

'I think the man who found it wondered if *I'd* written it,' she said. 'He must have thought the newspapers would be interested and told the *Western Mail*. They sent a reporter over to get the thing from him and then came out with it to where I was living then with my first husband. We had a flat not far from my parents' house in Marlborough Road. The memorial organizers had my address. The reporter must have got it from them. This newshound kept asking if I'd written the words and, if not, did I know who had? Did I recognize the handwriting? I said I hadn't and I didn't. He saw I wouldn't shift and said I could keep the envelope and its contents.'

'It's prized, I can tell you,' Stanton said. He moved off to talk to some of the other cadets.

'The reporter suggested that if I hadn't written the less than fond goodbye he supposed your dad, Laurence Charteris, must have. But that wouldn't make a news story, because it would appear malicious and petty and backbiting. They couldn't publish something that might diminish a hero.'

'Well, yes,' Ian said, 'I suppose it would have done that.' 'Malicious.' 'Petty.' 'Backbiting.' These were terms which would suit his father from time to time. Or more often. *Hi, Dad, I recognized you instantly.*

'It troubled me, that poisonous adieu. It was from somebody hurt and resentful. I thought, yes, possibly your father.'

'Oh, surely not,' Ian said.

'Possibly,' she said.

'I can't believe it.'

'The sight of that non-eulogy – anti-eulogy – in the envelope made me realize I'd been rather offhand about the rescue. Someone – Captain Corbitty – had died for me, and I think that became an enormous, engulfing idea in my head. Possibly rank came into it. I might have been impressed – stupidly impressed – because a ship's master had tried to save me, the captain of a vessel. Your dad – only a crewman. It was a disgusting attitude. My life had depended on your father. That was the positive side of the incident, and perhaps the more important. No two ways about it, I'd been foolish. I knew I'd better get in touch with Laurence again. Make it up to him, show I wasn't really someone bamboozled by rank – and by a death.'

'Get in touch with him? Did you?'

'I decided I had to thank him properly, put things right. I actually hung about in Hunter Street one day until I could nab him on the quiet. He was astonished to run into me there. I had to do it, though.'

'I didn't know about this,' Ian said.

'No, nobody did, except your father and me.'

God, what was she saying? She'd 'nabbed' him. What the hell did *that* mean? 'Oh, I see,' he replied.

'I didn't want my then-husband asking a lot of unhelpful questions, did I?'

'Unhelpful?'

'That sort of thing. Negative. Possessive.'

'I see.'

'And your father would have been careful not to speak of it at home, I imagine.'

'I expect so.'

'It would have been awkward. Unnecessary. But there were bound to be unique feelings between Laurence and me, weren't there? A bond, formed first in that grubby Penarth sea. There aren't many such bonds, you know.'

'Did Dad say he'd written the abusive cheerio, when you'd nabbed him on the quiet?'

'How is he?' she replied.

'Dad? He's fine.'

'Good. That first marriage broke up and then I met Frank towards the end of the war.'

'Broke up?'

'We had certain serious differences. That can happen in a marriage and I began this Service life, trying to fit it in with my own career.'

'Which is?'

'Government work, mainly in London. It's interesting, perhaps important.'

'A civil servant?'

'Government work, yes.'

'And have you any children?' he asked.

'In the RAF you never know when the next posting will come, nor where to,' she replied. 'As you may discover! Eventually, it became impossible to keep in touch with

Laurence.' She amended this familiarity: 'With your father. The demands of my own job, which could be quite severe, and then Frank's also.'

'No, I can see that.' This nabbing and the watery bond had caused Ian a bit of thought, and might have produced a startling revelation. 'Tell me, were you in a jail crowd at an execution in 1941?' he asked.

'I'd heard about the murder from your father, naturally, and read the papers. I thought he might have attended because of your connection – chance of an extra meeting. There had been some cherished interludes. I hope you'll look kindly on this unique closeness. There were times when I felt carried back to those moments under the surface near the paddle steamer and I'd see your father through the murk of the sea there and his hand, sure of itself, precise in its exercise and determined, reaching for the shoulder of my jacket to pull me up into the air, his face bold, certain of triumph. Yes, yes.' She seemed to de-trance herself. 'But it was your mother with you at the prison gates, wasn't it?' she said.

'And did she know you were . . . that you'd been in this special . . . this special, well, in touch with Dad?'

'My pictures had been in the Press, of course,' she said. 'Your mother would have seen them, I expect.'

'Dad has the cuttings. I think she spotted you and wanted to leave at once.'

'Yes? Well, obviously, I have to recognize that she might have heard rumours. These tales take on a kind of abounding strength and self-perpetuation, don't they?'

'What kind?'

'There'll almost always be gossip, won't there, Ian?'

'I was puzzled at the time,' he said. 'And disappointed, I think – pulled away suddenly from that jail-gate gang for I didn't really know what reason. I'd been getting lionized. I was a sort of exhibit, the one who'd made this occasion at the prison possible.'

'But I don't want you to assume Laurence – your father – was the cause of my divorce.'

'Your divorce? Certainly not.'

'Career pressures as much as anything. I'd done some

Government Service exams and tests and to my astonishment passed first place for my intake. All right, I think I'd always known I was reasonably bright, but this – well, imagine! I'd left school at fourteen, no college, yet I could come out top in a quite tricky lot of papers. I was offered a very desirable and demanding job. I grew up. Home life suffered. I'm still a consultant there, but am able to pick and choose when I work. That's necessary because Frank might get a posting to some far-distant spot.'

'Consultant where? Which part of Government Service?'

'I still feel for . . . I still feel very obligated to your dad,' she replied. 'Isn't it inevitable? And, of course, I'll do everything – shouldn't say this, should I? – but I'll do everything I can for you here, although I'm only the CO's missus, not the CO, and quite often his missus *in absentia*. It's a kind of contact with Laurence, isn't it – I mean, via you?' This time she let the name stand, the name she'd known him by. 'That's precious to me, even so long after.' She touched his arm very briefly. 'Now, I fear I must talk to some others. I have my duties! I'll drop you a note through your pigeon hole in the Mess if I have any further thoughts.'

'Well, thanks. But you mustn't inconvenience yourself.'

'I'll enjoy helping. I'm away a fair bit, but I should be able to make sure things go well for you.' She put two fingers to her closed lips, signalling that she shouldn't say or do this, but had said it, and said it twice, and would try to do it.

He considered it would be wisest not to tell his parents he'd run into Emily Stanton, née Bass, here. Old resentments might surface again in his mother.

SIX

I t wasn't quite cold enough to freeze the mud in the trenches up near the control tower. Trenches? These dimples in the ground hardly deserved the word, Ian thought: nothing like those deep, lived-in networks of the First World War he'd read about as a kid and seen sepia pictures of. There had been a song still around when Ian was a child making fun of the exceptional care for their own safety shown by some officers and non-commissioned officers at the front. It went:

If you want the sergeant major, I know where he
*   is, I know where he is;*
If you want the sergeant major, I know where he is,
*   I know where he is.*
If you want the sergeant major I know where he is:
He's down in the deep dugout.

It was a simple melody playable on that pocketable, popular Great War instrument, the harmonica. The tune might owe a bit to that nursery song about 'the big ship Ally Ally Oh'. But move forward a quarter of a century to another World War, the Second, and there'd been no deep dugouts for sergeant majors to hide away in during bombardments. In 1940, troops sent to guard this airfield from possible Nazi invaders had been hurried and careless about the digging. Blockhouses on the perimeter were supposed to stop the enemy. If they got this far, it would be only a matter of holding them for a couple of minutes so the tower could be sabotaged and evacuated. These basic, two-man, shallow ditches were considered enough for that kind of token defence. Most likely the walls had started to crumble before the spades were out.

Move forward again. The Second World War is over, too. The airfield and its accommodation blocks have been trans-formed into this Officer Cadet Training Unit (OCTU). Now a couple of months into his National Service, Ian already spends most of the time thinking far, far ahead to his release date, and to days and nights with Lucy Armitage again. Also, of course, to a job where he would not have to wear boots and linger in mud. Especially tonight he kept thinking about both good aspects of the future.

But there was this other war under way, though distant. And so there was the Korea call-up. Although the Lincolnshire airfield no longer needed defending even notionally, airfields in that new, distant war might. Ian and the rest were here to learn how to do it. Tonight's mock battle might help show them. Some graduating officers would get sent to the war; the RAF Regiment's job to keep installations secure so the aircraft would have somewhere to take off from and come back to. Korea was rough terrain – a lot tougher than Lincolnshire, but Lincolnshire would have to do for this training exercise.

Very little worth securing still existed on the OCTU airfield. It was a learning centre, a kind of outdoor academy. The control tower did remain and was manned off-and-on in case of fog diversions, but an aircraft putting down here in 1952 was an event, and then only small machines – an Anson or Tiger Moth: nothing operational since 1944, apparently. Instead, for six or seven years, in day exercises, night exercises, camouflage exercises, consolidation exercises, counter-attack exercises, the trainee officers had churned up the bottoms of these minor dents in the clay that Ian and the rest occupied tonight. In the winter, there would always be several inches of cold, thick mud to engulf your boots, smear and kill their gleam, and strike through to your feet, except when it had iced over hard. A driving, large-flaked blizzard blew across the field now and the trenches stayed gluey.

White Course, with Officer Cadet Ian Charteris in charge for this exercise, must play-act the backs-to-the-wall British, hanging on to an airfield menaced by enemy ground troops. Green Course, under OC Raymond Bain, were the attacking North Koreans, who wanted the field and the planes if possible, but, in any case, to put the airstrip out of use as a bomber base. Ian knew he and Bain were probable main contenders for the Sword of Honour – top cadet award – at the end of training. Bain might be a little ahead and a victory tonight could clinch it. He'd done brilliantly in orienteering and small-arms and rifle tests on the range. By custom, each Sword of Honour graduate stayed on here at the OCTU for a spell, to help train new intakes. It sounded a very nice, comfortable and safe number. Nicer and more comfortable and safer than Korea. In fact, though, almost anywhere would be more comfortable and safer than Korea. If Ian missed on the Sword and got Korea he would go, naturally. No option. He wasn't sure what Lucy's attitude would be. Emily Stanton had wondered, too. Perhaps any woman would wonder about the impact of such a long separation and such intercontinental mileage. Of course, officers shouldn't have these selfish, unsoldierly thoughts. Most officers probably did, though, and especially officers who were only officers because they'd been drafted.

'As a matter of fact, the snow and wind tonight make it more authentic, you see, valuably more,' the Wing Commander said with filthy enthusiasm when someone wanted the exercise ditched because of conditions. 'Damned harsh climate, Korea. No picnic. You need to get the feel of a place where it's no picnic. Absolutely. A mistake to imagine your time in the Service will be a picnic. If some of you are sent out there you'll look back and thank us at the OCTU for running this little show in less than perfect weather. Oh, yes. Acclimatizing. Hardening.'

White Course took up guard and resist posts in front of the tower at half-past seven and it was now just after nine. They'd heard nothing from the enemy all night. Green had until ten o'clock to make and complete their attack, taking five White Course prisoners how they liked, and removing them as hostages. Ian would have expected Green to get their assault over quickly, so everyone could scoot back to the warmth of the Mess bar. But, of course, *they* were not deployed and immobile, their feet gripped and chilled by mud. They had the excitement of their scheduled onslaught to keep them warm. They would be moving about. But *where* would they be moving about? Anywhere, and invisible so far.

Harry Nelmes, alongside Ian in the miniature trench, said

Green must hope the stretched suspense would get at White's nerves. It was typically Oriental: subtle, patient, attritional. And Ian thought, yes, and if the rest of their plan was as effective as this, they'd as good as won. No talking. No smoking. 'This is war,' said the Flight Lieutenant umpire, on a quick tour of White's positions. 'You must maintain that reality. You don't advertise your positions by chit-chat and tobacco glow. The enemy is redoubtable, ruthless, alert to any signs of relaxation in your unit, Charteris.'

Which reality? This was Lincolnshire. In the nearby town of Grantham, there were well-stocked, traditional-style shops run by people with traditional-style British names, like Roberts, Tomkins, Hardcastle. Korea was Korea, and possibly twice as awful, with the enemy knowing the land better than you. But the minor awfulness of Lincolnshire winter would do, thanks. Ian and Harry took it in turns to watch across the airfield. Nelmes had the duty now. Looking that way, you took the wind and snow in your face, and after a few moments' vigil, hostile, swirling devilkind seemed to be galloping at you, white on White. It reminded him a little of those smoke-swathed figures in the public air-raid shelter in 1941. But they'd been real. So far, charging warriors here were figments brought on by weather-driven optical illusion.

Crouched for shelter against Harry's feet, Ian wondered how Green would go about the actual rough physical business of getting their prisoners. He felt a bit weakened, worn down, by the cold, by girl-lessness, by dawn reveilles, and might not be much good if it came to hand-to-hand stuff. The trouble was that, even if you spotted the attack early enough, and let off all your blanks in roughly the right direction, the umpire didn't say who'd been killed until afterwards. By then, anything bruising and worse could have happened. Bain played prop-forward for a rugby club somewhere, and for the OCTU, and knew about intelligent thuggery.

Half-past nine nearly. Harry and Ian changed over. Thick snow crusted Nelmes' helmet and forehead and the shoulders of his greatcoat. Ian sighted his rifle into their arc of fire and the moisture where his elbow rested seeped through to the skin. The cold hurt him between the eyes and he started seeing things again. Occasionally the wind dropped and in the spell of near quiet he heard the gentle, moist amassing of snow on soil, and then on snow, a friendly, wholesome sound and a credit to Nature, but not one he thrilled to, and, really, only pleasant if you knew you'd be getting out of it soon.

And, suddenly, this subdued pitter-patter was drowned. Out of the white-dotted darkness came the raw blare of music: a jangling, combative din from some hugely amplified band and a woman vocalist, careering up and down the octaves without mercy. At first, Ian couldn't decide where it came from. Green had a wind-up gramophone with them, instead of the standard Bren? In a minute, though, he realized it must be roaring from the tower amplifier. This pointed out over the runways to sound a warning hooter for landing pilots who'd forgotten to get their undercarriage down. It had to be loud enough to register over engine noise. Someone had connected a record player to it.

The music seemed oriental – shrill, full of wailing and sing-song words from the vocalist. Obviously shocked and panicked by it, one White Course cadet in the trenches loosed off five blanks rapid, probably directed any old where. Ian did an all-round hard gaze, suspecting a diversion. Nothing came, only the blizzard.

It lasted three or four minutes and then the music stopped. A weird sort of laugh followed over the loudspeaker. 'What is it?' Harry Nelmes asked.

'A ploy.'

'What ploy?'

'Listen,' Ian said. 'Stay watchful.'

Someone started to speak in place of the music. The voice was male, disguised by an assumed, Far-Eastern, comic accent, but Ian thought he identified Bain from Green, commander of North Korea's foray team: 'You out there, poor bloody Blitish Tommies? In the snow storm and the dark we sneaked past your trenches. We clever tloops. We winning tloops. We in tower. You hear me OK, yes? We going fight you, give you nasty time if you don't surrender now. Hurry, please, to capitulate. We will see white flag, even on snow-white background. We would like to be kindly to you, oh, yes. War can be honourable. But war can also be velly savage. Oh, yes to that, too. No chance at all is what you have. You all nervous in cold? Tligger happy, yes? Bang, bang, bang. You velly fed up? Me have idea for your boss, OC Ian Charteris. All Tommies come here, be captured, yes? Velly, velly easy, yes? Leave guns behind. Hands in air. Hanky for that aforespoken of white flag. We not cold, not miserable. Having party in here. Plenty rum, plenty whisky. Party in dark because we have girls, too.' Ian heard a little scream and giggle, which might have been one of the canteen staff. 'You come see, give up before White nuts freeze off, OK?'

From somewhere out in the dark the umpire bellowed: 'Look here, Green, that's all very well, but I don't think we can accept this sort of ruse. Not legitimate. Not at all in the proper spirit of things. It makes the exercise absurd. You must see that.'

'All fair in love and war, yes? Old Blitish saying, I thlink. Must win. No good coming second. In war the ones who come second come nowhere at all. Sorry you White men can't attend party. Have something for you velly special.'

No one answered. Ian whispered to the next trench a command for absolute silence from White and maximum readiness and observation. 'Pass the message.' Green were not the only ones who could do subtlety and patience, the bastards. He felt quite good now. He and his boys would show that famous British – Blitish – resolve.

The loudspeaker crackled, then talked to White again: 'Letter here for OC Harry Nelmes from Angela, very sentimental, velly, velly intimate, velly, velly rude and lewd. One for OC Bernard Colley from Delphine, even ruder and lewder and with drawings.'

The umpire yelled: 'Damn it, you've stolen some of White's post from Mess pigeon holes, Green. Outrageous, contemptible, un-officer-like, *so* dishonourable. Such tactics cannot be valid. This would never happen in a true Korean setting. Not even such an enemy would stoop to that – akin to poisoning the wells.'

'Final notice from hire-purchase company for OC Wilson,' the loudspeaker replied. 'Several letters here, yes. Velly bad

mistake. Somehow, yes, somehow handful of White letters go
to Green for last few days. Often very poor postal service in
Korea, I will admit. Many mix-ups and wrong letter boxes –
or pigeon holes. Your great author, Anthony Trollope, worked
for Blitish post office and made things run so velly sweetly.
And it is still so. No Anthony Trollope in Korea so far. And
so bad system. Here is unkind "Dear John" farewell letter for
OC Ian Charteris from Lucy. Really sad. I call it "Dear John"
letter because that what goodbye letter from girl to Tommy at
Front always called, I believe. But, of course, it is "Dear Ian".
Begins like this: "Dear Ian, I have something serious to say."
Oh, yes, velly serious. Velly final. And so sad.

'But not everything for him too bad. Here another note for
OC Ian Charteris. Velly high-quality paper. Some pricey scent
on? No stamp or flanking on envelope. It says, "Grand to see
you. I'm sure I'll be able to help in some way. I must." Signed,
E. Just E. I wonder who is E? Help him how?'

Nelmes was out of the trench running towards the tower, a
good, swift, stylish run for this kind of ground, but also,
somehow, desperate and panicky. Through the pelting snow,
Ian made out Colley as he caught up with him and overtook,
despite Nelmes' elegant pace. Colley kept yelling, 'Surrender!
Unconditional. Give me my fucking letter, Green.' Ian couldn't
free himself from the mud at once. It sucked lovingly at his
boots, tugged at them as with a special form of gravity far
outside Newton's scope. Disgracefully, he stuck the muzzle
of his rifle down into the single hardish part of the trench floor
so the gun took most of his weight like a crutch, pulled one
foot free and then the other and joined the rush, the barrel of
his weapon useless, stuffed with muck, probably a court-
martial offence in real battle conditions.

SEVEN

And Lucy *did* have something serious to say. Once the formalities of victory by Green had been completed and the 'prisoners' listed, Bain released the letters in a touching little procedure, like dishing out rations to the starving. Ian saw from the postmark that Bain must have liberated his from the pigeon holes a week ago. Just for forward planning this lad might deserve the Sword. Ian felt too tired and fed up to read her letter tonight. He knew the bleak gist of it already. Thanks, Ray.

Next day, after morning parade, there was an Equipment Indenting lecture: how to order new blanco, new light bulbs, new bedding, new ammo, new French knickers for Women's Royal Air Force girls. The specialist Equipment Flight Lieutenant giving the lecture said the buttons-under-the-crutch knickers had saved more man hours than any other innovative piece of gear in the Service. After this, the session faded into dullness. Half of White Course slept, but Ian spread Lucy's letter out on his thighs under the lecture room desk and, before sleeping himself, absorbed most of the message. She said that in her view things between them had become too difficult – he far away in the OCTU, she preoccupied at the start of a newspaper career. It was Lucy's feature-writing job that had made Ian think about journalism for himself when he left the RAF. She believed they should both recognize these problems and end their 'understanding'. The relationship had become complicated and uncertain. He might be sent abroad soon. He didn't know what job he'd try for when demobilized. It would be better if they finished. He dozed but in half-waking moments thought she might be right. Perhaps things *were* too complicated and uncertain. Some aspects of a relationship could be simplified and improved at the same time, as with the knickers buttons. But only *some* aspects of a relationship.

He had invited Lucy to the passing-out parade next week,

when he'd collect his commission, maybe even the Sword of Honour, though he doubted that after the capitulation of White Course in the snow. Bain had shown he knew life was going to be no picnic and had toughened up and developed his no-rules warfare techniques to suit. Lucy's letter added that, in view of her changed feelings, and because of the distance and the time off work required, she would *obviously* not be coming. That *obviously* really hit him. As North Korea's Ray Bain had said in his airfield statement, the letter made things 'very final'. The *obviously* meant there'd be no point in arguing, pleading, replying. The letter was already a week old, anyway, so the time for an urgent answer had most likely gone.

In the Mess bar a couple of evenings later, Ray Bain approached Ian and asked if they could have a private chin wag for a few minutes. They took their beers to a corner table. Bain said: 'I've been thinking, Ian. Maybe the umpire was right and I went too far.' He was red-haired, plump faced and generally mischievous looking, chirpy, strongly put together, as a prop forward had to be. Now, though, he did seem regretful, a heavy frown in place, his eyes not meeting Ian's much.

'"All's fair in love and war", you said, Ray.'

'Yes. Oh, I think snaffling some of the letters was OK, only a sort of jape really, though the brass here might not think so. But, whether they do or not, broadcasting that brush-off from your girlfriend – poor, very. Harsh. Beyond the decent and playful. And then there's E. Is E of the distinguished notepaper who I think she is? How did you manage it? Blimey, Ian, that's some conquest, and so quick. Will the Group Captain come gunning for you? Anyway, that tactic of ours the other night, it was not "in the proper spirit", as the umpire said.'

'Well, what Lucy wrote would have been a kick in the guts whether it got pumped out over the airfield or read in private. Don't scourge yourself, Ray. You were only the messenger – amplified.'

'It was serious with her, was it?'

'I thought so.'

'I'm sorry,' Bain replied. 'Really, I am. Very wrong to have treated it flippantly.' He brightened, grew positive, constructive, more like Bain. 'Look, Ian, I know an address down in the town where there are some really sweet, cheery girls. OK, they're not Lucy, and not E, but they *are* nice. Why don't we get along there together tomorrow evening? I'll pay. I want to make some recompense. I should, after all that. You're not tied up with E tomorrow, are you?'

'What sort of address?'

'Really pleasant girls. They take an extremely favourable view of the camp, think of themselves as unofficial staff. Obviously, it's an all-ranks place, but some of the girls prefer officer cadet material.'

'Well, yes, I expect so.'

'They're familiar with cadets' troubles – love troubles and others. One of those girls, or perhaps more than one, will help you forget Lucy for a while. No strings. They understand they mustn't ever try to get in touch. They know we'll soon be officers, and that some matters must stay confidential.'

'Not broadcast.'

'Are you on?'

'I'm a free man.'

'Yes, I'll look after the money side.'

'I meant I'm free to look around.'

'Of course you are. Great. I'll see to everything. Everything. I feel a lot easier in my mind now.'

'Whiter than white?'

'That kind of thing. You know your way around the unit's Free From Infection facility, do you? The Service thinks of everything, doesn't it?'

In the middle of the following week, Ian had another letter from Lucy. This time he collected it for himself. She said in her bold, big handwriting that she admired *unstintingly* the dignified way he had reacted to her previous, possibly unkind letter. 'No, not just *possibly* unkind, Ian, *undoubtedly* unkind.' His silence and refusal to whine or protest or wheedle in reply had touched and impressed her, as they would have impressed any discerning woman. She thought of him now as 'really quite noble'. It would be absurd, even unpatriotic and cheap – despicable – to cast him off merely because he had to serve the country. After all, he hadn't volunteered. He'd been conscripted. It would be unjust to punish him for that. She'd like to go back on what she said previously. It had been thoughtless and negative. 'Please forget it, Ian. *Please.* I send all my love. And I'll be there to see you strut at the pass-out parade. Yours ever, and I mean it, Lucy xxx.'

He thought this letter pretty good. She put her excuses in a clear, convincing fashion. She'd probably make a very good feature writer for the women's page in one of the main newspapers.

Later that day he was called in to see the Adjutant, Training. He sported a Distinguished Flying Cross and two bars ribbon, white with diagonal purple stripes plus two silver circles for the second and third awards. 'Sit down, Charteris,' he said. 'The news is good. Congratulations! In the normal run of things you'd have taken second place on the passing-out list to OC Bain of Green. Strictly, as to workaday points tally, he leads. If this were the army he'd undoubtedly get the Sword. We do things differently, though. We try to look beyond mere totted-up achievement marks. We think of the spirit of the Service, the character of the Service, its . . . well, yes . . . its aura. Part of Bain's score comes from Green's extremely dubious victory in the war exercise. When I say "extremely dubious" I don't mean that the victory itself was not won. But it is the method that's in question. While, mathematically, Bain is out ahead, we don't feel he has abided by the standard gentlemanly, fair-play requirements of an officer, and – here is the chief matter – definitely not of an officer who gains the Sword, and who will return to instruct new courses of cadets in the ethos of leadership, its deeper nature, as well as its practicalities, which we certainly do not undervalue.

'But we have a certain discretion in making the award, and a certain wider responsibility. The Group Captain has thought it over and considers, on reflection, that it would be quite wrong to allow Bain to succeed, in the circumstances. Quite wrong. In the circumstances. We would be rewarding sharpness and mere trickery – rewarding, in fact, disorder masquerading as supreme competence. That would not – cannot – do, Charteris. You, therefore, are our Sword of Honour man. Congratulations!' He came from behind his desk. Ian stood. They shook hands.

'Thank you, sir,' Ian said.

'There's a wisdom and remarkable far-sightedness to the Group Captain. A splendid ability at taking the overview.'

'I hope I deserve them.'

'I'm sure you do, absolutely sure you do. The Group Captain has a brilliant eye for future leadership talent – embodiments of that ethos I spoke of. You're National Service, I know, but do you ever think of signing on for a full RAF career?'

'Probably not, sir.'

'Pity. Some people do very well, you know. A good Service spell can put you in touch with all sorts. I was on a night fighter station with a chap called Townsend, Peter Townsend. Before you could say "Six-Oh-Five Squadron" he was equerry to the King, deputy Master of the Household. All right, you'll identify a touch of flunkydom about all that, but these are not posts on offer at the Labour Exchange. Think about it, do.'

The Adjutant went back to his desk. He spoke confidingly now, like a worldly uncle. 'To other, more personal matters. I was sorry to hear about the finale letter from your girlfriend. My wife, too, felt a great deal of sympathy when some of her chums mentioned it. The unpleasant news has spread, as you'd expect.'

'Broadcast, sir.'

'Yes. The umpire heard it all, of course. But my wife asked me to tell you not to be too upset. "There are other fish in the sea." Those were her exact words: "There are other fish in the sea." And that's true, in my experience.'

'I think so, sir.'

'The town here is not without interest. But, clearly, one should be aware of risks – be aware of them, but not squashed by them.' Ian thought of the DFC and the bars. They'd have come from managing risk, though not the kind of catch-a-packet or crabs risk he meant now. 'This is *me* speaking for the moment, not my wife,' the adjutant said. 'One must be careful and . . . well . . . basically alert, in a corporeal sense. But these are things that can be seen to, given a little forethought.'

'Yes, sir.'

'Good. You understand. You won't have told her about

the . . . well, the publication of her letter in that rather improper fashion? Perhaps you are no longer in touch, which would seem to be the result of such a letter.'

'No, I haven't told her.'

'Good. Nothing to be gained by it.'

'There's been a further letter, sir.'

'Ah. From Lucy? I have her name right, have I? Did someone mention an E, also?'

'My girlfriend is Lucy, yes,' Ian replied.

'Ah! Making everything fine again, I suppose?'

'Yes.'

'I did wonder, of course. The time-span. Weeks. They can be like that, especially if confronted by silence. They find silence very unnerving. They like to hear a cry of pain. This confirms to them they have behaved properly. If it doesn't come, they start worrying, reacting. They wonder whether the man they've cut off really *wanted* to be cut off, and hasn't replied to the cutting-off letter in case she takes pity on him and reinstates things. So, they think they'd better reinstate things, anyway, because they only wanted to cut him off if it smashed him up for a while being cut off.'

'Women?'

'I don't say they're sadistic. Not all. There's Mother Theresa and Mary Magdalene. But most women long to be prized, and causing hurt to a man proves to the dears they have status and power. Did you give her some silence? Wise. Panic in them follows. They're so changeable. I'll tell my wife. She'll be pleased. Not surprised.'

After the passing-out parade there was a drinks and snacks party in the Mess for newly commissioned officers, their visitors and camp staff. Postings were listed on a board outside the Mess. At the start of proceedings, Ian had received the Sword from an air-vice-marshal, here to preside at the cavalcade. Ian led the march past. He reckoned he did the difficult salute with his Sword reasonably all right, and kept his stride moderate so short-arses behind could stay in step.

In the Mess now, Ray Bain came over to talk to Lucy and Ian, Lucy tall, composed, hard-headed, at ease with everyone, and closer to being beautiful than at any time Ian could

remember. Of course, he realized he might value her looks
more now because he'd almost lost her. The Adjutant and his
wife probably had things blandly wrong. There were *not*
plenty of fish in the sea, not like Lucy, anyway. He'd been
able to give her the big ignoral treatment only by accident:
Bain had sat on her letter for a week. Ian didn't think he
could have stayed unresponding if the get-lost letter hadn't
got lost like that, or held up. Didn't Hardy build half his plot
in *Tess of the D'Urbervilles* on a letter that failed to get to
someone on time? If Lucy's letter had reached him the day
after posting, he would have felt he had to argue, even plead,
by return – although the rational side of him might consider
her right, and there seemed too many difficulties in their love
life.

He introduced Lucy and Bain to each other. Her attendance
here would show him she must have changed her mind about
ditching Ian. He wouldn't know, though, whether she'd heard
the letter was promulgated in Korean English on the wheels-
up warning system to Whites, Greens and the umpire, and
from them to who knew where? As Ian had said to the Adjutant,
he hadn't told her. And he hadn't told Bain he hadn't. Let him
guess.

Emily and Frank Stanton were together on the other side
of the room. Chatting to guests. She didn't come over, but
silently mouthed 'Congrats!' as between conspirators. She
gave a discreet, low-level thumbs-up. He had won. *She* had
won?

'Didn't Ian and the Sword make a grand sight out there?'
Bain asked. 'As if they were made for each other.' He did a
quick all-elbows imitation of the Sword carrying posture at
the march past. 'If I may say so, Lucy, I believe the thought
of you inspired him to greater efforts, motivated him, for the
whole time we've been here, and so he pipped me into second
place. But no hard feelings. Or only a few! Wonderful to
meet you at last. He constantly spoke of you throughout the
course to anyone who'd listen and some who wouldn't. When
a few of us went out on the town he'd invariably stay behind,
saying, No thanks, lads, he'd rather remain in camp. We
guessed he wanted to write to you, or read over again letters

you'd sent to him. I'd see one in his pigeon hole next to mine – B and C, you know, Bain, Charteris – woman's handwriting on the envelope, and I'd know Ian would be so pleased and happy. I felt some envy, I can tell you.' Bain had obviously decided Lucy was ignorant of the snowscape broadcast. So he could fantasize; so he could spout his lies with a benevolent, constructive, lovey-dovey intent.

'What's your posting, Ray?' Ian asked.

'Attached to K-4 as starters.'

'K-4? What and where is that?' Lucy asked.

'An airfield,' Bain replied. 'Mainly Yank. Well, the war's mainly Yank, on our side. I report there, if we and the Americans are still holding it, which I'm warned is not at all certain, then get sent where most needed.'

'An airfield in Korea?' Lucy asked.

'Yes, it's Korea, isn't it, Ray? Airfields are K-coded there,' Ian replied.

'North Korean ground troops target our fields,' Bain said.

'Not a picnic,' Ian replied.

'Why do you say that?' Lucy asked.

'Someone here mentioned it,' Bain said.

'And mentioned it,' Ian said.

'But what does it mean?' Lucy asked.

'Not a picnic,' Ian said.

'Oh, do stop stiff-upper-lipping, will you?' Lucy said.

'Yes, it does make sipping the drinks difficult,' Bain said.

A couple of months later Ian heard from an Air Ministry officer visiting the OCTU that Bain was back in Britain short of both legs from above the knee. There had been a night battle for an airfield and its control tower. 'One of the K spots out there, you know. Bain and his unit held on. This was quite a little victory in its own way,' the Ministry air commodore said. 'I wouldn't be surprised if he got recognition. I gather he did well when he was here.'

'Well, yes.'

'Came out second in his intake.'

'Yes,' Ian said.

'They sent him to somewhere offering a real challenge. He was considered up to it. That must have made him proud and fulfilled. And so he went to K-4, and then to an even tougher spot. He's a credit to the training here. Know him, did you?'

'My intake. A different course.'

'Ah, so the fact you're here on the staff . . . Did you beat him into second place?'

'It was touch and go.'

'These things are always chancy. And do you get on all right with the top people here – Group Captain Stanton? His wife, Emily? An impressive woman. Some unspecified government work. Very unspecified, yes?'

'I believe so.'

'Formidable couple. She's a strength to him. He produces the goods, such as Bain.'

And, as the Air Ministry bigwig had guessed, Bain did get recognition. Ian took a phone call from him. Male voices clattered and boomed behind Bain's. It sounded as though he might be in a big common room with several other wounded men and a couple of three-sided telephone booths. Charteris found he didn't want to visualize it too fully. 'Guess what – they're giving me a gong,' Ray Bain said, 'so show some due respect, would you, please?'

'Great, Ray.'

'Distinguished Service Order.'

'That's high. Brilliant, Ray.'

'Yes, brilliant. There are one or two others here who are getting similar.'

'Great, Ray.'

'Yes, great. Do you know what I'd like?'

'What's that?'

'I'd really like it if you could be at the Palace for the presentation. It's going to be quite a do, I hear. I should think they'd give you a day's leave for that kind of thing, wouldn't they – hero alumnis of the outfit? We're entitled to invite parents, spouse and children, or a couple of friends in lieu. I haven't got a spouse or children, so you could come, in lieu. Perhaps bring Lucy? You see, Ian, I have the feeling that you're really very much part of it.'

He tried again not to visualize Bain in a wheelchair making

the call from the get-together room. What would those nice girls in the town make of him now? Ian wondered how he could be 'very much part of it'. Or no, he didn't wonder; he had an idea why Bain could see him as 'very much part of it'. This wasn't an idea that Ian felt all right about. He hadn't felt all right about it since he first heard what had happened to Bain. 'That's very kind of you to ask me, Ray,' he said. 'I'll see if Lucy can make it. In any case, I'd be honoured to come.' He let rip with some falsity. He wanted the grotesqueness confirmed: 'But I don't understand what you mean when you say I was part of it.'

'Very much part of it,' Bain said. 'But for you, I might not have been sent out there and given the chance to filch a medal. If things had gone the other way, I'd have been an OCTU instructor with no hope of combat, except maybe umpiring night attack exercises, which we both know a bit about! I'm not running down the instructors there, but it's a limited scene, a rather academic and abstract scene, isn't it, Ian? Suppose I'd been there, Sword-proud and stay-at-home, *you* might have gone to shovel up decorations in K country, instead.'

'I doubt the last bit.' God, Ian felt dazed, sickeningly troubled. What was the flavour of this conversation? Could it possibly be taken straight or did enough irony, rancour and bitterness lie in the words to sink the fleet? Were there bad and crippling wounds behind them? Did Ray Bain have in mind that letter on fine notepaper lifted as a ploy from Ian's pigeon hole? There'd been no sender's address or letterhead, but it had come in an unstamped envelope, because E, the writer, must live in quarters on the camp. An E, domiciled on the station, equipped with classy notepaper and most likely, from the letter's style, a woman. Ray had made guesses: congratulated Ian on his correspondent. The note promised to do whatever E could for Ian, as if he were very special to her.

And Ian *was* very special to her, though not in the way Ray probably thought of it. Did the 'whatever she could do for Ian' include fixing the Sword of Honour by biased, repentant pillow talks with E's husband, the unit's commanding officer, so ensuring Ian Charteris a staff place here at a hearteningly

safe distance from K dangers and the absence of picnics, where
DSOs could be won and lives or half legs lost?

'That deep midwinter attack and defence exercise we had,'
Bain said. 'Almost an absolute model for a scrap I was in out
there – though without those control tower elements in poor
taste, of course. This is what I mean when I say you were part
of the real action, and a factor in my luck at finding situations
where I might shine.'

'Where are you now, Ray?' It would presumably be some
hospital or recuperation centre, perhaps full of shattered
veterans in wheelchairs or worse, some setting the loss of a
limb, or limbs, against a gong award and calculating whether
on the whole they were in credit.

'I'll get the Palace people to send you the invitation then,'
Bain replied. 'It will be really great to see you and introduce
you to my parents. Naturally, I've told them plenty about you.
How's Lucy?'

'She's fine. Everything's fine there.'

'Great.'

Ian had received another letter on excellent-quality notepaper from Emily Stanton. He was a commissioned mentor
member of the camp retinue now and the letter didn't go into
a pigeon hole but was brought to him in his room. She wrote:
'Of course you'll remember an officer cadet who was in
training at the same time as you, called Raymond Bain – red
hair, pushy, runner-up in the Sword list. Well, Frank has it
on the grapevine that he's to be presented with the Distinguished
Service Order for bravery in Korea. Isn't this wonderful news
in so many ways? I can almost forgive him for that disgraceful
trick he pulled during the mock attack, when he loud-speak-
ered those messages from me and your girlfriend. Yes, almost.
The word was bound to get around, wasn't it? Frank and I
will be going to the award ceremony in Buck House. It's a
special invitation from Royalty to mark the good work done
here by Frank and his team, as so magnificently exemplified
by Bain. We'll certainly pass him your best wishes and
congratulations. E.'

She'd most probably discover soon from her husband that
Ian had asked for leave to attend as well. No mention of

injuries again. Off and on Ian allowed himself to think that maybe the air commodore had this huge detail wrong: but much more off than on. You wouldn't get to his rank if you made mistakes of that size. Perhaps not to talk about wounds was ingrained practice, a way of hanging on to good morale. Focus on the positive: in this case, Ray's DSO.

EIGHT

The air commodore hadn't made a mistake. From a back row of the audience chairs in the high, cream and gold ballroom at Buckingham Palace, Ian watched as Ray Bain's name was called and he went forward in his wheelchair and stopped in front of the Queen. Lucy hadn't been able to come: newspaper duties. The Queen bent to talk to Ray briefly and seemed to laugh at something he said. Did he mention how he'd paraded not so long ago with fixed bayonets to mark her accession? Then an attendant handed her the medal and she pinned it on his tunic. Decorous applause. Bain wheeled expertly away. He learned fast at most things. Another name was called. An army sergeant marched the few steps and received his medal. He looked undamaged.

A reception in a side room followed the ceremony. Double mirrored doors caught the light from chandeliers and gave the notion of extra spaciousness where there was already bags of space. *Wider still and wider shall thy bounds be set.* Waitresses in black and white costume moved about among the crowd offering drinks and small nibbles. Bain's parents, the Stantons and Ian grouped around the wheelchair. Bain did the introductions.

Stanton said: 'You seemed to get on nicely with Her Majesty, Ray.'

'She's remarkably well up on the fighting out there, sir,' Bain said. 'In fact, most Palace people seem to be. Before the ceremony, one of her aides asked me if I'd been anywhere near the Scottish Black Watch contingent of the Commonwealth Brigade. I said yes, they weren't far away. He follows up with did I know the area called the Hook, a ridge in very inhospitable, hilly country? I said I'd heard of the Hook, but because my job was airfield protection I worked mainly on the flat, such as there was of it. He had a little giggle about that.'

Oh, God, the pleasant, informed conversation around this warrior's indispensable chariot.

Emily announced, 'Previously, a DSO was reserved for officers in the higher ranks. Obviously the top brass consider your achievements knock a hole in that snobbish tradition, Ray. Good. Very good indeed. And I'd say, judging by the enthusiastic way she behaved, the Queen approves, too.' She spoke with what seemed to Ian a lively mixture of warmth and authority. She had taken over the occasion. First there'd been the Queen, then Emily. Yes, both had obviously decided to ignore the injuries and concentrate on the positives. Leaders did concentrate on the positives – that's how they got to be leaders. They led. It was as though Emily recognized and knew well the customs of the military game and would normally excel at applying them, but also acknowledged there would come times when these customs should be set aside, and if necessary flung aside. Ray Bain's gallantry flung them aside. He'd been only a Flying Officer – equivalent of an army lieutenant – but had earned the DSO. Emily approved, and seemed to feel her endorsement important.

Ian recalled that description, or half-description, she gave of her career after the sea rescue. She had soared in what she called 'Government Service'. The Air Ministry officer had described her job in the same way, and hadn't been able to specify what kind of work. Ian thought he'd asked her which section, because, as a term, 'Government Service' covered big and undefined areas. Yes, 'covered' might be the apt word in Emily's case. He couldn't remember getting any answer to that, though. Hadn't she skipped off to another topic – to inquiries about Ian's father? So, why skirt a reply? Why the secrecy? 'You must be very proud of Ray,' she said to the parents.

'Proud?' Bain's mother said. She paused for at least ten seconds, gazing down at Ray in the buggy. She seemed to struggle to bring together two utterly different aspects of her son's life. Then she replied, 'Yes.' That word, 'proud', had seemed to bamboozle her, shock her. She spoke as though holding it up in front of herself for inspection, and also as though it had never occurred to her before this to be proud.

In the matter of her son, she had other feelings to cope with. She was above average height, as Ray Bain had been, and wore a mauve silk suit over a white blouse, with a thin gold necklace. Also like Ray, she spoke with a slight Birmingham accent. 'We have him at home with us now. That's something,' Mrs Bain said.

'For a while Ray was in a mobile army surgical hospital out there,' Mr Bain said. 'It seemed such a long way off, not a place we could visit.' He was the same height as his wife, heavily built, in a burgundy-coloured cord jacket and navy flannels, fair hair thinning, a look of constant puzzlement on his face, as if he couldn't believe Ray was as he was, and couldn't believe Ray was as he was in Buckingham Palace talking about Korea to the Queen. They had a son who'd never intended joining the armed forces, but who'd been directed into the RAF for a limited interlude before resuming his preferred way of life. And that limited interlude had produced events which would permanently condition his preferred way of life, quite possibly make it impossible. This was a bucketful for his mother and father to swallow.

'Yes, a MASH unit,' Ray Bain said. 'That's what they call the hospitals. It was run by crazy American doctors – crazy but brilliant at snuffing out pain.'

'Ray always speaks well of them,' Mrs Bain said.

Ian could tell that Emily didn't like the way this conversation had turned. Wounds had started to dominate. Wounds were negative. Pain, even snuffed-out pain, wouldn't do. She said: 'This might not look like a war of immediate concern to us here in GB, but it is a United Nations matter, and we must be part of that.'

'We can't allow the whole peninsula to fall,' Frank Stanton said. The four rings nicely stacked on the arms of his tunic shone very fetchingly under the chandeliers. 'Where else in that region would be lost next?'

'And you were a friend of Ray's at the officer training unit, were you, Ian?' Mrs Bain said. 'He used to mention you.'

'A friend and an enemy,' Bain replied. 'He was defence, I was attack, in an imitation battle one night out on the airfield. Waterloo wouldn't come anywhere near it for intensity.'

'The various courses competed – sort of war games,' Emily said. Keep it general, keep it matter-of-fact, keep it playful.

'I was White, Ray was Green,' Ian said.

'And you stayed at the OCTU afterwards, I gather,' Mrs Bain said.

'Yes, that's the convention,' Frank Stanton said. 'I think it's quite a valuable practice. Ian can help by passing on to new intakes what he has learned, and what he has excelled in.'

'Ray could have done that, if he'd stayed, could he?' Mrs Bain said.

'Certainly,' Stanton said.

'He could probably teach them something else now,' Mrs Bain replied.

'The luck of the draw, I suppose,' Mr Bain said.

'Not exactly that,' Stanton said.

'No, as I understand it from Ray, it's a kind of reward, a kind of distinction,' Mrs Bain said.

'One could describe it so, yes,' Stanton said. 'But also a very practical business. We – the Service – benefit.'

'Ian overtook me quite late on in the merit table,' Ray Bain said. 'He was the Sword of Honour.'

'By a very narrow squeak,' Ian said.

'Quite often narrow squeaks are what shape our days, aren't they?' Mr Bain said.

'Ian will have to move on to a new posting eventually – so as to make way for future Sword of Honour officers,' Stanton said.

'Move on to where?' Mrs Bain asked.

'That will only be decided at the time,' Stanton said. 'Where the need is. Needs change.'

'Airfields here, there or anywhere,' Mr Bain said.

'Yes,' Stanton replied.

'Certainly,' Emily said, as if she would have some influence in the choice.

'When you say "a very narrow squeak", Ian, what does that mean? What counted towards the squeak, I wonder?' Mrs Bain said.

'All quite complex,' Stanton said.

'Always at the end of these courses it's a problem sorting

out the top people in order,' Emily replied. 'Many are excellent but one of them has to emerge as supremely excellent.
Obviously, I know this only from the strain and worry I detect
in Frank at these times. I'm not consulted. No backseat driving.
It's a Service matter.'

'But it must be very stressful for you,' Mrs Bain said.

As Ian saw it, a kind of egomaniacal, very belated gratitude drove Emily. She'd been saved from the sea by his
father and come to believe she had failed to show proper
thankfulness towards him, by piling most of her farcical
praise on dead Corbitty that day at the memorial service,
and perhaps generally elsewhere. So, as one way of compensating, transfer the thankfulness, direct it to the rescuer's
son. Help get him a cushy, unendangered posting where he
might oversee mock engagements on the airfield, but dodge
being part of a real, bone-smashing, potentially slaughterous
engagement on another airfield on foreign soil. She'd try to
skip the fact that someone had to go out to that other airfield
and take the hurt. It would taint her generous policy of
recompense. Ian was her generous policy of recompense.
His legs proved it.

He hated the role, felt subjugated by it, wanted to resist
it; loathed the notion of getting selected, elected, as stand-in
for his father. He saw himself as caught in the noose of her
gratitude. Emily didn't owe him – Ian – anything. He'd
prefer it like that. She'd had a goofy, girl-like adoration for
a ship's captain who'd died for her. OK, understandable.
Now, she'd matured into somebody else, and saw that the
man who saved her might be just as entitled to hefty thanks.
In fact, she'd matured altogether, as her important, deeply
unspecified job seemed to prove. She didn't have to go on
making it up to Ian because she'd slighted his diving dad
for a while. She was continually looking for means to reward
those she'd injured. He recalled words in her letter about
Ray Bain's medal. 'Isn't that wonderful news in so many
ways?' The 'in so many ways' meant, did it, the DSO might
help make more tolerable the wrecking of his body? Could
she really believe that? Final whistle on his prop forward
games.

If I should get half my legs blown off,
Think only this of me: that there's some corner,
Of a foreign field where I needn't have been,
But for dirty work behind the scenes at OCTU.

'Of course, we'll move on from this posting ourselves at some point,' Stanton said. 'Different type of stresses then, I expect.'

'When Ray used to come home on a break from the OCTU he'd sometimes refer to what are termed, I think, "officer qualities",' Mrs Bain said. 'OQs, as he called them. He told us nobody could quite define them, but crucial to have plenty. I wondered if it was because of officer qualities that Ian did best. Rather vague matters, hard to pin down, still important, though.'

'But Ray has shown he has those qualities in abundance,' Emily replied. 'Nobody gets a DSO without them.'

'Well, yes, that's what I might have been getting at, I think,' Mrs Bain said. 'Who decides who has the most OQs? Is it a committee or one person? Do the candidates have it explained to them how exactly they scored and how exactly they fell short? But can it be done exactly, if the OQs are so hard to define? And perhaps there are other subtle, undisclosed factors – undisclosable factors? He didn't ask us to the passing-out because he wasn't the winner. Typical! He has to be Number One or he thinks himself a failure. He might have been ashamed of his low OQ count.'

'Not at all,' Emily said. 'In fact very high.'

'But not high enough,' Mrs Bain said. 'He used to joke about it sometimes, didn't you, Ray? He'd tell us that the main test of someone's OQs was if he could go into a crowded bar and get served at once.'

'That's it,' Ray said.

'But, anyway, here we are now, in Buckingham Palace,' Mr Bain said.

'Exactly,' Emily said.

Ian had done another censorship job as far as his own parents were concerned. He hadn't let them know that they and his brother could have attended the passing out. He'd feared this might lead to difficulties. It would probably have involved a meeting at the after-parade party between his mother and Emily. Mrs Charteris wouldn't want that. His father might have been embarrassed by the occasion, too, and this could turn him ratty. Ian had to serve at least some more of his National Service at the OCTU, and he'd rather his father didn't sour things here for him. In any case, his father didn't like occasions where someone else got made a fuss of for an achievement, even one of his sons – or perhaps especially one of his sons. Mr Charteris admired the family as an institution, as long as in the case of *his* family the members realized he was the one who brought its excellence and distinction. Swords of Honour could be shoved up somewhere *dis*honourable.

Ian felt a little relieved that because of her new job Lucy wasn't able to come to the Palace. She wouldn't have put up with the evasions and blank-offs in the talk. She'd have said something awkward and bleakly truthful. He reckoned she'd have to get out of that way of thinking if she intended to survive in journalism; though at that time in his life he knew nothing about journalism at first hand, of course.

NINE

And then there came a temptation that could have taken him away from journalism altogether and into something . . . into something potentially murkier but with, possibly, more status, though secret status. During the last months of his National Service, Ian Charteris had a couple of visitors, a man and a woman in good civilian clothes, who carried very high-grade Defence Ministry identification. One or other of them had overdone the scent. Ian didn't know much about scent but he thought this one smelled quite decent, not the kind of stuff you could win at a fairground. 'In some respects we are making a routine call,' the man said. 'It's standard in our work for people to function in pairs. Oh, let me present Lorna-Jane Underhill. I'm Charles Fisher. We operate as a unit in this kind of procedure. Very much so. A harmonious unit, I might say.'

'Which kind?' Ian said.

'A very reasonable question! We like to talk to people who are about to be demobbed,' Fisher said. He had a big voice that came across as not too far off rage, or possibly hysteria. He somehow made 'reasonable' sound as if it meant offensive or insulting or footling. It was sort of *'Don't fucking quiz me, matey 'cos I'm the fucking one who does the fucking quizzing. Well I and she.'*

'We talk to *some* people,' Underhill said.

Fisher growl-laughed. 'Yes, not *all* people who are about to be demobbed. That would be a huge list. A certain selectiveness does operate. A quite considerable selectiveness, in fact.'

'Rigorous,' she said.

'Which people?' Ian said.

'I think that will become plain during the course of things,' Fisher explained, or not.

'This is a very secure establishment, isn't it?' Underhill said. 'One can't just drift in. Or, for that matter, *two* can't!'

'Fairly secure,' Ian said. 'We and the RAF police do our best. But you didn't have bother drifting in, did you – not with those papers?'

'Of course, we'd heard of this station before we learned you were here in an operational role,' Underhill said. 'As you'd expect, such places float into our purview to some degree.'

'No, I'm not sure I'd have expected that,' Ian said. 'What *is* your purview?'

'There'd almost certainly have been some guidance about your posting to this category of station after the OCTU staff,' Underhill said. 'This wouldn't be chance.'

'Hardly,' Fisher said. 'Anything but. The very reverse of chance.' He did a thoughtful lip purse. 'Now, I wonder what would be the reverse of chance, the very reverse.'

'Planned?' Underhill said. 'Designated?'

Ian wondered how often they'd performed this bit of chit-chat for an interviewee, harmoniously together.

'A kind of unobvious but nonetheless powerful influence would have put you on such a particular type of station,' Fisher said.

'Certain philosophers and clerics argue there's no such thing as pure chance, anyway. They maintain there is always some scheme, some meaning, however much concealed,' Underhill said. 'A variant on "God moves in a mysterious way his wonders to perform". Those wonders may seem simply that, random wonders, but the theologian would argue that the "mysterious way" is, in fact, a coherent, purposeful way, if only we could discern it. But our brains are not attuned to this pattern, are not adequately perceptive. This is what these scholars would say.'

'Some guidance about my posting from whom?' Ian said. 'Not God, I take it.'

Fisher had a fractional laugh, the kind of laugh that said he'd heard this sally fifty times previously, and hadn't thought it funny even the first time. 'This connection with service matters of a confidential, secret category will be as relevant to your CV as the Sword of Honour – on the winning of which very post-event congrats, by the way,' Fisher said. 'I'd love to have seen that passing-out show.'

'Oh, yes,' she said.

'All that gallimaufry put into brilliant order,' Fisher said. 'Some people in our business abhor all uniforms and display. For them, brass bands are anathema, swinging arms a farce. That's understandable, I suppose, though narrow, negative. Our objective has to be achieved – if it can be achieved at all – and too often it can't! It has to be achieved in shadowy, even subfusc style. But, for myself, I love a good parade and the brilliant concerted subordination in that "Eyes right!" to some gold-leaf chieftain. People having to look one way and march another! This is flair. This is potential shambles. This is induced skill. Would there have been a band, too? Did you have to shout commands above its rotund din while flashing your indisputably earned Sword? Resplendent! Cohesion! Cohesion is the *sine qua non* in such displays. I believe in cohesion, but rarely see it.'

They would both be in their late twenties, Fisher's accent educated Midlands, Underhill's very educated cockney. He had on a suede jacket, made-to-measure Ian would say, tan trousers, brown lace-up shoes, white shirt, beige and green striped tie; she was in a navy skirt, navy hip-length jacket over a light-blue silk blouse, moderately high-heeled glossy black shoes. When Fisher spoke about the parade and the band his face became suddenly animated and slightly flushed, as though the pleasure he took in imagining it might be depraved. Part of that harmoniousness between them must come from a shared, illicit pleasure in military ceremonial. He was dark-haired, small-featured, square-built, thick-necked. He'd be another front-row prop forward if he played rugby, with possibly a nasty side to his game, perhaps eye-gouging and/ or ear-biting. Ian thought Ray Bain would not have gone in for those, except retaliating, of course.

She was about his height but slimmer, auburn hair cut fairly short, straight though not prominent nose, blue, intent eyes, pleasantly uneven teeth with a minor gap to the right, probably not the result of a punch or catapult ball-bearing in the school yard, but kept like that because she thought it distinctive and intriguing. And Ian did like it – thought of it as the kind of opening you'd love to squirt something through. Also, the space caused a certain delightful, muted whistling around some of her spoken consonants, like the sharp whirr of a well-spun cricket ball. 'We've worked out you'll quit the Air Force in fifty-seven days unless you re-engage,' Underhill said.

'I'm not counting,' Ian said.

'And we gather you've no intention of re-engaging,' Fisher said, 'although we're sure they'd like to have you.'

'Gather where?' Ian said.

'You're thinking of journalism,' Underhill replied.

'Pathfinding there already done by the girlfriend, Lucy Armitage, and her effectively caustic writing style,' Fisher said. 'We're happy that relationship seems settled again and satisfying after some differences. There are bound to be episodes of uncertainty.'

'I'm glad you're happy,' Charteris said.

'Now, I'm certainly not going to argue that there aren't good careers in the Press – if you can put up with a double negative,' Fisher replied. He made it sound as if Ian had better put up with it or he'd trample his balls and put the relationship with Lucy in peril once more.

'Journalism, though, is what it sounds – of the *jour*, as the French would put it – of the day. Immediacy, nowness, is its essential and its strength, its *raison d'être* no less,' Underhill said. 'These are certainly not qualities to be totally discounted. The instant report has its value. Think of Hemingway in the Spanish Civil War, reporting what he saw. Merit, too in the kind of considered "think piece", as a comment article is often described. Lucy is very telling with her think pieces. Here is intelligent opinion, here is well-based attitude vigorously expressed.'

'Undoubtedly,' Fisher said.

She changed tone. Her voice got touched by super-rationality, and by contempt. 'Yet some might allege journalism gives only extremely short-term gratification to its practitioners,' Underhill said. 'The word "journalism" can be derogatory, can't it, equating with opportunistic, shallow, sensational? Literary critics, for instance, condemn material as "mere journalism" in work that is trying unsuccessfully to be something deeper. My brother was a barrister and not making much at it. My mother – not highly educated, but bright – said that whenever she heard the word "barrister" as a youngster it was accompanied by the word "impecunious" – an impecunious barrister. Skint. Likewise, I think, the word "journalism" is tied to the word "mere" – mere journalism. There are, Charles and I believe, those who seek a return on their work which is more lasting, more solid, basically more worthwhile.'

'True,' Ian said, 'and they wouldn't have to learn shorthand.' The three were in his office overlooking the patrolled gates and double-layer, twelve-feet-high barbed-wire fencing below. For this tail-end of his service, he'd been posted away from the OCTU and to a camp in Yorkshire. RAF Norton, Gleadless, Sheffield had no airfield to guard, but a very high security rating – 'matters of a confidential, secret, category' operated from here, as Fisher had said.

'Obviously, Lorna-Jane doesn't want to pile on the flattery, but she feels, as I do, that you might be wasted in the journalistic game,' he said, 'even supposing you could get on to the kind of paper you'd like. It's not always easy, and Lucy's advice and influence could only help up to a point. This is why we're here.'

'It's not the first time we've been to Norton,' Lorna-Jane said.

'Hardly,' Fisher said.

'Norton is what you might call our sort of hunting ground,' she said. 'Its officers tend to be our kind of people.'

'Which kind?' Charteris said, but he could make a guess.

'Norton's record with us is exemplary. Its people are naturally accustomed to the clandestine,' she said. 'The role of Norton demands it. This and its sister outfits around GB lie outside the general three-tier command structure of the RAF – Fighter, Bomber and Coastal – don't they? Norton, and its sister establishments, stand separate, a bit shady, even – confidential, secret, as Charles puts it. These units are Ninety Group, a title which calculatedly tells nobody anything about the nature of its members' work: not fighter, bomber or coastal duties; not to do with aircraft at all in fact, or only the potential enemy's aircraft. The urgent role of Norton and its comparable stations is to prepare, extend and service the country's network of radar defences against a Cold War Russian threat.'

'You're not supposed to know this,' Ian replied.

'It's the type of thing we *do* know and specialize in,' Fisher said.

'We've advised on some of the security,' Lorna-Jane said. 'I don't mean your Alsatians. But, for instance, the Ninety Group's headquarters is in that delightful, innocent-seeming, seventeenth-century former country manor house with high, ornate ceilings and glowing mahogany panelled doors, at Membury, near Marlow, in Buckinghamshire, yes? We suggested that as an unnoticeable spot. I expect you've been there for a briefing pre-Norton. Of course you have. We laid it down that every new joiner at Norton should be given a thorough preparatory Membury session first. You'll have noticed that the travel warrant actually named two stops beyond where you left the train, so as to prevent evidence in the rail company offices of a slinky visitors' build up at HQ. That's a routine precaution recommended by us.

'You and your contingent of RAF Regiment troops, plus the military police platoon and their doggies, look after Norton and the radar installations its technical crews set up and monitor in north-east Britain. That would probably be the airway route for any Soviet plane or rocket attack. If possible, the existence and location of Norton and the other linked stations should be concealed from the Russians, as well as the areas of Britain where the radar fields are at their most effective. You'll surely see what we mean when we say you're already accustomed to operating in an area of vital and sensitive State secrets.'

'You're a natural,' Lorna-Jane put in.

'No, not exactly a natural,' Fisher said. 'He's been shaped and directed towards this kind of work, and has grown to be efficient at it.'

'Perhaps more than efficient,' she said.

Ian said: 'Perhaps. But I—'

'But you think a newspaper future,' Fisher said. 'Sure, sure the Press does useful work now and then. Naturally, we've undertaken quite a bit of research into your early days, including a dedicated scan of old newspapers in your locality then, and—'

'Dedicated to what?' Ian said.

'And we'd have to admit – and I'm sure I speak for Lorna-Jane as well as myself here – we'd have to admit that the Press reporting of that air-raid shelter murder and the trial back in 1941 certainly covered very significant ground,' Fisher replied. 'And, of course, you figured notably there as a witness. You, in fact, made the nationals as well as the town Press. I don't know whether in your boyhood that helped turn your thoughts towards a newspaper career – rather *writing* the material, not being its subject. The crime and trial were given considerable space, despite the shortage of newsprint in those wartime days. And, naturally enough, you followed up that sequence of incidents to the end, and joined the jail gate crowd for the hanging, also covered by the newspapers.'

'How do you mean "*dedicated* scan"?' Ian said.

'An affection for and interest in the Press from that kind of experience might seem far-fetched,' Underhill said. 'But the idea struck both of us, Charles and myself. Quite often these seemingly minor, even quirky, factors lead to very substantial decisions.'

'And then again, even earlier than this, came the heroic sea rescue by your dad,' Charles Fisher said. 'That had great Press coverage, too, didn't it – and justifiably so? I expect he'd keep the cuttings and you saw them as a child. You might have developed a sort of subconscious link to the admittedly exciting world of newspapers.'

'Many are fascinated by that world – the smell of printers' ink and so on, the green eyeshade, "Hold the front page!" – even without your special, emphatic connection to reportage by participation in the shelter case,' Underhill said. 'Emphatic connection to reportage' came out slightly, intriguingly, shrill through the teeth cleft, the consonants busying themselves around his ear drums like special, excited messengers. 'And yet is this more than a superficial romanticizing of what is basically a run-of-the-mill trade, like many another run-of-the-mill trade?' she said. 'Urgently relevant on one day, perhaps, and fish-and-chip wrapping the next. I ask once more, can it

provide long-lasting satisfaction for someone of mature
outlook? And we take leave, Charles and I, to judge that you
are of mature outlook. We don't have to rely on our own find-
ings to form that conclusion; we also get extremely credible,
reliable advice along those lines.'

'Journalism's detractors always do the fish-and-chip paper
bit,' Ian said. 'But, by the time yesterday's paper is a wrapper,
there's another issue out full of new, topical reading.'

'I wouldn't say we are *detractors* of journalism,' Underhill
replied.

'Oh,' Ian said.

'No, indeed,' Fisher said.

'Are you recruiters?' Ian replied.

'Recruiters in which sense?' Underhill said.

'Recruiters in the recruiting sense,' Ian said.

'It's an interesting suggestion,' Lorna-Jane said.

Ian kept it general for the moment. 'You go around talking
to selected National Service people near the end of their time
and try to persuade them to stay on – switch to a career
commission? I suppose the Sword of Honour would help put
me on your shortlist. You're not in uniform, though. Does the
RAF farm out the job to Management Selection firms? Anyway,
it's not going to work. I'm leaving. Anyone who's asked about
it I've told at once, I don't want that kind of life. Your research
into my childhood and so on is brilliantly accurate, but irrelevant – a time-waster, I'm afraid.'

'No, not that kind of recruiting,' Underhill said.

'Which other kind is there?' Ian said. He thought he knew,
though.

'Yes, there are other kinds,' Underhill replied. 'I think you'll
come to see what we mean.'

'Your pal has already said that. I still don't know what it's
about,' Ian said.

'I think you possibly do,' Fisher said.

'We've given plenty of indications,' she said.

'We're not here to propose a twenty-two-year commissioned
career in the RAF Regiment, excellent as that regiment and
career might be,' Fisher said, his cadence branding the regiment and a spell in it as unholy shit.

'But it *is* about a career, is it?' Ian said.

'We don't think of it as simply a career,' Underhill said. 'That might do for journalism. It's too narrow and ordinary a word for what we're talking about.'

'But I don't know what you're talking about,' Ian said. He did, but enjoyed giving them the tease. He had an electric kettle in his office and some mugs and made tea now.

'That research you kindly spoke of threw up something else apparently irrelevant – to use your word – yes, irrelevant in a workaday sense,' Fisher replied. 'Yes, flagrantly irrelevant in a workaday sense.' He waved an arm to give extra force to 'workaday sense' or 'flagrantly irrelevant'. The movement made it obvious he wasn't responsible for the nice scent. 'But perhaps in a mysterious, even mystical way this research finding provides a pointer.'

'We like to build from available information a personality profile of those we're going to talk to,' Underhill said. 'A completeness, in so far as that's possible.'

'Did someone do it to *you*?' Ian said.

'What?' Underhill said.

'Concoct a version of your personality before they offered you a job,' Ian said.

'It's routine in our sort of activity,' Underhill said. 'One doesn't resent it. Indeed, one recognizes it's for the best; there will be a matching of work with the operative's character. "Character" here to mean inner resources, flairs, aims, ambitions.'

'Which one doesn't resent it? I do,' Ian replied.

'There are more things in heaven and earth than are dreamt of in standard-issue thinking, Ian,' Fisher said. 'I'm referring to your illness when you were four years old.'

'How did you get on to that?' Ian said.

'Yes, we got on to it, to use your phrase,' Fisher said, with a comradely smile. 'This is part of what we mean by a "dedicated scan", you see. One can't know what might be turned up.'

'Diphtheria,' Ian said.

'You were whisked off to the sanatorium,' Fisher said. 'An emergency ambulance job, you torn away from your parents.'

'The sana, as it was known,' Ian said.

'An isolation hospital,' Underhill said.

'Luckily, its medical records are still archived and available in some circumstances,' Fisher said.

'Which circumstances? I thought medical records were private, even a child's,' Ian said.

'Well, yes, in a sense,' Underhill said. 'Definitely.'

'Which sense?' Ian said.

'We *make* the circumstances. Fortunately, we were able to get sight of them,' Fisher replied.

'But how?' Ian said.

'That's the way things go sometimes, isn't it, given a degree of know-how in procedural matters?' Fisher said. 'We discovered that every patient in the sanatorium had a number, and twice a week in the *South Wales Echo* – previously the *News* – a bulletin gave the state of all patients, but, for confidentiality, using these numbers, not their names. This appeared as a grid under one of two headings: "Condition Unchanged" and "Progressing Satisfactorily". Given the fatality record of diphtheria then, "Condition Unchanged" looked funereal.'

'There was a blackboard over each bed with the number chalked on it,' Ian said.

'You were two-one-three,' Underhill said. 'They kept you in the sanatorium for six months, so you must have got very used to those figures.'

'Yes,' Ian said.

'It would have taken over your name,' Fisher said.

'In a way, yes,' Ian said.

'This must have been nearly impossible for a child of four to comprehend,' Fisher said. 'An identity, as it were, lost. Older patients might realize their name had been put aside temporarily for admin reasons as much as anything. Normality would return once they were discharged. But a child of four might think he'd permanently ceased to exist as he had been previously. Not death, but a total morph.'

Underhill said: 'I spoke of building a personality. Sometimes we have to *re*build.'

'That was ages ago. My personality has been OK lately,' Ian said. 'I've got an RAF number, but it's not me, it's a number.'

'There are memoirs by prisoners in German concentration

camps or Russian gulags who became reduced in their own minds to an institutional number, as might have happened to you – almost certainly did happen to you – in the hospital,' Fisher said.

'And then, of course, the Charles Dickens novel *A Tale of Two Cities* shows this sad mental state in a character called Dr Manette,' Underhill said. 'Freed from the Bastille prison in the revolution of 1789 for a while he can think of himself only as his cell label, "One-Oh-Five North Tower". He slips back to that identity if suddenly stressed even long after release, and restarts the job he had there mending shoes. Perhaps you felt something like that.'

'I've never mended shoes,' Ian said. 'I hated the way cobblers kept the nails in their mouth. A bit of an indigestion twitch and they'd swallow the lot.'

'Of course, we called at the public library and looked through bound copies of the *Echo* covering your "sana" months checking for mentions of two-one-three,' Fisher said. 'We had a real thrill when, between Tuesday's and Friday's editions of the *Echo* one week you moved from "Condition Unchanged" to "Progressing Satisfactorily". It seemed to say more to us than your health had improved. We felt we could reach out to you now, and you to us.'

'Look, what's all this jabber about, then?' Ian said. 'Why so much digging? Who told you I had diphtheria?'

'It must have come to be almost second nature for you to drop your name and the identity that went with it and become this number two-one-three instead,' Underhill said. 'The self you'd been born with and brought up with for your first four years could be discarded, and this new, sort of anonymous, featureless, individual took over. You'd become a chalk mark on a board.'

'That is a very useful asset in the kind of work we're here to discuss with you,' Fisher said. 'The uniforms, and the band, and the *gloire* and the Sword are all very, very fine. Who'd deny it? But they are not, decidedly not, everything. Our impression is that even though you took the Sword of Honour you knew this.'

'Of course I fucking know life is not one noisy parade,' Ian said.

The three of them were seated around a small conference table near the window in Ian's office. He had taken the chair he usually occupied for meetings at the table's head. Anyone looking in would have assumed he was running things. It didn't feel like that to him. More like things were running away from him.

Underhill had made an occasional note in a small pad she carried. Now, she read some words from it. 'You mentioned our possible interest in "selected National Service people near the end of their time." I think we can plead guilty to that. But I'd like you to notice above all the word "selected". And Charles referred to it, didn't he? You'll probably have gathered from what we've said so far that selection is not at all a pushover. We know what we are looking for and those who haven't got it will be excluded. In fact, it's very unlikely we'd even approach them.'

'For instance, we've recently brought aboard a one-time colleague of yours, Raymond Bain,' Fisher said. 'Now, as you'll know, in some respects he might not seem suited to the kind of career we've been discussing.'

'You mean the wheelchair?' Ian said.

'He has certain very palpable limitations,' Fisher said. 'There's no getting away from that.'

'Some try,' Ian said.

'But he has, too, the kind of character and mind and background that we seek,' Fisher replied. 'This is someone with a very worthwhile medal, not all that far down from a Victoria Cross. Reports on him showed he has intelligent aggression and considerable inventiveness. Well, you'll remember the airfield broadcast, I'm sure. This was in some senses *outré* and maverick, not in the properly play-fair mode favoured by the British officer class – at least until their backs are to the wall. But nuts to that. The ploy had propulsion. It had zing. Possibly it lost him the Sword. You'd know more about that than we do. But nuts to the Sword, too, if I may say so in the presence of one of its holders. We are folk – Lorna-Jane, myself, our workmates – who respect, who crave originality. Bain, in our view, exudes it. His family looks fairly ordinary at first sight but on the father's side had a distinguished man of letters who became a notable professor of Deccan College in the University of Poona, India, and wrote on Aristotle.'

'This should be a help,' Ian said.

'Ray Bain is very happy in his present post,' Underhill said.

'Emily Stanton told you to give him a job, did she?' Ian said. 'She has that kind of power? What is she exactly? Where in the heaven and earth scheme of things? She's always trying to compensate for mistakes she's made. She thinks she helped get Ray's legs blown off. Perhaps it should have been mine. But she was compensating to me, as well, in place of my father.'

'This is another aspect of chance,' Underhill said.

'Look, Emily's got some big position in one of the secret service outfits, has she?' Ian said. 'Is she your boss, then? My dad told her about the diphtheria and so on, did he?'

'People think of our kind of work as gumshoeing enemies, breaking and entering in a search for evidence, occasional rough-house encounters with spies and/or traitors,' Underhill replied. 'And, of course, there *is* some of that kind of thing. But we have a place for planners, too, for desk men and women, for gifted folk who will interpret and set in a context what those officers out in the field produce. We're convinced Ray will execute that kind of sedentary function very, very well.'

'You could say he's made for it, or *re*made,' Ian said.

'It's often the case in nature, isn't it, that where a living being loses part of itself, that loss is made up for by an increase in some other part of the body or faculties,' Fisher said. 'We cut back a rose, for example, to make it flower in due course even more strongly than before, because it feels its existence is threatened and it must defend itself by a sort of attack. Ray Bain will be like that, I know.'

'Because his legs were pruned?' Ian said.

'He will concentrate on the possible, and by that special concentration make up for certain other lacks,' Underhill said.

'Did Emily have me moved here, to acclimatize myself to secrecy?' Ian said. 'And to get the mention on my CV? It doesn't matter too much, I suppose, that I'm not at Norton long. What counts is the mention. It helps with the profile.'

'The profile *is* important, for reasons that have been mentioned,' Fisher said. 'We prefer a more comprehensive term than "profile" though, such as "portrait" or "life narrative".'

'The Bain family has its creditable past in the nineteenth century, while you, Ian, are from a family that excelled itself more recently through the gallantry of your dad,' Underhill said. 'This sort of thing is an impressive factor. Couldn't be more so.'

'I understand from Emily that my father was having it off with her for a while,' Ian replied. 'My mother might at least suspect. It would thrill Dad to know a paramour could have been dead but for him.'

'We don't expect you to give us an acceptance of the job offer now,' Underhill replied, 'but that's what this is, an unconditional offer. You have those fifty-plus days to go and then a month's paid resettlement leave. Charles will let you have a card. It's as if for an accountancy firm in the City. There's a number to ring. Ask for the Receivership Department. The Receivership Department. Charles or I will be there, most probably. If not, it's quite likely you'll go through to Ray Bain. In that case, you'll discover for yourself how content he is, and how suited. We'll let him know he might be talking to you soon. Say within the next couple of weeks?'

TEN

Ian Charteris didn't ring the Receivership Department of the nominated Coldstream, Fay and Partners accountancy firm in the City, but he did take a telephone call at home from Ray Bain. Ray wanted a meeting, urgently.

This would be getting on for three years later, though. By then, Ian was out of the Air Force, into freelance Fleet Street journalism, living in London, and married to Lucy, with a child due soon. There had been no echoes of that long-ago brush-off letter. The Adjutant, Training, had been half right: women could be changeable, but also not.

'Ian!' Bain said. 'Grand to hear your voice. Actually, I was expecting to hear it quite a while ago. Lorna-Jane said you'd be in touch. I gather she and Fisher visited when you were at Norton, back end of 'fifty-three. We were disappointed here in the office. They'd been very much impressed.'

'By . . .?'

'You. And all that barbed wire. Lorna-Jane gets the hots from bright, unrusted, triple-furl barbed wire.'

'Grand to hear you, too, Ray.'

'I understood they made you one of their propositions.'

'Well, yes.'

'They're not ten a penny, you know.'

'I did think about it.'

'But?'

'Not my sort of thing.'

'How could you be sure? *They* believed it was. They're personnel experts. They don't often pick wrong 'uns. Time justifies them.'

'I reckon they'd decided before we ever met. Or they'd been told to decide it – told from above.'

'That's a possible, I'll admit.'

'I got the impression they were run by—'

'Absolutely.'

'I didn't like it. I felt I was being dragooned. Lucy did, too. Choices removed.'

'*I* was dragooned,' Bain replied. 'Benign dragooned.'

'But you like the job, don't you? They told me you were very happy.'

'I had *limited* choices, didn't I? Factors that don't apply in your case. Two of them. The Regiment said goodbye, naturally, and they arranged a bit of a disability pension. Then, I was glad to get welcomed into another career, with the backing of someone at the top. That could have been the same for you.'

'They said not to call it a career. More like a vocation. I was set on the journalism, though, Ray. I wanted something a bit more frivolous. And some fame. I must have got that taste from my father. What you definitely can't have in your kind of work is fame. A bullet comes with fame.'

'Journalism – so chancy.'

'For a while it was, yes.'

'I see your byline in the papers – a lot of different papers.'

'Best like that. I didn't plan it this way. It just happened.'

'Spread your talents?'

He'd done the statutory learning year on a provincial daily then came to London. It had been hard, and occasionally he regretted turning down the Underhill-Fisher-Emily invitation.

Bain said: 'Could we meet? I've got something to discuss. Not on the phone, though. There's a Mooney's pub in Fetter Lane. Serves the true Guinness, plus Gorgonzola with crusty bread.'

'Yes, I know it.'

'I have a driver. I can get dropped and picked up there. It's quiet in the evenings. Near the *Mirror* building, opposite side of the road, but the staff all go to Barney's – *The White Horse.*'

'Yes, they do. You keep informed.'

'What my job is about.'

'Mine, too,' Ian said. 'I do some work for the *Mirror* now and then. When they want a particular kind of reporting.'

'Which?'

'Celebrity-based, emotional, sympathetic, dramatic.'

'So how did you crack all these papers?' Bain said.

'I had some luck.' It had been a little slow arriving, though.
At first he'd had to grab casual, holiday-relief, sickness-relief,
maternity-relief reporting shifts on most of the Fleet Street
papers, broadsheet and tabloid, 'quality' and popular. None
had asked him to join their permanent pay roll. The work was
sporadic and now and then absent altogether. Of course, this
worried Ian. There had certainly been times when he almost
rang the accountancy number to activate the Underhill-Fisher
unconditional offer. Gradually, though, the rather frantic,
unpredictable work opportunities became a plus. The sheer
range and enormous variety of assignments across the whole
national Press output built him a terrific spectrum of contacts.

'Yes, luck, Ray,' he said. 'Things started to improve fast
during that wonderful, doomed romance of Princess Margaret
and Group Captain Peter Townsend. News and magazine
organizations all over the world were avid for stuff about a
possible heiress to the British throne and the fighter plane ace
– the divorced, and therefore markedly unsuitable suitor, fighter
plane ace. And I got some of it for them.'

That Adjutant, Training, who'd given Ian benign, superfluous
advice about prophylactics, had mentioned that he'd served
with Townsend and used to speak about him and his flying
career occasionally in the Mess, a long time before the
romance. The ex-adj had been posted elsewhere now and was
himself promoted Group Captain but Ian traced him and got
more insights into the Townsend, Distinguished Service Order,
Distinguished Flying Cross (twice), he'd once known. Ian
plumped out reports on the royal tale with these extra, exclusive
bits. 'The thing was, Ray, I managed to become a specialist
on the sex life of Maggie and Pete. Some news editors abroad
who discovered I'd been in the Air Force obviously thought
I'd known Townsend myself – and possibly Margaret as well.
I tried not to mention that my feet had stayed very safely on
the ground and that I'd been trained like a soldier, not a dare-
devil pilot. My reputation as someone who had access to more
or less everybody soared. Editors like correspondents with
access, especially access to royals.' By spring 1956 he had
established a sound, freelance service to a growing market and
couldn't have afforded to join any paper's salaried staff.

'Lucy OK?' Bain said. 'Getting near her time.'

'You keep informed.' She did have a regular post as an Economics Correspondent on one of the heavies, and had helped support him for the first few London months. She'd take time off to have the baby, and wasn't sure she'd go back to her paper afterwards. She thought of working with Ian. He approved. She'd bring gravitas.

'This phone number of yours – a flat in Russell Square still?' Bain said. 'Home and office. I don't blame *you* for the colour of your front door. It must be the landlord's taste. But bloody mauve!'

'You keep informed. Ray, this meeting – you and me – is it . . . is it, well . . . is it to do with your sort of game? Shades of Lorna-Jane and Charles Fisher?'

'They're still with us. Mooney's nine p.m.,' Bain replied.

Although he wasn't sure he liked altogether the idea of a meeting with Bain, he knew he'd go. Oh, of course, he'd be glad to see him as a former mate cadet and rival, and especially if he seemed content; or as content as his state allowed. But Ian wondered what Bain was after, and perhaps what someone above Bain was after. Ian didn't fancy getting pulled into the kind of official shadows Ray Bain must permanently inhabit these days. Secrets dominated: they were due to discuss something that couldn't be mentioned on the telephone; and they'd talk about it in a secluded, very off-Broadway pub. Ian still resented the power of gratitude. And he knew gratitude was what made it certain he'd turn up. After all, he had his own legs to walk on. Matters might have been reversed – and fates.

Just the same, he didn't care for the way Bain obviously relished showing how much he had on record about Ian and Lucy's life and location. Some serious work had been done. Why? To intimidate? And, by intimidating, to persuade? Underhill and Fisher had pulled the same kind of ploy. There'd be ruthlessness as a routine in their game. He described the conversation to Lucy. She found it funny and childish, as he'd known she would. She despised anything to do with furtiveness and surveillance. Just the same, though, she agreed he had to go to the meeting. She'd realized why he felt obligated. 'It's absurd but inescapable, love,' she said. 'They're having

another go for you. She must be really . . . really obsessed.'
He sensed a moment's sexual jealousy in her. A long time
ago, he'd told her the Emily story from the paddle-steamer
rescue on, through the OCTU to her RAF Norton emissaries.
Lucy obviously sensed that the Bain call might continue the
campaign.

'Did he mention, hint at, recruitment?' Lucy said.

'Sailed near it. Claimed the people who came to Norton
were positive about yours truly. Their orders told them to be
positive – that was my impression.'

'Tread carefully, love. These are tricky people.'

Ray was on tin legs now and using a cane. Seated, he looked
pretty much as he had when Ian first met him at the training
unit, though it would probably be wrong these days to describe
his face as mischievous: more like strong, responsible,
purposeful. Devious? Possibly. His red hair was as thick and
shiny as ever, worn longer than at the OCTU and with no
retreat from his forehead. He'd be around twenty-seven or eight.

He was already in the pub when Ian arrived. Two pints of
Guinness plus the food stood on a table in front of Bain, his
stick propped against it. With a bit of an effort he stood to
shake hands. Ian saw this was important to him: the ability to
get up on cue. 'Welcome, welcome famous Blitish journablist,'
he chirped. Ian grinned. But was it funny, or did it recall an
episode that helped send Ray into battle and then crippledom?
Had he ever discovered what happened in the occult tallying
of points, and the Sword award, with its safe and guaranteed,
non-K, OCTU posting? He and his new colleagues seemed
able to find out quite a lot, didn't they? He had a black briefcase which he lifted in his left hand when he stood. It was on
a chain locked to his wrist and would have dangled very obviously otherwise.

There were two elderly men drinking and talking at a table
on the far side of the room; no other customers. A barman
appeared, disappeared, appeared again. The Guinness exuded
dark charm, compromised a bit by the drink's sharp tang, but
only a bit. The cheese exuded, too – a rich, penetrating, slightly
foul pong, the way Gorgonzola should, young or old, and he
thought this might be oldish.

'We're looking for some help, Ian,' he said.

'Help from me?'

'It's to do with this Suez invasion muck-up.'

'Which "we" do we mean?'

'There was quite an argument back in the office about whether to try you,' Ray replied.

'Which office – that accountancy outfit?'

'Coldstream, Fay and Partners? They went into liquidation.'

'An accountancy firm in liquidation? Does this happen often? If they can't make a go of things, who can?'

'But, of course, others took over their practice and offices.'

'That's a relief.'

'Some people there, headed by Lorna-Jane, said that since you had conspicuously ignored the original approach, it would be "unwise, even perverse " – those were the words – to seek contact with you again, especially when the country's in a war situation with Egypt over the canal. Lorna-Jane has gone up a peg or two since their visit to Norton, despite the failure to land you. She's management now, only a notch below me. Gets a car and a PA. Her opinions rate for something.'

'But not as much as yours, and those of—'

'Of the famous E. No. As I see it, Ian, Lorna-Jane's only real knowledge of you is through that Norton encounter and the dossier material they dredged, which is admittedly considerable,' Bain replied, 'but one or two of us there can bring something markedly deeper.'

'Two.'

'And Charlie Fisher, who accompanied Lorna-Jane at Norton, gave you true support. He lacks her new departmental clout, but his views are not negligible. Not negligible at all.'

'I took him to be the thug side of things.'

'He's been in therapy and the improvement is startling. The job paid for his treatment, naturally. Quite a few staff need something of that kind. Nobody would have mentioned consistency as one of Fisher's qualities before but now, yes, he's more often consistent than not. But even so we're talking about his own style of consistency, I admit. You've got to settle for what you can get, haven't you, and therapy is expensive. Charlie took up Lorna-Jane's words – the "unwise" and "even perverse" – and did quite an analysis of them, regardless of her rank, a really aggressive taking apart.'

'He'd be good at that. But I thought they worked harmoniously together.'

'Before the promotion, yes. Charlie's intervention – very much to your advantage. He said he thought that "unwise" in this context suggested you could not be regarded as discreet, secure, able and willing to maintain confidentiality. He wouldn't have this. He considered that by declining the offer made at Norton and, instead, going for the journalistic career you'd always wanted, you showed strength and focus. Whether your choice was "conspicuous" or non-conspicuous didn't matter a toss, in his opinion.

'He argued that if we came to you for assistance and asked for this request to remain covert, at least temporarily, you would have the discipline and resolve to accept such a condition. I, naturally, endorsed that, Ian. As to "even perverse", Fisher said he believed this actually meant Lorna-Jane felt insulted by your refusal of the offer and that it would be degrading, humiliating, to come crawling to you for aid, even if you could provide it. This he considered a negative, vengeful, illogical, arrogant response. In not quite such blunt terms, we endorsed that, of course.'

'Which we?'

'As in any organization there are disputes. Occasionally, it can appear as though our people are more intent on fighting one another, rather than the outside enemy. This impairs efficiency. I sometimes think I'd like to write a book about it. Call it, say, *The Looking Glass War*. I won't, of course, but I offer the idea.'

Was all the verbiage a sales pitch? Ray Bain wanted him to know there'd been a squabble over whether he should be asked for help. And so the strung-out baloney about what Lorna-Jane had done, and what Fisher had replied, despite his inferior rank. And so, also, the quibble about Ian's 'conspicuous' ignoring of their invitation, or non-conspicuousness. Those in favour of an approach to Ian, including Bain, had won the dispute. Therefore, the reasoning went, Ian would see how much he was prized by some. He should feel gratitude – and agree to what they asked – since some had fought so gallantly for his suitability and right to be asked. More gratitude. Another noose.

He found it hard to guess how he could help, anyway, if it was to do with 'this Suez invasion muck-up'. He didn't know much more than anyone else about this Suez invasion muck-up, except that it *was* a muck-up. The basics were simple, and the basics were all he had: Egypt's President Nasser recently decided to nationalize the Suez Canal; Britain had sent an army and war planes to stop it happening. Some people here and abroad were outraged by Prime Minister Eden's decision to attack. There had been near-riots around Whitehall and Westminster. Ian had gone to report on one of them and was just able to skip out of the way of a police horse charge. His familiarity with the issue extended no further than that.

Or only a bit further: one night he'd been hanging about the newsroom of the *Mirror* when the editorial director, Hugh Cudlipp, cigar alight, breezed in, bright with an idea. Ian had been glancing at some pictures of youngsters in a club obviously enjoying a new kind of high-spirited music and dancing brought over by Bill Haley from the United States. The *Mirror* would use one of the photographs and a couple of deskmen were trying to pick the best. Jack Porter said: 'So what is this rock 'n' roll, Henry?'

'I don't know, Jack, but I bet they fuck afterwards,' Henry said.

Cudlipp wasn't concerned. He suggested to Ian a trawl through right-wing newspapers for anti-Eden comment. It was important they should be Rightist, Conservative sheets. Cudlipp wanted to show that even Eden's pals thought him wrong. Ian had done the scan and a couple of days later the *Mirror* came out with a string of the quotes and a front-page, upper-case, big-type headline EDEN MUST GO. Maybe it had been a foolish mistake of Eden to have the kind of short surname that fitted easily on to page one in those massive, unmissable letters.

Ian and Bain drank and ate. Ian had his back to the pub's street door and was aware of someone light on their feet entering behind him. Bain, facing the other way, put down his glass and stood again. 'No, don't, Ray,' Emily Stanton said. Ian stood, too. She took a chair next to him. He and Bain sat down once more. 'Don't blame Ray for not warning you I'd be along,' she said. 'I didn't tell him. In fact, I wasn't sure I would come. But then I thought I should, since it's mainly about me and mine.'

'Oh, Ray said it was Suez,' Ian replied.

'Me and mine and Suez,' she said. She asked the barman for a red wine. She didn't touch the food.

'You and your what?' Ian said.

'Daughter,' Emily replied. She said the word without special emphasis, almost throwaway, but in her face he read pain. At that OCTU reception party he'd noticed her easiness and poise in company, plus plenty of vivacity and humour. Perhaps she could still turn all that on when needed. But he was seeing something different from her tonight, a deep nervousness, impossible to conceal. She had on a long beige coat with a large pointed collar. She wore no hat. Her hair, like Bain's, was longer than Ian remembered, on to her shoulders, and still free from grey. How could he connect her with that tactless, blurt-prone creature at the memorial ceremony? Or with that noisy, careless girl on the *King Arthur*'s second-up deck cable, come to that? He couldn't. People progressed. The wine arrived and she took a sip.

'You and Group Captain Stanton have a daughter?' Ian said. 'I hadn't realized.'

'The Group Captain has a stepdaughter.'

He thought around that. 'Ah, a daughter from your first marriage?' Ian said.

'I have a daughter,' she replied. 'She was away at school at your OCTU time.'

'You've probably heard of her,' Bain said, as if to shift the topic sideways fast.

'She's an actress – stage, some television, a film. She uses the name Daphne West,' Emily said. 'Just turned twenty.'

Ian said: 'Well, of course I've heard of her and seen her in things on TV – the *High Circle* adaptation. Great. She's a bit of a star. A very attractive girl. Perhaps I do see a resemblance.'

'Kind,' Emily said.

'Was West your first married name?'

'She chose it. Stage name.' She cut that strand of talk. 'What's your feeling about Suez then?' Emily replied.

'Probably a mistake. Very unpopular. In the way of work I've joined a few protest crowds. Atmospheric, but not comfortable.'

'We detect a growing disgust with government,' she said, 'and especially with the PM.'

'Maybe,' Ian said.

'This is not like the World War or Korea,' Bain said. 'By and large the people backed our fighting services then. The moral case was strong, irresistible. The country was willing to rally round.'

'Whereas now, the opposition could grow to a dangerous level,' Emily said. 'I mean an unmanageable level, very focused hate, very organized. Serious.'

Ian thought it did seem to be personalized on to Anthony Eden. That's probably what came from winning a Military Cross in the Great War and looking like a dandy.

'Eventually he'll have to go,' Bain said.

'But what comes next when he does?' Emily said. She didn't wait. 'I'll tell you: we get a political vacuum. There'll be outfits who see their chance to move in and take over – some of these outfits not at all desirable. So perilous, Ian. That's our worry.'

'Your job – jobs – mean you two *have* to worry about this, do you?' Ian said.

Bain said: 'Why we exist. Many worry about it, though.'

Ian didn't bother now to ask which 'we' that might be.

'But your daughter?' Ian said. 'How is she touched by all this – an actress, and successful?'

'Yes, she's caught up in it, indirectly caught up in it,' Emily said.

'Part of a protest group?' Ian said. 'I would think a lot of young people feel that way. The average age in the demonstrations I've covered has been low. It's probably normal for idealistic teenagers and twenties. Remember that Oxford University union vote in 1933 against fighting for king and country as Nazidom began to gallop ahead?'

'Yes, as a matter of fact, history does come into it. Can I digress a minute?' Bain said. 'This might sound a little far out, but let me give you the outline: some of us see this present situation as comparable with 1936.'

'1936?' Ian said. 'No Suez crisis then, was there?'

'I'm talking about the run-up to the abdication of Ed Eight, our playboy king. The country badly, grievously split and, in any case, struggling hopelessly with prolonged economic slump and widespread unemployment. Our archive material shows real fears began to sprout that the poverty and despair – the lockouts, dole queues, soup kitchens, miners' marches – might lead to an out-and-out people's revolt. Life was intolerable for so many. We know now that some highly placed, wealthy/aristocratic figures felt amazed – and vastly lucky – that this hammered, deprived working class hadn't already tried to overthrow a failed system – a system which, even when running properly, did so only by exploiting the poor and weak.'

'Revolution?' Ian said. 'Oh, come on, Ray.'

'They had 1917 Russia in mind – less than twenty years earlier. Very frightening,' Bain said. 'See any parallels, Ian?'

'You mean with now? But—'

'Some time early in 1936 rumours, whispers, hints, multiplied concerning a strange, organized – yes, possibly, revolutionary – force in Britain. It's all documented,' Emily replied. 'Our predecessors in the job carried out a very capable research mission and wrote it up. We have the records, as you'd expect.'

'I've never heard anything of it,' Ian said.

'Well, you wouldn't. The material can't be made public for years yet,' she said.

'But you've seen it?' Ian said.

'We have a certain access, yes,' Emily said.

'Like Underhill and Charlie Fisher with my medical records as a kid?' Ian said.

'They got into those, did they?' Bain said.

'Didn't you know?' Ian asked. 'I assumed one of you cleared that for them.'

'I say this force was strange because it seemed based on a remarkable – no, not just remarkable; on a unique – alliance,' Emily replied. 'As you'd expect, one side of it were workers, trade unionists and extreme Socialists, representing the people who suffered most, were most deprived. But the other part is possibly more interesting and astonishing. It was made up of major upper-class figures, some of them authentic, blue-blood nobility, even courtiers. I mean, Britain leads the world on class division, and more so twenty years ago, but this was a partnership that managed to bring together the suffering, disaffected, ground-down Left and the anxious, self-interestedly patriotic, fiercely enraged Royalists. Documents show our forerunners in this trade—'

'The secrets trade?' Ian said. He'd decided suddenly on a moment of frankness at last.

'They believed that the new King Edward, known as David to chums, provided the link between these two kinds of unlikely confederates,' Emily said.

'It went like this: both lots, for different reasons, vowed their faith in this mesmeric sovereign,' Bain said. 'The Left regarded him as a symbol of possible benign change, a saviour of the working class. Remember his promise that something would be done about unemployment, when he was confronted by the poverty and distress of his subjects in South Wales? It was regarded as a sensationally political statement for a Royal to make. Ordinary people had apparently come to believe the supposedly very modern, progressive, bold but sensitive royal night-clubber could work some sort of wholesale improvement in the wrecked state of the country. They'd forgive the gadabout image as long as he saw their condition properly and sympathized. They thought he, individually, on his own, might pull it off.

'At the same time, you see, Ian, the Right wanted him to guard the political structure and traditions that had done them so fine for centuries and, in their view, should go on doing them fine for ever. Think of Hobbes.'

'Which?' Ian said.

'Thomas Hobbes, the seventeenth-century philosopher,' Bain said.

'Oh, him,' Ian said.

'He thought people were basically so much alike in ability that they would always be fighting one another so as to get one step or two steps ahead. Only a strong leader could prevent this chaos by becoming so obviously superior that the population would kowtow to him or her, and behave properly towards everybody else. Thus, a monarch.'

'Fascinating,' Ian said, 'but so? What's it to do with now?'

'Note the 1936 to 1956 similarities,' Bain said.

'You're telling me Eden is like Edward VIII and, if he, Eden, goes there'll be a coup, a revolution?' Ian said. 'Only Eden holds Britain together?'

'Stability is something we can't take for granted,' Emily said. 'Most of our citizens do take it for granted. They expect the streets to be reasonably safe; they expect the electricity and the water to reach their homes. They suppose the country is able to defend itself against foreign aggressors. But, as we've seen less than twenty years ago, such confidence can be challenged. We have to work for it and actively protect it. That's one reason Ray and I hold the kind of jobs we do. It's a responsibility.'

Perhaps the weight of it was what had helped change her from that unthinking piece at the pier memorial, that silly kid on and then off the *King Arthur.*

'The trouble in 'thirty-six over the King's wish to marry Wallis, the American divorcee, was kept out of British newspapers,' Bain said. 'They agreed to censor themselves so as not to disturb national stability. But some crafty, ambitious figures, mainly on the Right, did know the frailty of the King's position, and they spotted rich possibilities, incorporating massed working-class power as an element in their own armament. There's hefty evidence that a junta was in preparation, ready to take over. And, the point is, we get whiffs of the same possibility now.'

'A sort of re-run,' Emily said.

'Junta!' Charteris said.

'There were people in 1936 who reasoned that, if Edward were forced out because of Mrs Simpson, unrest in the country might grow uncontainable, triggered finally by the loss of this man, Edward, who seemingly understood the pain of the masses in the slump, and who might have brought widespread hope and relief,' Emily said. 'There had already been occasional public protests about unemployment and hardship, but without any real central drive. Some considered the displacing of Edward could provide this. I've seen a photograph of a protest banner in Oxford Street as the end of Edward's reign approached that warned: "Abdication Means Revolution". It may sound pat and vacuous to us now, but the possibility existed.'

'And now you believe Suez could mean that?' Ian said.

'There are always opportunists,' Emily said.

'What opportunists?' Ian asked.

'Power opportunists,' she said. 'Political people, wealthy people, business people, trade union people, anarchist people, military people,' Bain said. 'A country falls into anarchy. It happens abroad. Do you think we're immune?'

And, perhaps yes, Ian did think that, did believe the governance of Britain usually stayed fairly comfortably on a safe and moderate track. So was he naive, outdated? Had his time in the Regiment, with its spit-and-polish, discipline and obedience, convinced him that things in GB would always sort themselves out?

'We are for ever alert for groups ready to grab control if things look likely to break down,' Emily said. 'They could break down now. And we've already seen signs. The rioting you mentioned, Ian. The Suez crisis of 1956 is potentially as bad for Britain as anything in 1936. The volatility is very comparable, very equal. And you newspaper people are not helping. Some negative, even provocative stuff gets printed.'

'"Eden Must Go", do you mean? All my own work,' Ian said.

'Oh, people imagine there'd be an orderly transfer of power to RA Butler, if Eden is toppled,' she said. '*When* Eden is toppled. A tactical illness seems probable. Perhaps a real illness. In Press pictures, he looks bad; and worse, because he had always been so effulgently dapper. I can tell you, the Conservative Party won't have Butler. He's forever tainted as a Hitler appeaser. Who then? No obvious candidate. This is the point, isn't it, Ian? This is the peril. An inviting emptiness for those quick off the mark and resolute. Power could be snatched by forces outside the usual party system, a putsch. For instance, there are toffs who believe in a strong, orderly, strictly hierarchical regime, with themselves holding favourable, entirely secure positions in it, of course. Compare Mussolini's Cooperative State. Or compare Magna Carta.'

'I thought Magna Carta was a statement of the people's essential, inalienable rights,' Ian said.

'Did you?' she said.

'It's not?' Ian asked. *Was* he naive, outdated?

'A crowd of barons looking after their own interests, as barons always will. A few gestures towards protection for the general populace were crocheted in as disguise,' Emily said. 'Likewise the Glorious Revolution of 1688 and the Parliamentary party in the Civil War – on the face of it early democratic movements, but really the rich and noble perfecting together a tidy deal for themselves.

'The thinking we have to fear now is in line with these earlier conspiracies – precise and dangerous thinking, Ian. The 1936 situation didn't come to anything because Edward suddenly quit and did a bunk. Both sides, Left and Right, felt abandoned, disabled. The 1956 version might not be so easily seen off.'

Ian went to the bar and bought another glass of wine and two more pints. Did these tales from twenty years ago, and from deeper history, colour and distort Emily's and Ray's views of the present? Were they slaves to their secret archive, searching for parallels and echoes, half-crazily predisposed to find them, because finding things was their forte? After all, what was the use of an archive if you couldn't tickle it into life now and then? Too much theory, too much guess, too many imagined echoes and reruns – the way generals might think in terms of a previous conflict, instead of the one they had to fight now? All kinds of huge changes had taken place in Britain between 1936 and 1956: the impacts of a six-year world war, two Labour governments, a new Queen. Was it anything like the same place?

When he returned with the drinks, Emily said: 'You think it's all waffle, don't you, Ian? Theory. Speculation. And, yes, there's some of both, possibly. That's unavoidable. It's not the whole picture, though. Let's get to particulars then. Consider my daughter. She's having a relationship with the stage producer, playwright and occasional impresario Milton Skeeth. He's a member of the building and property development family. But he wanted a theatrical career, so isn't active in the

company. He's got a lot of Skeeth Construction loot and shares
behind him. Big capital.'

'I think I might have seen something about your daughter's
career in a couple of the gossip columns,' Ian said, 'but, obviously, I didn't know who she was then.'

'"The fascinating and pert Daphne West" as one of them
called her,' Emily said.

'What do *you* call her?' Ian said.

'Just Daphne,' Emily said. 'That's her real first name.'

'But not West?' Ian said.

'Skeeth and his brother Leonard – MD of Skeeth Construction
– are two of the people we think could be interested in a coup,
the sort we're talking about,' Bain replied. Their motives might
not be entirely bad. They want stability; they need guaranteed
order for the Skeeth interests to thrive in. They seemingly
don't believe the government, or even an alternative government in present circumstances, can produce that stability, that
guaranteed orderliness.'

'Ah, I get it,' Ian said.

'Milton and Leonard are under what we hope is covert
watch,' Bain said.

'You see, Ian, I get reports from some of our operatives
about my own daughter,' Emily said sadly, 'as one of several
women Milton Skeeth is seeing. It's not sweet. And she talks
about him to me. I don't mean she deliberately informs, but
she discusses their relationship and, of course, she's occasionally telling me more than she realizes.'

'It's all very delicate,' Bain said.

'Sounds agonizing,' Ian said.

'Yes, it is,' Emily said.

'What we have to take into account is that some people –
some business people, for instance, some moneybags people
– agree absolutely that Eden must go, not at all because he
committed Britain to an unlawful war in Suez,' Bain said.
'The reverse. They gun for him because he turned pathetically
indecisive once the fight began,' Emily said. 'They consider
the invasion entirely justified. As obligatory, in fact. The Suez
Canal they regard as vital to Britain's, and therefore their own,
wealth. As they see it, Nasser will interfere with the canal's

free flow of shipping. So, attack and get rid of him. To them, the logic looks simple. If you've got a lot of boodle and assets and someone seems to be threatening them, the reaction does tend to be simple: you try to protect yourself by any means you can. One of those means ought to be the Prime Minister of Britain, in their view. This Prime Minister has failed, though – also in their view. He was, apparently, a gallant soldier in the Great War, but has either lost his touch, or isn't suited to taking the great policy decisions and following them through.'

Emily said: 'They believe Eden has buckled pathetically. Even treasonably.' She seemed to have switched back to the large political picture as a relief from discussing Daphne. 'They think he's turned yellow because the United States hints it might refuse support for sterling unless Britain pulls back her troops. I've heard talk of impeachment. Not a real option. But, in any case, they want him out and someone tougher – someone who understands business and trade better   they want a replacement like that to take power temporarily, until the crisis is settled in our – GB's – favour. And above all, *their* personal favour.

'It wouldn't necessarily be a substitute produced by conventional democratic methods – almost certainly would not be – but a grand *vizier* used to leadership, perhaps with royal connections, a figurehead capable of decisive thought and action in defence of traditional British interests, the traditional British interests being mainly, though not totally, commercial. There's also a pride aspect. "Can a country like GB get messed about by Egypt, for God's sake?" they ask. "By Egypt! No, sir, never!"'

'Lord Mountbatten, for instance,' Bain said. 'Or Lord Mivale, the Oxford Economics don.'

'It seems preposterous,' Ian said. But, repeat question, was he naive, outdated?

'My daughter doesn't know the kind of work I do,' Emily said. 'Obviously, she does know I've a government consultancy job and that my line is Personnel, but not the *kind* of Personnel. I can't tell her what we have on Milton Skeeth, or think we have, and that we'll be trying for more. Even if I did, it probably wouldn't make her drop him. She's strong-minded and independent, not disposed to take that kind of advice from her mother. Few girls would. They'd see it as meddling by a *croulante*, an ancient old wreck. I'm not sure whether Daphne knows about the other women. In any case, Skeeth's love life is not our concern, even if my daughter's involved. We are interested in him for other reasons.'

Ian thought she might like to believe this, but it was obviously not true. Although she and Bain *were* interested in Skeeth for other reasons than his love life, the fact that Daphne West figured as part of that love life troubled Emily, perhaps even affected how she would run the department's investigation of Skeeth, maybe tied her hands.

And this might be why she and Bain needed Ian. He thought he could see how they would want to use him. He thought, too, that Emily might guess he'd pick up on Daphne's age, apply some simple maths and start wondering – feel compelled to help. Family. Noose.

ELEVEN

Saturday morning, dawn start, Ian went on a badger hunt, most likely illegal under animal-cruelty laws. Badgers shouldn't be persecuted with dogs. They were amiable, handsome animals loved by everyone who'd read Kenneth Grahame's *The Wind in the Willows*, where Mr Badger came over as a wise, gruff, solid, kindly character. Didn't he welcome Rat and Mole into his home when they were lost and desperate in the Wild Wood? There was even a move to make badgers a protected species. To dig for one, let alone kill or injure it, would be a crime. Not yet.

The badger setts – their elaborate, wide-mouthed and obvious burrows – were strung out on a long grassy bank near a small wood on the edge of a cooperative farmer's land. He blind-eyed these hunts. To him and his neighbours, badgers rated as pests, bringing TB to their herds. The four hunters carried a couple of spades, a locater instrument like a Geiger counter, and two long steel probes to push into the tunnel network and listen.

Ian didn't reread *The Wind in the Willows* as preparation for the hunt, but a pamphlet on the kind of dogs used. He had to get familiarized. He had to blend with the badgerers. On the face of it, he'd be the hunters' guest, keen to learn. He'd discovered how much the dogs were revered, and once he'd watched what some had to do, he understood why. They starred. They carried the risk: the pair of Jack Russells, Belle and Daisy; a Border terrier, Kate; and two Patterdales, Napoleon and Bert, kept on the leash. Kate wore a special collar that signalled from underground so the huntsmen could guess the dogs' position: vital once they cornered the prey, because in any prolonged scrap below the badger would win and the dogs get bitten or clawed to death; or shoved under soil and suffocated. It was bred into badgers how to deal with invading dogs deep down and in the dark, and sometimes the quarry would triumph.

At first they put the Jack Russells in – undreamy, short-legged rough-house dogs who'd obviously seen it all before. They'd take on anything, and pushed down hard and quick into the sett. The badger might turn and clobber them, finale blows. The prey was bigger than them, hefty in the paw with jaws that didn't mess around, a wily subterranean, used to the lack of light.

Immediately the men on the surface knew the target animal and dogs had met and where, the hunters rushed to dig a vertical shaft down to it. When the badger was exposed like this at the bottom of the hole, the Patterdale surface dogs, bigger animals, could pitch in and help. It might take ten minutes or more to reach the underground battle, all four men working hard in relays with the spades.

So, the two Jack Russells – short-legged, bandy, fearless, frantically energetic – had raced into one of the sett's openings as soon as they arrived. Kate went down soon after. For a couple of minutes, there was no noise as the underground search started, then barking followed by a heavy thumping sound. It must mean one or more of the dogs and the badger had joined and were sparring. Len and Malcolm listened on the probes at two of the sett entrances trying to pinpoint. The locator, held by Jeff, started a loud, continuous buzz. He moved about like a diviner until the din got to what he regarded as maximum. Ian guessed the badger was cornered in a cul-de-sac tunnel and had turned to fight off the terriers.

Len and Malcolm forgot their probes and very urgent, almost feverish, excavating started. Norman Vernon Towler helped. If the shaft wasn't absolutely accurate they'd have wasted that much time and that much energy and would have to try another dig at once. By then, the dogs would be near exhaustion and at big risk. The badger was on its natural ground, in its private domain, and could smash intruders as of right. A badger's home was its castle. Jeff had told Ian how they'd lost a Jack Russell in a sett not long ago because the locator failed and they were forced to operate by instinct; wrong instinct, as it turned out. They'd found the dog smothered.

Jeff was Jeffrey David Dill, thirty-one, burly, fresh-faced, fair-haired, no criminal record, unmarried, school leaver at sixteen, trade-union shop steward, two younger brothers, no criminal records, father and mother living on a council estate in Bristol, no criminal records, Baptists, lapsed.

When Ray Bain had ultimately unlocked his chained briefcase and opened it in Mooney's bar, he brought out a file of the Skeeth operation to date. Jeffrey David Dill was one of the names recorded and backgrounded there. 'We believe the revolution/coup planners have people in various parts of the country who'll run anti-government, anti-Eden, protests when the time's considered right to signal general unrest. The aim is to make a takeover appear justified and necessary, even inevitable,' Emily had said. 'The coup chiefs will look like saviours. It's a traditional ploy by insurgents: Robespierre, Musso, Adolf. Dill's one of these potential stirrers. We've watched him for a while. He works in an automotive parts factory and is used to organizing the workforce. Probably best to get to him when he's relaxed, off-duty. Some weekends he goes badger hunting with pals.'

'Len Gale, Malcolm Ivins, Norman Vernon Towler,' Bain said.

'If you could talk your way into joining them you might be able to get on matey terms with Dill,' Emily said. 'I don't pretend it's simple or easy. But they're very proud of their dogs. Ray has the names and breeds. Throw the pooch praise around. They'll accept you, maybe. Then you can sneak on to wider topics with Dill.'

Ian had sensed from near the start what Bain and Emily hoped to get from him. It was devious and clever. Ian might have expected something like that from Ray. Emily could manage it, too, apparently. They wanted Ian, as a freelance reporter who necessarily knew all the Press markets, to follow up leads from their investigation. They'd like him to publish in one or more newspapers an article, or articles, about the organization of a projected putsch. This sudden, unforeseen and basically hostile exposure would ruin its timetable, identify and target its leaders, probably kill it off. And if Emily's daughter didn't already know of Milton Skeeth's involvement she'd find out about it now, without Emily herself having to breach security rules of the trade to tell her. It was personal, but it was professional, too.

'This would make a splash newspaper piece, wouldn't it, Ian?' Bain said.

'Or more than one,' Emily said. 'You could bring about immense political and even military change. It's what a responsible Press in a democracy is for, isn't it?'

Possibly. But it wasn't the role of a responsible Press to do fetch-and-carry dirty work for the security services. He felt as though Emily and Ray Bain had wanted to recruit him in straightforward, 'unconditional' style to their outfit, and, having got nowhere, were now trying a more devious, compromise method.

'Law and order, Ian,' Bain said. 'Democracy can function properly only when those essentials are in place. You and your newspaper of choice will be helping to preserve these. It would be a vital contribution.'

Yes, this was probably true – if, and triple if, their reading of the political crisis made sense. They did present a good case. And then, also, and very weighty, there was the matter of the mighty debt he owed them both. The noose again – gratitude. *He* could follow a badger hunt over no matter what kind of ground. He had both his legs in full.

But he hadn't felt like committing himself, just the same.

'L-J. – Lorna-Jane Underhill – wanted to give the tale to Sefton Delmer on the *Express*, but we stopped that,' Bain said. 'It seemed so right for you. Charlie backed us.'

'It's good of you all,' Ian said.

'Make a start with Dill and his friends,' Bain said. He returned the file to its briefcase and re-locked the chain to his wrist.

'You'd be helping us, Ian,' Emily said, 'and doing yourself some good as a brilliantly vigilant and constructive reporter, wouldn't you?'

Maybe. Not if their scenario of future events proved to be only that – a scenario, prompted by a half-baked, half-daft urge to see the crisis of 1956 as a repeat of something allegedly – very allegedly – similar twenty years ago. He was fond of Emily and Bain, and did owe them something. But that must not mean he had to shut down his mind, ditch all sensible judgement. And his judgement said that no editor would buy their idea. If a paper did show a morsel of interest and the whole business then turned out to be eyewash and impossible to verify, the blame would stick for months, or for ever, to Ian. A colourful account of his stupidity would get around Fleet Street to every national paper via bar talk at the Press Club. Future work would get to be very scarce. Credibility in his byline would be terminated.

Bain's car and driver were waiting when they left Mooney's. 'We'll take you home,' Emily said. 'I want to see that mauve front door.'

'I'm going to think about things,' he'd told them. As he felt then, he meant he would think a little more about things, and then forget their scheme. It was too woolly, too basically unlikely, too damned imaginative. He'd try to find a more polite way to put it, of course. It would still be a refusal. They'd be hurt and probably angered. He was sorry, but this looked to him like the only reasonable decision.

A couple of days later, though, he had to back off from that supposedly rational decision and think again. He had a call at home from a work acquaintance, the Labour politician and former *Daily Express* writer Tom Driberg: Delmer now, Driberg then. In the 1930s his articles under the pen name William Hickey, after the eighteenth-century diarist, had revolutionized gossip column journalism. Driberg had often featured ordinary people as well as royalty, the aristocracy and show-business stars. He must be into his fifties, half a step or less from decrepitude on London newspapers, unless you actually *owned* a title or two, of course.

'Could we meet, Ian?' he said. Driberg was an ardent and questing homosexual but didn't take offence if you let him know you preferred something else. Rumour said he was writing an autobiography to be called *Ruling Passions*. It would be withheld from publication until after his death. People assumed the *Passions* were politics and fellatio. He would probably describe it as such himself. He named a pub in the Strand, walkable from Fleet Street, though not a journalists' spot and reasonably private.

Did Driberg feel he must struggle to stay in the game? Fleet Street crawled with one-time greats trying to sell exclusives to the papers, and so resurrect their names for a day. Not long ago, *The Morning Sentinel* had asked Ian to look at a political tip from Driberg, and Ian met him a couple of times then. This potential tale had never got off the ground, though. Ian had the notion that Driberg felt guilty about the failure and wanted to compensate somehow. It was the lesson he'd got from that kind of flop that had made Ian plan to sidestep the Emily-Bain project.

'It's re the Suez situation,' Driberg said near the end of the phone conversation.

This had almost made Ian back off again. That same old topic. Well, not so old, perhaps, but ever-present these days. 'What about it?' he said.

'Not for phone talk,' Driberg said. He fixed a time and ended the call.

Oh, God, more semi-secrecy. But Ian had some sympathy for this former journalistic big wheel, some fellow-feeling. Who'd be next to tumble, next for the tumbril? National newspaper offices and staffs could be very rough, and also very sentimental, could be unscrupulously competitive, yet sometimes mildly considerate to those once mighty in the trade and now shrunken. 'Never send to know for whom the bell tolls.'

It was a sedate, panelled pub, with comfortable, discreet booths. Driberg possibly approved of booths. He looked a booth person, somehow: suave, plaid shirted, bulky, dew-lapped, pondering. He'd put on some pounds since Ian last saw him. He uttered a big, comic groan. 'I've been in news-papers for – oh, Lord, who's counting? I've seen all sorts.' He appeared eager to drop into reminiscence. It was natural. It was enforced. He had excelled in the past. He needed to boost himself and impress Ian with prestige bygones. But did he have anything for now? Now was the Press's favourite period. For the sake of Driberg's ego, Ian would let him get recollec-tive for a while, though. He wanted to be kindly.

'I've run into all sorts, you know, Ian.'

'Well, I expect so.'

'Statesmen. Actors, actresses. Kings. It's kings I wanted to talk to you about.'

'Which?'

'Or at least *a* king.'

'Which?'

'Edward.'

'Which?'

'Which? Which would I have been concerned with?'

'Edward the eighth?' Ian tensed. Echoes of Mooney's.

'Prince of Wales, then short-term king.'

'What about him?'

Driberg didn't answer at once. He gazed at some of the panelling. When he spoke again it was as though his mind and its topics had drifted. Or had they? This was an accomplished storyteller. Perhaps he'd give a fragment – enough to tweak the listener's attention – then shelve that and switch temporarily to something else: tease tactics, salesman's tactics. 'Who was it said history is doomed to repeat itself?' Driberg asked, sipping.

Of course, he was the sort who wouldn't put the question if he didn't know the answer. Best get in before the pretentious old plaid-garbed prick: 'Marx quoting Hegel. Not quite those words, though.'

'Well, yes,' Driberg said. 'How splendid that reporters read books and have degrees these days.' He gave the panelling some more scrutiny. 'Have you heard of a Lord Mivale?'

Yes, he had heard of a Lord Mivale, from Emily and Bain: someone who might be installed as head of a ruling clique, in their portrait of the future. He said: 'Should I have?'

'Yes, you should have.'

'In what connection?' Ian asked.

'A connection between 1936 and 1956.'

'I don't follow,' Ian said, half-following and not liking it, half-longing to get out of this bar, away from this meeting, before he fell beaten unconscious by boredom.

'When I was on the *Express* in 1936 I began to pick up rumours, whispers, hints, about a strange, organized, potentially insurgent force that was ready to step in if the king's abdication threw the country into chaos. I say strange because it was an alliance between Left and Right, even extreme Right.'

'Yes?' Ian said.

Ageing, maybe, but Driberg remained quick, perceptive. 'You've heard something of this already?'

'Never.'

'Why I referred to the tag about history doomed to repeat itself.'

'You see something similar now?' Ian said.

'Mivale is an Economics don at Oxford,' Driberg replied.

'Yes?'

'You note the parallels between 'thirty-six and 'fifty-six, do you?' Driberg said.

'You want me to believe, and get an editor to believe, that Eden is comparable with Edward and that if he, Eden, goes the country will slide into revolution? You think Eden holds Britain together, and Eden only?' Hell, Ian realized he was more or less quoting himself from that session in the Irish pub. He felt knocked off balance to have this bit of nightmare thinking put to him from two different sources – different and distant. Had he been stupid to dismiss what Emily and Ray Bain said about the possible future?

'You think Mivale has been lined up as likely Supremo?' Ian said.

'Mivale or perhaps Mountbatten. This is the word that reaches me.'

'From?'

'Some sources still consider me worth contacting,' Driberg said, with a great chortle of self-pity.

'Which?'

'I think you ought to try and talk to Mivale. He's probably an easier target than the arrogant, posing Mountbatten.'

'Why don't you? You're a newspaper man, an eminent newspaperman still.'

'Still? Was. I wouldn't get near him. I'm a politician, a Left politician. This would be a Rightist conspiracy, one that made use of the disaffected masses, but allowed them no sniff of the leadership. He'd see me as dangerous, a kind of spy. He might talk to you. No form. Reasonably open, smiling face. An innocent.'

'That's me,' Ian said. Was it? He longed to be considered as worldly, capable. How could this bloody has-been see into him like that? So, all right then. He wouldn't approach Mivale yet. But he'd upend his resolution to ignore Emily's and Ray Bain's suggestions. And so, the badger hunt.

As Ian and Driberg left the Strand pub, Driberg had said: 'I sense a grand, powerful nothingness at the centre of you, Ian, a polished, powerful negation. I had some of that once. Guard it. This is the one essential for a great reporter. People observe the void in you, as they did in the former me, and subconsciously feel challenged to fill it. And so they talk all their secrets at us. I'm doing it myself, don't you see? Something compels me to chat away to you. All you have to do is listen. You're wonderfully null, inconstant, uncommitted, unstable, opportunist. Yes, negative capability. You'll excel in newspapers.'

Ian hated it when people who seemed so obsolete and discarded could suddenly produce such glistening, offensive, accurate insights. Walking back to Fleet Street alone he felt fierce resentment at Driberg's profile of him as a nothing. *Could* a nothing get profiled? Moneywise he was not a negation, was he? Oh, no! Ian – or, at least, the paper – paid for all the damn drinks, yet Driberg had called the meeting. He told Lucy about Driberg's civic chaos thesis, and about the character picture he'd drawn of Ian Charteris, reporter. She'd raged for a while about that last bit, called it 'filthy backbiting and vilification'. This brought some comfort to him, but he recognized she might be biased. Ought to be.

TWELVE

The log extract read out in Mooney's by Bain mentioned a country pub where badger hunt lads went and Ian had been there one evening and did what Emily suggested: talked himself into bogus friendship with Dill and the others by showing a good, intelligent affection for their dogs, tethered outside in the pub yard. Ian's work seemed suddenly centred on pubs. He would go carefully. He'd let the hunters assume he might want to become one eventually, if he liked what he saw today.

Playing the eager learner he'd asked which sort of dog he should get and train and how the men shared costs for the equipment. He said badgers were certainly very handsome and interesting animals, but a menace to health. He'd been going to describe them as 'fascinating' rather than 'interesting' but decided this would be flowery, soft talk and censored himself in time.

Investigative reporters could get badly knocked about, or worse, if the people they meant to expose came to suspect the game. Ian had glanced around the country pub's customers, wondering if one of them had Dill under surveillance, and Ian, therefore, under surveillance now, too. He didn't see anyone who fitted, but could he really know how one of Emily's people might look? They didn't advertise. Could he have told from her looks what Emily excelled in, or from Ray Bain's now, either?

On the Saturday hunt, Ian could suddenly make out at the bottom of the hole the grey and off-white, blood-streaked pelt of a big badger, and Daisy with her teeth fixed into its neck. The badger's paws flailed, trying to knock Daisy away. Malcolm let this contest go on for half a minute then leaned down and pulled the badger out by the tail. He held it high for a few seconds. 'Over twenty pounds,' he said. He was judging that by sight, not the weight on his arm, because Daisy still had her jaws clamped and was dangling. Malcolm dropped the badger. 'A tough, ferocious sow,' he said. 'She's pregnant. We'll let her go. Unsporting not to. Have to keep up the supply. And above all else, we're sportsmen.' They didn't unleash the Patterdales. Daisy released her bite and fell to the ground on spread paws. The dog had obviously done this often before and perfected the landing technique. Belle and Kate came out barking from the mouth of the sett and seemed to recognize the fight was over.

The sow stood dazed for a moment, then ambled off, no basic hurt. It had a kind of dumpy dignity, like someone playing a dowager in a theatre piece, and gave a sort of groan or sigh as it went out of sight in the undergrowth. Ian could guess what would have happened if they hadn't let her go. Most likely all the dogs would have been put on her. They'd be better able to subdue and kill her above ground. Malcolm said: 'It's simply a chance for dogs to flash their skills and courage. That's their nature. They *need* the thrill. They *deserve* the thrill. It's what they're for, just as Frank Sinatra has to sing. A Saturday morning outing in the fields, like golf.'

THIRTEEN

'Enclosed please find classified documentation. Return registered to PO Box 17. No name of addressee needed or wanted. I've lifted this lot from the office safe. FOR YOUR EYES ONLY. Ray's in hospital for routine check-ups etc lasting three days. Send back by time he returns. Repeat, send back by time he returns. There are no duplicates. Ray hot on security and redacting and a bit tight with information at Mooney's I thought. I shall hand deliver. Why I wanted to make sure there was an adequate letter flap in your mauve front door. Repeat: FOR YOUR EYES ONLY. E.'

When Ian pulled the investigation file from its large white 'Exclusive to Addressee' envelope, the postcard had been drawn out in its wake and fluttered to the floor, her written message uppermost. She would have avoided stapling the card to the file cover, or even paper-clipping it, because either way a mark would be left, and Ray was sure to notice and know there'd been some fancy work. He might already feel there was something unusual in the Ian-Emily relationship.

No 'might', in fact. At the OCTU, and over the airfield loudspeaker Bain had speculated about the letter from 'E'. He'd seemed to assume an affair between her and Ian, regardless of age difference, and speculated about the reactions of a cuckolded Group Captain. He'd had that wrong, but he was right to identify a special closeness. The Sword of Honour adjustment away from Ray despite the points tally, and then what happened to his legs in Korea, would probably set him wondering even more strongly about the Emily and Ian connection. And, if Ray spotted Emily's need to make recompense with the job in her select gang for having committed him to danger and the wheelchair, he'd realize more strongly still that she'd craftily favoured Ian, and now felt some shame for it. Maybe she should. Ian wouldn't press this, though.

It was an ancient sepia picture postcard, showing on its

other side the *King Arthur* at what looked like full speed ahead
in the Bristol Channel, flag flying, crowded with passengers.
The caption gave the ship's name, but no date. The envelope
must have come overnight. He found it with the rest of the
mail when he got up first to make a cup of tea for Lucy and
him. He assumed the file was the one Ray had brought to
Mooney's locked to his wrist. Then, he must have restored it
to the safe. Ian thought he wouldn't mention the file or card
to Lucy, as if they came from a lover and must be kept secret.
They *were* secret, but only workaday secret, only Her Majesty's
Government secret. Had this project begun to make him furtive,
sneaky?

He scanned the file before going back to bed for ten minutes
with the tea. He looked for the report on Dill, in case Ray
Bain had cut out some material when talking about him in
Mooney's. Ian himself had discovered next to nothing of any
use from Dill. After the hunt they went back to the country
pub and Ian had made sure he sat and drank with him. Ian
had tried to lead the conversation on to something like those
wider topics Emily spoke of – wider, that is, than their sport.
But it had been difficult. It had been impossible. And perhaps
this impossibility did tell Ian something. He felt a calculated
resistance in Dill to let their chat move away from the contained
and containable matters of the day – from *this* day and the
badger episode. On the return visit to the pub, Ian had still
noticed nobody who might have been doing a surveillance
stint. Perhaps Emily had withdrawn the watch so he wouldn't
feel supervised.

He wondered if he had been too hurried, perhaps clumsy,
in trying to get to other subjects with Dill, and eventually to
one other subject. He was friendly enough when they first met
and for quite a time afterwards, but then appeared to grow
wary, even hostile. That might mean he had something to be
wary about, and hostile about to anyone who seemed to get
nosy. So, could Ian regard this as a discovery? Did the non-
disclosure amount to a kind of disclosure? That looked a vague
and slack deduction, but most likely the best he would get.
Dill was clearly someone acute, subtle, tuned-in, probably
capable of a big and special and confidential assignment. Might

this be another of those half-discoveries for Ian, a positive from the negative? Not, however, the kind of revelations that would make a newspaper story stand up and earn publication.

Some file details for Dill were as Bain and Emily had given them to Ian at Mooney's: the factory job, the union position, bachelorhood, the weekend badger hunts. But these basics were preceded by what seemed to be a tabulated report from a surveillance team. It answered a major and obvious question in Ian's mind: how had Dill been selected in the first place?

OPERATION TITLE: Wallflower
LOCATION: Outside 12 Feder Road, Chelsea, London, home of Milton Skeeth and subsequent visitor tracking.
OBJECTIVE: Note and identify all callers to the house.
ACTION TAKEN: Clandestine stalk of male visitor upon leaving. Subsequently identified via electoral register and local Post Office as Jeffrey David Dill. His name and biographical details already known to us. (See Paper Ht 834 /L, recording past interviews with two civilian inform-ants coded Jimmy Cagney and Attila the Hun – first intimations that Dill might have role in potential nation-wide junta scheme.)

Ian thought he understood why Bain might want to conceal for now the bond between Dill and Milton Skeeth. Ray prob-ably feared this would be to tell too much. After all, Ian was merely a journalist, untrained in the delicacies and careful, variable pace of the secrets business. In fact, journalists were trained in the opposite: if they wanted something from someone they went bull-headed to get it, because if they didn't an opposition paper might swoop and scoop and leave them behind. How did these voices, Jimmy Cagney and Attila the Hun, know Dill, and realize he might qualify for the attention of people like Emily and Bain? Did they work with him, and hear some of his views? Did they go after badgers with him and hear some of his views? Did they drink with him in the country pub and hear some of his views? Did they decide these views might be dangerous and should be referred to the authorities?

And, dwelling on the difference between Emily's and Ray Bain's type of work and his own, he changed his mind about showing the file and card to Lucy and discussing them. The concealment would be wrong, divisive. He'd decided a long time ago at Norton that he didn't want to get sucked into the secrets network. He still felt like that. He disliked the melodrama and autocracy in those repeated injunctions, FOR YOUR EYES ONLY. They sounded like the trite, teasing title for a new James Bond spy book. He flipped through a few more pages of the file and noticed further names he recognized: Lord Mivale, Daphne West, Anthony Eden, another actress, Fay Doel, additional insiders' whispers from Cagney and Attila.

As Lucy supped tea and read the card and some of the file alongside him in bed, he knew he had done right in not hiding the stuff from her. Pregnancy suited Lucy. Her skin glowed. She didn't deserve to be blanked out from any part of his life. He wasn't in that sort of career, and still didn't want to be. She obviously liked the way he had ignored the FOR YOUR EYES ONLY label. It showed Lucy he considered his first loyalty was to her, and this brought comfort and reassurance. She would see that Emily was part of a possibly important and startling newspaper tale, and that the connection didn't go beyond this. Lucy, herself a journalist, clearly shared in the excitement of a potentially enormous exclusive. By showing her the papers, Ian had invited her in to the assignment with him. That's how a marriage ought to be. And, of course, it was about more than a possible page-one newspaper splash. The future of the country might be involved. This sounded inflated, maybe, and alarmist. Just the same, it was true. And they'd have a child's prospects in that country to consider soon.

'Did she buy up a sackful of these cards d'you think, Ian, to commemorate that escape from death?' she said.

'She thinks she commemorated it wrongly at first – crowing about the drowning of Corbitty for her sake. She put my father into second place. She's been making up for that for years.'

Lucy pointed at the file. 'She takes risks on your behalf. Classified material slipped to you on loan.'

'Yes, but she's also looking for a benefit. Her daughter's apparently tied up with one of the people they suspect. That's Daphne West, the actress. We've seen her in plays on TV, haven't we?'

'Pretty girl, hardly out of her teens?'

'Yes.'

'From a previous marriage?'

'Perhaps.'

'What does that mean?'

'It means no.'

Lucy sipped some tea. 'Oh, I see. My God, Ian. Your dad's?'

'Quite. I'll probably have to interview her, as part of the inquiry.'

'That will be strange for you, won't it?'

But he felt curious, naturally. Apprehensive, also, naturally. 'Possibly a bit strange, yes.'

In the afternoon he'd take the file into the box room he used as an office/study and go through it thoroughly. Now, sitting up in bed, Lucy did the kind of page skimming he'd carried out himself a few minutes before. 'Here's something fascinating,' she said, 'a note by Emily in person, I think. At the end comes her majestic "E", like something from the Queen. It's apparently an assessment of three informants on their list, someone called Jimmy Cagney, another is Attila the Hun, and another, Ivor Novello.

'I think I might have met one of them out on the badger hunt.'

'Which?'

'Don't know. There's probably an informant at his works, and maybe another on the hunts – Attila and Jimmy Cagney. The hunt voice feeds them the insights, and then they want me to follow these up, find what else I can and sell it as a Press story – which would most likely kill the conspiracy. You can't have a conspiracy when its existence is a splash in the Press.'

'Attila she considers "enthusiastic, determined but inclined to fabricate and oversell". He gets a B-plus. Cagney is "scrupulous but indolent" and is awarded only a B. Ivor Novello she finds "factual, bright, wide-visioned, systematic" and earns an A/B.'

'I wonder how she'd rate me?' Ian replied.

'Oh, an "Incomplete" I expect.'

'Are we told the genuine names behind the aliases?'

'No.'

'She doesn't trust me that much.'

'Not yet,' Lucy said. 'I told you, you're an Incomplete. You've some way to go yet.'

'Do I want to?'

'Do you?'

'Probably not, but I've been snared, noosed.'

FOURTEEN

Working at home on the Emily-Ray file with its mentions of secret names, celebrity names, clandestine projects, Ian had a phone call, the voice educated, male, not unfriendly, but not friendly: a touch of *Got-you-at-last-you-sod-and-don't-imagine-you-can-do-another-toddle-off.* 'Mr Charteris? Mr Ian Charteris, journalist and possibly more?'

'No.'

'Not Mr Ian Charteris and possibly more?'

'No.'

'No what?'

'Not possibly more.'

'Mr Ian Charteris, journalist?'

'Speaking.'

'Forgive me for speculating – the "possibly more". Guesswork.'

'In journalism we don't do guesswork,' Ian said. 'Facts are the thing. Facts are treasured. Who was it said "Comment is free but facts are expensive"?'

'Yes, all that travel and bribery.'

'First-class travel,' Ian said. 'It's journalism's attempt to look like a profession, not a trade.'

'It's facts I wanted to talk about, facts which to date might have been concealed. Or disguised as something else.'

'Facts can be like that. Evasive. Hidden. One man's facts are another man's speculation.'

'This is Milton Skeeth.'

'Milton Skeeth?'

There was a pause as if he didn't believe in Ian's show of puzzlement, felt riled by it, considered it not based on fact as recently boasted about by Charteris, wondered why the fuck it was necessary, but, OK, whatever game he – Charteris – wanted to play, Skeeth would go along with it for now. Patience.

Tactics. 'I work in the theatre. I think I can claim it's a name known to the Press.'

'Ah, Milton Skeeth, of course,' Ian said.

'That's it. I hoped it would register.'

'We get rung up by so many people,' Ian replied.

'Who?'

'Who what?'

'Who get rung up by so many people?'

'Journalists. We're well known for it. Folk telephone to tell us things, or to tell us that things other folk have told us are not true. A hell of a lot like that.'

'It must be arduous.'

'Most of us wouldn't have it any different. We live on these calls. They are our oxygen.'

'I'm glad to learn this. Plainly, I am now making such a call.'

'Quite often there's preamble. We don't complain. It gives us time to get the notebook open.'

'I hear you've been talking to a friend of mine.'

'This has to be a possibility. As I've said, we talk to many. It's of the essence in our trade. Our profession, would-be. Heard from where that I've been talking to a friend of yours? This might help me narrow things down, because I'm sure you will have a great number of friends.'

'I gather you've spoken lately to Jeffrey Dill,' Skeeth replied. 'Does that narrow it down?'

'Oh, obviously, it does more than that! It immediately reduces the field to one.'

'I believe it's so, isn't it? You met him?'

'Well, yes.'

'The meeting took place in a situation quite normal for him, but perhaps less so for you.'

'Journalists get into all kind of situations. Think of Stanley tracking down Livingstone. That would hardly be customary ground for Stanley – if reporters, in fact, *have* a customary ground.'

'Jeff mentioned it.'

'You're on those kinds of terms with him, are you?' Ian replied.

'Which?'

'Shortened first names – "Jeff". Would he call you "Milt"? When he mentioned it – the meeting – did he refer to it in, as it were, passing, or make a special point?'

'He wouldn't normally trouble me with that kind of thing. I deduced he felt anxious.'

'Anxious?'

'He wonders.'

'About what?'

'Oh, definitely he wonders. He's a worrier. You wouldn't think so to look at him – he seems so hale and solid and attuned to badger hunting. Would you have suspected he was a worrier?'

'These would be the terms I'd use about him myself – hale, solid, remarkably attuned to badger hunting, as I can personally testify – not something third hand. Most probably you'd need someone of that nature. Not someone good specifically at badger hunting, but of that general quality.'

'Need in which sense?'

'It's quite difficult for someone outside to visualize the kind of friendship you have – how it ever came about: you prominent in the theatre and, as I recall now, there's a mighty family business. These on one side, and then Jeff and the badgers. Democratic and seemingly classless, a wide acquaintance with life, yes, yet a puzzle.'

'When you say "outside" what exactly were you getting at there? "Outside" presumes a kind of inside, doesn't it? I'd be interested to know how you see this inside from outside.'

'In a sense journalists are always outside, trying to discover that "inside" you spoke of. It's rather like barristers. We have to make ourselves specialists for a while in some topic, brief ourselves, so to speak, then probably forget all about it and move on to something else.'

'Which topic are we talking about here? Which topic have you been briefing yourself on, and, possibly, getting briefed on? That's why I added those words, "journalist *and possibly more.*"'

'I don't get that.'

'The briefing. Not the briefing of yourself *by* yourself but by knowledgeable figures from a separate organization, a separate discipline. Possibly you are privy to exceptional information, exceptional in regard to its confidentiality, its secrecy, in fact.'

'It was a terrific morning out with Jeff and his colleagues in rural surroundings,' Charteris replied. 'An eye-opener. No other term will do. Such luck to get their invitation and help. It's quite a recherché sport.'

'Colleagues, certainly. I don't see why you shouldn't call them colleagues.'

'Oh, are you worried about one of them?'

'"Worried" in which particular?' Skeeth said.

'You seemed troubled by the word "colleagues" – as if you had reservations about one of them, perhaps more than one. When you said, "I don't see why you shouldn't call them colleagues," this seemed to set up some uncertainty, some tentativeness. Perhaps "partners" is better. They back one another up so well. This might be one of their chief strengths: they act instinctively together. Would you go along with that, or are there still some doubts about one of them, or more?'

'Nailing a badger has to be a team thing, I gather,' Skeeth said. 'Cooperation of a high degree, men and dogs.'

'You've never been on one of their hunts? This is the reason I felt perplexed slightly concerning the basis of your friendship. That side of things is so important to Jeff, isn't it? You're not up on dogs, yourself, are you – terriers?'

'Malcolm was there, as well, I understand. That's Malcolm Ivins. Rock-like is how I think of Malc.'

'So you have met him, as well as Jeff?'

'Some surprising facets to him as well as Jeff,' Skeeth said.

'Yes.' Ian naturally remembered Malcolm holding the swollen sow high, declaring the pregnancy test positive, and issuing his statement about the need to be good sports and ensure a supply of more badgers to set the dogs on. Malcolm seemed to embody the spirit of Olde England.

'Malcolm is a character,' Skeeth said.

'In fact, all of them seemed vivid personalities,' Ian said.

'"Vivid" is another appropriate term for all these lads.'

'It was a privilege to tag along.'

'Some I know better than others. But that's only natural.'

'Do you mean one or two actually hid their real personalities from you? You're in the acting pursuit, so you'll be used to people substituting another personality for their real one – that is, if any of us *have* a single *real* personality. Aren't we all rather more protean than that?'

'Malcolm, I have to tell you – in confidence, if you don't mind – but Malcolm doesn't always show proper respect for the rules,' Skeeth replied. 'For the law, in fact. That's the other side of *him*, just as Jeffrey has his less obvious side, too.'

'Why I said protean.'

'Malc's in useful touch with someone who's in touch with someone, who's in touch with someone else, who has the means of tying a vehicle's registration number with unchallengeable accuracy to the owner's name and address.'

'Through police records?' Crooked. So, it didn't sound as though Malc was Jimmy Cagney or Novello or Attila the Hun.

'Police records, yes, that line of country, I believe,' Skeeth said, 'but this is between us only. Malcolm is Malcolm.'

'It's wonderful you can be so categorical and definite. You see Malc as a sort of self-contained echo of himself, despite all we've been saying about human variousness.'

'That kind of research into cop records is costly and takes a while. Payments required at each stage, cash only, of course, and not chicken feed. I don't suppose I need to tell you where the expense falls. On yours truly. But it's worth the outlay. How else would I get finally to chat with you? Anyway, the result is that, although I'm told Jeffrey and the others on the day knew you only as Ian, perhaps by design – I mean, yours, and you're absolutely entitled to partial anonymity if that's what you wanted – yes, although you were Ian and nothing more, Malcolm was able to take things further by passing the details of your Ford into this – I'm afraid it must be admitted – this rather illicit system. I don't believe he meant harm. I hope you're not offended. I'd hate you to feel you've been . . . well . . . I'd hate you to feel you've been victimized or callously exposed by illegal means.'

'I have been, but you'd hate me to think so,' Ian replied.

'But Malcolm does like information, authenticated

information. The fact that in this case the information was about you – your full particulars, of course – is almost a by-the-way matter. Simply, he has this thirst for data *per*, so to speak, *se*. A hobby, you could call it, an applied hobby. In many ways it's an asset. Most ways. Considerably so. Some people are good at one thing, some at another. Information is Malcolm's bag. Occasionally he will go rather too far in seeking to collect it. One has to concede that. There is a persistence to his work that may become obsessional. His motives can be misinterpreted – though I don't say by you. Certainly not.'

'Thanks.'

'Of course, when Jeffrey told me your full name, as secured by Malcolm, I instantly recognized it from bylines in the Press, and, like all good journalists anxious for tip-offs, hints and whispers, you are in the telephone book, so we had a further guide to your address. You work for the *Daily Mirror* sometimes, don't you? I've seen some of your reports there.'

'Now and then.'

'A tabloid and brash, but also with a very responsible, serious aspect. I love the *Mirror*.' Suddenly, Skeeth went into acute excitement, or pretended to. It was as if he hoped to keep the conversation light and lulling and semi-rambling, so he could turn it gradually, imperceptibly, to what he wanted to know: the sort of technique Emily had suggested to Charteris for the Dill interview. 'But, look, you've probably seen and even talked to "THE MAN THEY CAN'T GAG" – Peter Wilson himself, the paper's sports writer, have you? That really must be something.'

'Oh, yes. He's easy to recognize at the office because anyone can see he hasn't got a gag in.'

'And Driberg – doesn't he do some stuff for them occasionally, now the *Express* glory days are over? Such a distinguished commentator in his day. Rather promiscuous, I hear, and frank about it. He's never given you trouble, has he?'

'At the *Mirror* I'm known as "THE MAN THEY CAN'T SHAG".'

'Perhaps understandably it did perturb Jeffrey when he

discovered you were a Press man. And Jeffrey perturbed and angry can be frightening. Extremely. His words to me were, "This bastard came pretending to be interested in rural sports and dogs, and all the time he's a fucking journalist. At least a fucking journalist. He could be severe trouble." This is verbatim. I can memorize lines as well as any actor. That "at least a fucking journalist" explains my "possibly more" gloss earlier. Jeff wondered what your purpose might be. And as this call would indicate, I suppose, I share that curiosity, would wish to ask you an explanation.'

'Purpose?'

'Your "underlying purpose" was how Jeff phrased it. He's got a vocab, despite leaving school at fourteen. This would be an allusion to that duality we have been discussing. There is purpose – in its obvious, superficial meaning, namely badgers, and there is additionally and importantly a concealed aspect, such as the journalistic, and whatever else.'

'Which whatever else?'

'Yes, whatever else.'

'You know him pretty well, do you?' Ian replied. 'I still find it perplexing when you're from such different areas of life.'

'He's the kind who does look for underlying purposes,' Skeeth said. 'It's his nature. Some people have only a surface concern for others' purpose. But Jeff will always seek to unearth what underlying purpose lies beneath that surface purpose. He can't be satisfied with appearances. This might be deemed a flair or, on the other hand, if disapproved of, a compulsive, objectionable invasive twitch.'

'I simply had a great curiosity to see how the dogs worked in these conditions. Such a revelation!'

'I told him it would be something of the sort – that you were probably a through-and-through terriers person and were keen to see the range of terrier activities. I had to try to allay his nervousness.'

'Odd you should put it that way, because there have been occasions when an absolute stranger has come up to me and said, "I can tell from your face you must be a through-and-through terriers person."'

Skeeth had a small laugh, the kind to indicate harmlessness and a wish for notional comradeship, as long as it led to some gain or gains for him. 'Which terriers interest you most?' he asked.

'Jack Russells.'

'Bonny, indomitable creatures. I'd have guessed these were your favourites.'

'How? You couldn't have read my face. We've never met.'

'That's a fact,' Skeeth said.

'The Patterdales are handsome,' Ian replied.

'I assured Jeff it would be this love of dogs that brought you into their company, but I have to tell you, Ian, he remained apprehensive. And he becomes difficult to cope with when he's apprehensive. He can fall into extremism. He has great talents, but also this latent, unhelpful tendency. So I said I'd see if I could make contact and have a chat about things – see if I could sound out your thinking. I gather you first bumped into Jeff and others via a pub, correct me if I'm wrong, do.'

'More the yard and car park of a pub.'

'Its yard?'

'I saw the dogs tethered there, and thought to myself, *This looks promising*. As anyone might have. I don't claim this as in the slightest degree a unique reaction. Anyone interested in terrier breeds, that is.'

'You just happened to be passing this country pub, out in the country – well, obviously a country pub would be in the country – you just happened to be passing, did you, when you saw the dogs?'

'Luck, also known as serendipity.'

'I take it you'd have been in the Ford when you spotted the dogs. You'd be gazing around on either side, but also, obviously, watching the road ahead, as a matter of safety?'

'There they were and quite noticeable, though not barking or fighting one another. Well behaved, like troops on a landing craft, keeping themselves in readiness for a fray. What one would expect from first-class terriers – confident their owners would return in due course, untether them and remove the group to a more terrier-like, active kind of situation. They'd know they had to save themselves for real conflict underground, not fool about squabbling or showing off. Yet there was nothing cowed or, as it were, hangdog about them. Dignified.'

'What exactly made you think sight of the dogs was *promising*?' Skeeth replied. 'That's how you described your reaction, I think. You declare anyone interested in terriers would have responded similarly, but I'm not so certain. This might be a flair special to yourself, but you are too unvain to regard it as such. You do not distinguish yourself from others, yet your – let's call it affinity – yes, your affinity with these dogs in the yard – your immediate insight – does that: it *does* distinguish you from the majority.'

'You wouldn't ever see a covey of dogs like this in the yard of an urban pub. I can't imagine it.'

'Do you get into the country a great deal?'

'It's such a bracing change from London life, I always feel. Nature is so fulfilling.'

'And noticing the dogs, you pounced on the chance?'

'That would be a very apt description.'

'This touched off something in you – the seemingly banal collection of dogs, yet, in your thinking, supremely meaningful? Or, perhaps "thinking" is not the word. This would be an instinctive response, rather than a methodically rational one.'

'What might be called in religious lingo an epiphany, a revelation. These dogs took on a symbolic character for me. Does that sound pretentious, mystical? Sorry, if so. I can't say whether all others would feel similarly. You could be correct on that. Country folk would possibly be quite used to such a sight and regard the dogs simply as . . . well, simply as dogs tied up in a yard while their owners have a pint. They might be sceptical about the attempt to give the experience overtones.'

'Yes. But it's like so much in life, isn't it – an opportunity shows, such as your glimpse of the pub car park dogs, and one either takes it or sees it disappear, perhaps for ever. Had you gone back a day or two later there might have been no trace of the dogs.'

'Yes, the postman *doesn't* always ring twice.'

'Jimmy Cain. A great film and book.'

'Or then again, as to literature,' Ian replied, 'there's "a tide in the affairs of men which taken at the flood leads on to fortune," but, not taken, the result is shallows and misery.'

'Good old *Julius Caesar.* The theatre can often deliver a truth. Think of this new play by John Osborne, *Look Back in Anger*, with its obvious flaming, bitter disgust at the Britain we live in now. The flagrant lack of good leadership, the absence of a philosophy to live by. The loss of an empire and nothing to take its place and conserve our collective pride. How many does he speak for, I wonder?'

'Yes, do you find Britain disgusting, Mr Skeeth?'

'Milton. How I wish I'd been offered the privilege of producing that play.'

'It chimes with your thinking, does it?'

'There'll be other works along the same lines from different writers, I expect,' Skeeth said.

'You believe this is a general view, do you, contempt for the way our country is governed at present?'

'A prevailing dissatisfaction.'

'Warranted?'

'It's certainly there.'

'Perhaps we should meet?' Ian said.

'I wondered if you might call at my house for a drink.'

'Where do you live?'

Again there was a pause as if he thought Ian knew the address but wouldn't admit it, because that would indicate research into Skeeth had already been done. And it had been. Did he suspect this? Did it scare him? 'Feder Road, Chelsea, number twelve,' Skeeth said.

'Fine.'

'We'll be here all this evening.'

Which 'we' would that be? Was Jeff with him – Jeff who could be unhelpful and frightening? But Ian didn't ask. He'd prefer not to sound confrontational. Skeeth might be frightened off. Charteris recalled that sketch Driberg did of him as a great null, uncommitted nothingness which the customers were conned into thinking they should transform into a something by coughing all their intimacies to him. Yes, a smart old printman, Driberg, and political with it.

When the phone call had ended, Ian talked to Lucy about it. He would like another view. Correction: he wanted not just another view; he wanted *her* view, which was sure to be wise and sharp and to do with basics. 'What exactly is it that Emily and Ray Bain suspect him of?' she said. 'It ties in with what you told me Driberg hinted at, does it? I mean Driberg's state-of-the-nation analysis, not his scabbily slanderous analysis of you.'

'They believe that if the Suez situation keeps on going disastrously wrong for us, as seems likely, the country will slip into chaos and become more or less ungovernable – bad for everyone, but especially bad for those with a lot to lose, such as Skeeth and his family and the family boodle, properties and business. There'd be a small but formidable part of the population like that. They favour strong governance – thrive under it, are cosseted and protected under it, hold peerages and knighthoods and courtierships under it – and if it's not available they'll try to supply it.

'To get what they want they might form alliances with working-class folk like Dill and the folk Dill represents, who could erupt on to the streets and make trouble, but trouble that remains controlled, so no factories or plant belonging to the Skeeth family and similar are arsonized. Some of the Dill brigade have special talents – one called Malcolm dug out my name from a supposedly secure police source. This is infiltration on quite a scale. They can discover supposedly secure data, including the ownership of my car. Hence, the Skeeth phone call. I get an inkling of an organization already in place and functioning effectively, frighteningly.'

'The Dills and Malcolms will be cut adrift, of course, once power is secured, will they?' Lucy said.

'Naturally. Emily, Ray Bain and Driberg think something like this Right-Left line-up of forces was rumoured in 1936, at abdication time. They believe there could be a repeat now, but with a much better chance, because they don't have to depend on the king, who bolted in 'thirty-six. Although Skeeth's tone was sort of jokey and flippant on the phone just now, he spoke seriously about chances that might be caught or missed. I said the postman doesn't always ring twice. Sometimes he might, though.'

'But any putsch would need the military wouldn't it? Or at least the threat of the military.'

'Of course. Many of the people on the Right would have experience of command. Perhaps the plot already *has* some of the military. Maybe there are generals, and admirals, and air marshals who feel disgust at the prospect of an illegal invasion and Suez war – Operation Musketeer it's called, I hear from a *Times* Whitehall correspondent. Eden and the government know how unpopular the idea of conflict is. How could they not know? There are continuous battles inside the government about the legality or not of the war. As Mr *Times* describes it, the attorney general, Manningham-Buller, has decided an invasion is unlawful. But Eden ignores his views, and the Solicitor General's, Harry Hylton-Foster. Kilmuir, Lord Chancellor, will try to cook up some sort of justification instead. Confidential, so far.'

'Is that a job for a Lord Chancellor?'

'Doubtful. Manningham-Buller, Hylton-Foster and some of their staff are livid. There are resignation threats.'

'Provable?'

'Possibly not. In any case, it's the way Prime Ministers have always behaved, I suppose, leaning on subordinates for an OK, and probably the way a Prime Minister will behave in the future if we land in another illegal war. Mr *Times* says there are officers in a basement office at the Air Ministry planning an Allied Air Force Task Force. The room is so hidden away they're known as "the troglodytes". They are very unhappy, he tells me, about the confusion of political and military objectives. This uneasiness might be widespread in the armed forces, and exploitable.'

'But the 1936 element?' Lucy said. 'What's a supposed plan – very supposed – what's a supposed plan for an uprising then got to do with now? Have Emily and the others galloped to see resemblances? It's as if they've concocted a new shadow situation from a past state of things that nobody's altogether sure about, anyway. To me it sounds like figments on figments, guesses on guesses, fantasy on fantasy.'

'It's possible, though.'

'Likely?' she said. 'Could Emily, Bain and Driberg all have

been listening to the same source – the same faulty source? They seem to confirm one another, but actually they're all starting from the same wrong spot.'

'I've thought of that.'

'And?'

'There's a new, 1956 factor. Skeeth mentioned the Osborne play *Look Back in Anger* and its raging suggestion that there's something rotten in the state of present-day Britain. OK, it's probably bullshit: most likely Britain is more or less the same as it always was. But the accusation gives a writer something to hang a nicely worded tirade on. I asked Skeeth if *he* agreed about the rottenness. I don't think he answered. Do they want to clean up – in all senses, get once glorious GB back on track, ruling the waves etcetera? Do we detect a kind of perverted patriotism?'

'The conversation wasn't total playfulness and banter. And where it seemed to be playfulness and banter I got the idea occasionally that he was terrified. He couldn't understand how I'd located Dill and the others, nor what the result might be. He kept on with what sounded like farcical questions about the country pub and my noticing the dogs, and being a terriers fan, but which really weren't so farcical. He thinks my knowledge of their scheme is better than a journalist's.'

'And he's right, isn't he?'

'Of course.'

'The file shows plainly enough how you got on to Dill and the others. It's simple.'

'Yes, Skeeth's under watch and Dill is noted calling at the Chelsea house. But, of course, Skeeth doesn't know this. And neither does Dill,' Ian said. 'Dill still thinks Jimmy Cagney was a film star, and that's all.'

'You hope. Ah, and you think Skeeth is afraid Dill will suspect he – Skeeth – mentioned them to you, pointed you towards the dogs and Dill?' Lucy asked.

'He's scared of Dill. The upper-crust are always scared of the lower crust, and the lower crust never fully trusts the upper crust. There are fine historical precedents.'

'But why would Skeeth betray them?' Lucy said. 'That's what it would be, isn't it, betrayal?' She was lying on a settee, wearing an old sweater and elastic waisted trousers. She spoke to him over the good mound of her pregnancy. Her brain was, as ever, fully directed at his problems, ordered, alert to all the possibilities, entirely clear. She frowned a little through concentration, grinned occasionally when she got a kick from the kid, but generally looked as serene, confident and lovely as ever. 'In the chat after the pub, Dill turned suddenly very reticent, virtually hostile,' Ian said. 'Next step, Malcolm does a check on me. They become vigilant, disbelieving, they examine all the likelihoods, none comfortable – for them.'

'Well, of course they'd be vigilant – some obvious, officer-qualities city lad descends on them and wants lessons in the art of badger hunting. Credible? Likely? It's more or less preposterous, isn't it? As you say, they probably think you're one of Emily's lot, doing some would-be subtle penetration.'

'Yes, they might. And they'll ask how this one of Emily's lot found them in their country pub. They'll wonder, won't they?'

'By a tip-off from Milton Skeeth? You think that's what they decide? But I come back to the same question, why would he betray them?'

'In fact, he wouldn't and hasn't. Of course he hasn't. He told me nothing except he knew Dill, and, of course, he's coughed nothing to Emily or Bain or their people.'

'You're one of their people, aren't you?'

'For the moment. But he's done no coughing to me, either, just a sort of PG Wodehouse chit-chat, though with undertones.'

'It's not negligible that he's told you he knows Dill,' Lucy replied.

He delighted in that precision from her, the 'not negligible'. It was like a seminar. 'But he thinks I know already that he's matey with Dill. He deduces that's why I'm out badgering.'

'Yes.' She wagged a finger at him. 'You *have* come to sound like an undercover agent.'

'I am. Skeeth will also believe that Dill and co. won't be able to see any other path to them but dear Milt. They probably sensed from the beginning that the toffs and tycoons might ditch them when they felt like it. They're not stupid.

Most likely they'd know some of that relevant history – wars
bringing death and suffering to ordinary folk, and riches and
lands to the high-born and the arms dealers. The Workers'
Education Association probably points out that kind of dire
process, and so it should. Perhaps Dill and the rest imagine
the conspiracy has been rumbled by Emily's squad, and Skeeth
under questioning sang and sang, involving everyone. The
conspiracy, if it exists, *has* been rumbled by Emily's squad,
but Skeeth hasn't done any singing, as far as I know. He's
done some waggish conversation with me.'

'Yes, as far as you know. But wouldn't Skeeth explain to
Dill you were a journalist, not a spy?'

'He might. He's not convinced of that himself, though. In
any case, a journalist is just as bad from their angle, isn't he?
What do journalists do? Expose people. They want to get
front-page headlines that start with very upper case,
REVEALED: and then the dirt in detail on whatever it is –
secrets laid out for their readers' enjoyment. I think it's all
partly a class thing. Dill and friends are working class.
Journalists, Skeeth and those with Skeeth, are at least middle
class and perhaps higher. The working class is used to being
screwed and let down by their supposed superiors.'

'I don't think you should go round to his house,' Lucy
replied.

'It'll be all right. You don't get violent skulduggery in
Chelsea. This is the home of a famous theatre man, and member
of an eminent family. Anyway, Emily's people are in the street,
watching.'

She grimaced, didn't even get near to swallowing this. 'How
would they know if things had gone wrong inside the house,
gone wrong for *you?* The outside of the house would look as
it ever did. And it might be too late if they did eventually
suspect something was amiss inside.'

'I think I ought to see him. I feel a sort of duty.'

'Who to?'

'Not sure.'

'Always, darling, you're imagining yourself in moral debt
to someone.'

'It's my nicer side,' Ian said. 'Emily obviously feels a debt to me because of my dad. So, I get the Sword of Honour and now the file. I have to do a bit of reciprocity. That Driberg sketch of my personality – the perfect reporter because a total blank, a great fillable emptiness, inconstant with no positive drive or—'

'Don't. I'd rather not hear anything else from the rude swine,' Lucy said.

'I'd like to show I'm not like that,' Charteris said.

'Show whom? You don't have to show *me*. I know it's bloody rubbish.'

'Show myself. I'd like to be rated good at coping with a big newspaper story, but something beyond that, too.'

She shook her head. 'Egomania. But, OK. You can't go alone, though. I'll come with you.'

'I don't think he'd talk in front of you – suppose he's going to talk plain at all, which is doubtful.'

'I'll stay in the car and keep an eye on things from the street.'

'There are already people keeping an eye on things from the street.'

'Yes, but they won't be interested in *you*. They're present to chart what Skeeth does, and where he goes, and who his visitors are.'

'I'll be one of his visitors.'

'I meant dubious visitors.'

'I'll be a dubious visitor. Very dubious.'

'Not as dubious as some.'

They drove to Chelsea. 'Might Emily's daughter be here with him?' Lucy said.

'I don't know who might be. He did say "we".'

In opulent-looking Feder Road they saw several high-priced and elegant parked cars and a silver van that nominally belonged to 'Gerald Smart and Sons, Carpet Merchants and Fitters' according to red lettering on its side. There appeared to be nobody in the driving cabin. Ian would have liked to get closer and check whether any of the wordage disguised observation holes – the o in Sons and all those a's. For now, he'd assume they did. He drove the length of the road slowly, then went around the block and came back. Nothing seemed to have changed during this absence, no sign they'd been noted, no adjustments made.

He decided not to go to the house at once. It was well-lit. He wanted to watch for a while. And he needed to prepare some sort of plan to deal with all the possibilities – Skeeth in the house alone, Skeeth with Jeff and perhaps the other hunters, Skeeth with Daphne West, Skeeth not there at all. He and Lucy waited. It was a midwinter evening and dark. Lucy said: 'Will Gerald Smart and his sons be inside one of the big houses doing a bit of carpet laying?'

'Perhaps Gerald Smart lives there. Carpets might be booming. He can afford Chelsea.'

'They wouldn't like him leaving his work van in a street like this.'

'Perhaps Gerald doesn't care.'

After about ten minutes, a taxi turned into the road and stopped outside number twelve. Only the driver was in the car.

'This doesn't seem right,' Ian said.

The driver left the cab and was about to go through the front garden and knock on the door. Before he reached it, though, all lights in the house were switched off simultaneously, as if by a mains switch. The driver paused. After a moment the door was opened by a man who must be Skeeth, of middle height, slim, grey-haired, nimble. He seemed dressed in outdoor clothes. 'He's very, very ready,' Lucy said.

Alongside Skeeth was a young woman Ian did not recognize. She, too, had a street coat on. The driver picked up two large suitcases. Skeeth carried two more, the woman one. Skeeth pulled the front door to and with a key locked what seemed to be a mortise. He looked up and down the road, perhaps taking in Gerald Smart and Ian's Ford with the known Malc-retrieved number plate. They loaded the taxi and climbed in. At once, it moved swiftly away.

Immediately, the rear doors of the Gerald Smart and Sons van opened and a couple of men emerged from the back. Gerald and a Son? Unlikely. One of them closed the doors and they both ran around to the driving cabin. The vehicle started up and seemed to follow the taxi.

'Skeeth's baling out,' Lucy said. 'He's decided he doesn't need to meet you. He knows enough already.'

'Panic.'

'He's become certain they're in danger,' Lucy said, 'either from Emily or Dill or both.'

'Who's the woman?' Ian replied. 'Not Daphne West.'

'It's Fay Doel, isn't it?' Lucy said. 'I've seen her face on film posters. And wasn't she in that *Importance Of Being Earnest* we saw last year? She's mentioned in the file, I think, as "actress, a sometimes companion" of Skeeth – meaning, I imagine, sometimes Fay Doel, sometimes Daphne West, sometimes who knows?'

'He's more scared of Dill and crew than I thought.'

'Should you try to get after them?'

'No, I'll hear where they've gone. The airport, probably. Gerald Smart and Sons will report to Emily and Ray Bain. We'll hang on here a while.'

'God, but so masterful. I think you really, really *have* turned into a secret agent.'

After about half an hour a much older and more battered van than Gerald Smart's, with no lettering on the side, drove into Feder Road and pulled up about twenty yards from number twelve. You could imagine terrier dogs travelling in this kind of grubby banger. The distance must be a tactic: they wanted to reach the house without a warning noise directly outside. Dill and Malcolm Ivins came from the front and walked as though casually back towards the house, chatting, arms swinging in true relaxed style, though not truly relaxed. The absence of lights in twelve would probably unsettle them. Did it speak of finality? A man Ian recognized as Norman Vernon Towler got out from the back of the van and ran down a service lane, obviously to reach the rear of the house, perhaps to try for entry there, or to stop anyone from escaping that way.

This seemed the same sort of swift, planned, coordinated operation as that badger hunt, but lacking terriers. Dill went to the front door and rang the bell. Ivins stood back on the pavement looking at the upper storeys. When nobody answered the door Dill stepped over a low fence and stared in through a downstairs window. He and Ivins spoke together, not chat now, something more urgent and committed. Dill came back over the fence and he and Ivins returned to their van. Ten minutes later Towler reappeared and climbed into the vehicle. It didn't move off.

'They've decided Skeeth is out somewhere and they'll wait and surprise him,' Lucy said.

'Weeks? Months?'

'You think he's abandoned the plan – afraid too many know about it, such as you and those who sent you, and scared also of Dill?'

'Like that, yes.'

'Would it be courteous to go and tell them Skeeth will not be back for an indefinite while?' Lucy said.

'It *would* be courteous, but we won't.'

'You should sit low,' Lucy replied. 'They might spot you. This is a sensitive street tonight. Parked vehicles will get attention now. Dill wouldn't like it at all, would he, if he finds you waiting near Skeeth's house? It will confirm everything.'

'I don't think it needs confirming.'

'All the more reason to sit low and unobserved. But it's awkward for me to sit low with this belly bump.' She did a minor groan as she tried to ease herself out of sight.

'We'll move soon, I promise. Only, I'm wondering where the fourth one is.'

'Which fourth one?'

'By my count, a chap called Len Gale, who was one of the hunters, is missing tonight.'

'So?'

'So, I worry about him.'

'Why?'

'He might have been rumbled.'

'As Attila or Jimmy or even Ivor?' she said. 'Yes, that's bad. Potentially bad.'

'Yes. We bring trouble. Or Emily does. Always.'

'Just the same, I think you've delivered Britain from a putsch in this year of uncertain grace, love,' Lucy said. 'I know Skeeth and Dill etcetera would only be part of it, but very likely an important part, a crucial part. You should get an OBE to accompany the Sword of Honour.'

'We undercover people don't go in for that kind of decor-
ativeness.' So, neither Mivale nor Mountbatten would be
getting the summons to power. Regardless of Skeeth and *Look
Back in Anger* and Jeff Dill, things would drift on as ever. Ian
couldn't be sure whether that was good or not. He drove out
of Feder Road and gave continual squinting to the mirror. But
the ancient van didn't appear there.

At home he took a call from Emily. 'You were in Chelsea,'
she said. 'That wasn't really scheduled you know. We don't
like loose cannons.'

'Which we is that?' Ian said.

'But probably no serious damage done.'

'We didn't have time to say hello to Gerald. Lucy thinks
the threat is over, if Skeeth was a central, substantial part of
it. They probably won't be able to go on without him. They'll
imagine the whole thing is known about. Well, it *is* known
about, isn't it?'

'Yes. We believe it's *kaput*, too,' Emily said. 'Skeeth's
waiting for an air flight to South America.'

'Down Argentine way?'

'Vamoosed. He thinks you're on to him. Incidentally, does
Lucy want a job, after maternity?'

'*You're* on to him,' Ian replied. 'I go where pointed.'

'Not always.'

'It leaves me with nothing to write about,' Ian said.

'Something else is bound to show, isn't it?' Emily said.
'That's one of the first principles of journalism.'

'Perhaps.'

'But some things are bound *not* to be shown. Or not in full.'

'Oh? Which?'

'We think we lost a very valuable informant tonight. Or very
valuable at least until this Skeeth project collapsed – and of
which, in fact, we think the particular informant did much to
cause the collapse. We're waiting for identification of the body,
but I'm fairly certain who he is. Beaten to death in a country
churchyard, not all that far from the pub where you bumped
into Dill and so on, thanks to the dogs. You can't write about
this death either, though, not the confidential background. A
brief elegy would be OK. There's a precedent for that.'

'Who?' Charteris said.

'We called him Attila the Hun. You'll have seen his name in the file.'

'Len Gale?' Charteris said.

'Attila the Hun.'

'My God,' he said.

Lucy was listening to his side of the conversation. 'What?' she said.

He covered the mouthpiece: 'The fourth man I mentioned tonight.'

'What about him?'

'Killed. Murdered.'

'Get out of this line of work, will you, please, Ian?'

'Are you there?' Emily said.

'Did he have family?'

'We'll look after them, of course,' Emily said.

Charteris said: 'Emily, as to family . . .'

'You wonder about Daphne?'

'Skeeth's exited with another woman, hasn't he?'

'That's how it looks.'

'What will she make of it?'

'Yes, I've been wondering,' Emily said.

'Was it a serious thing with her?'

'Yes, very serious.'

'She might harm herself.'

'We must hope not.'

'I worry,' Ian said, and almost added 'as a brother', but didn't.

'I know you do,' Emily said. 'We both do.'

FIFTEEN

As Skeeth said, Ian often took on freelance work for the *Daily Mirror*. He had a call from Percy Lyall on their News Desk. 'Here's a possible tale that's very much your sort of thing, Ian – a poignant mix of near tragedy, possible thwarted romance, glamour. Can you get over there? Needs sensitive but, of course, dramatic treatment. And, it goes without saying, so I'll say it, depth. I immediately thought of you.'

'How right you were.'

'Daphne West,' Lyall said. 'Heard of her?'

Ian Charteris paused for a moment, or a moment plus. Yes, say three moments. The shock deserved that.

'Heard of her, Ian?'

Well, yes, sort of. She might be my sister.

Emily had it right and some other usable news topic would always show.